Billoughby

Saving Grace

by
D M Roberts

Copyright

Copyright ©2024 DMRoberts

All rights reserved. No part of this publication may be reproduced, distributed, or transmitted in any form or by any means, including photocopying, recording, or other electronic or mechanical methods, without the prior written permission of the publisher, except in the case of brief quotations embodied in critical reviews and certain other non-commercial uses permitted by copyright law.
Any references to historical events, real people, or real places are used fictitiously. Names, characters, and places are products of the author's imagination.
First printing edition 2024
Billoughby©2020

Acknowledgements

Thank you to all that have spurred me on to write a further story on the life of Inspector Billoughby and his family.

My special thanks to Sheila K, I am sorry I have kept you waiting so long and hope you enjoy this next chapter in Billoughby's life.

Thank you Kent for such a beautiful setting, the countryside in the garden of England is truly inspirational.

Dedication

Maragaret, Lorraine and Laura
Always in my heart, never far from my thoughts.
In Loving Memory
Michael Lyons, I will miss you my friend.

Copyright	2
Acknowledgements	3
Dedication	4
Foreword	6
Chapter One	8
Chapter Two	25
Chapter Three	41
Chapter Four	60
Chapter Five	77
Chapter Six	95
Chapter Seven	110
Chapter Eight	132
Chapter Nine	147
Chapter Ten	162
Chapter Eleven	180
Chapter Twelve	198
Chapter Thirteen	213
Chapter Fourteen	228
Epilogue	245
About the Author	246
Other books in this series	247
Books by this Author	248

Foreword

Billoughby – The Long Shadows
Inspector Milton Billoughby is called upon to solve a murder in the sleepy village in Kent, England.

Billoughby – Petticoats and Bowler Hats
Billoughby heads to London in the search for Grace's cousin, Henry, where he uncovers a much more sinister plot

Billoughby – Lost Souls
Billoughby is in a race against time to find a youngster that has been snatched from the village.

Milton Billoughby lives in the sleepy Kent village with his wife Grace and their 2 grown sons, Adam and Tom. Adam has a wife whom he met in Ireland and a daughter, Maisy.
The Reverend Tobias Moore is the vicar of the parish.
Elsbeth Stanhope is the lady of the Hall, a large estate left to her after the unfortunate death of her second husband in somewhat macabre circumstances.
Mary Stanhope is the sister-in-law of Elsbeth, Mary lives with her new husband Robert on his farm.
Daisy Harvey is a female constable that assists the Inspector in his work.
Mr and Mrs. Nash run the local grocery shop.
Geraldine is a longtime friend of the Reverend Moore and a frequent visitor to the village.
Joseph Lyons is the medical examiner; Joseph is the man called upon when a death is suspicious.
Connie was raised in and around the village, she recently moved to Maidstone where she married.

Saving Grace | D M Roberts

Chapter One

Tom was nervous, and he had every right to be. It wasn't every day that you introduced your soulmate to your mother, especially a soulmate that was nearer your mothers age than your own.

"Stop fussing, Tom. If you bite your nails much more there will be nothing left of them."

He wondered how she could be so calm about the whole thing; whereas he was quietly going into a spiral of stress that he had never before encountered. Elsbeth leaned in and kissed the nervous young man on his forehead then got back to the business of sorting out the sandwiches and cake assortment on the table.

"She isn't happy about it, dad told me. He said he would talk her around but I'm not so sure." Elsbeth said nothing; continuing in her task, for there was nothing she could add to make Tom feel better and all they could do was take the 'wait and see' approach.

Across the village, Grace was still wondering why she was expected to take this news in her stride when it went against everything that she believed in. Grace wanted nothing but the best for her family, that was undeniable. Tom had always been at the forefront of her mind, he was a solitary character unlike his brother Adam. Grace had hoped that Tom and Daisy would have made a go of things but that didn't work out and as a mother, Grace was quietly disappointed.

"Ready, love?"

Milton was standing in the doorway wearing his best suit, looking up at her still handsome husband, Grace sighed.

"No, I'm not ready. Oh, Milton I'm not sure I'll ever be ready for this. They won't ever have children, you know that don't you? Then there's the people in the village, what will they say about all of this? It's going to cause such a stir."

Milton held his hand out to his wife, she had always been the kind of person that let others do what they did without judgement, but this was different, this was her baby boy and where her sons were concerned all judgement faded into the background.

"Come on my love, let's get this cracked and then we can figure everything else out as it comes."

Grace could see no figuring this out but go she must.

Adam was fidgeting with his tie.

"Why do I have to wear this? It isn't Sunday and we're not going to church, he's my brother not the vicar."

"Because you do, it's polite and your Ma said you have to, so stop messing about with it."

"I really don't see what all the fuss is about, she's good for our Tom. I've never seen him so happy. I know Ma is worried about the age thing and what people may say, she's definitely not happy that they won't give her grandchildren but like I told her, we're not done yet."

His wife shook her head, Cate knew what a simplistic way of thinking Adam had.

"Oh, and how many more do you think I'm going to be popping out?"

"I was thinking at least 6 or 7, you're healthy enough and still not a bad looking woman."

Adam ducked as his fiery Irish wife threw a cushion at him.

"Cheeky man. Come along now before your dad eats all the cake. Come here little darling, we're going to see Uncle Tom and Aunty Elsbeth."

Picking up their daughter Maisy, the pair headed off to the family pow-wow that was English afternoon tea.

David met Grace and Milton at the door on arrival with David as excitable as ever.

"Hurry up, we have cake. Ma says we can't have any until the guests arrive."

"Hm. are we the guests then young David or are there to be other guests?"

David screwed his face up at Billoughby's remark, he hadn't thought about this.

"How many guests are we going to have Mr. Billoughby? There isn't that much cake."

"You can never tell lad. Tell you what I'll do, I'll let you have a bit of my cake if we run out." David shook his head, he hadn't considered they might run out of cake and that thought didn't bear thinking about.

"Are you having a joke with me Mr. Billoughby, is Mr. Billoughby joking Mrs. Billoughby?" Grace laughed, such innocent thoughts must be a wonderful thing to have. The sounds coming from inside were that of children laughing and chattering and Grace couldn't help but wonder how her boy would cope with such a large and expanded household, heaven's it was hard enough with one child but 8! That would take some doing.

Sally came to the door now, shaking her head at the young lad for keeping them outside.

"Please, do come in. David, would you like to show our guests into the parlour?"

David was more than happy to go into the parlour where he could keep a watchful eye on the table.

"Mr. and the Mrs. Billoughby are here Mrs Stanhope, I've had young David take them through to the parlour. Shall I bring in the tea?"

Elsbeth was now wondering if this had been such a good idea and was pacing back and forth in the kitchen. The cook smiled at her.

"Get yourself in there, Miss You were friends before and you'll be friends again, I'll finish up here."
Elsbeth nodded gratefully and taking a deep breath she walked through the large hall. It had been a strange few months and the woman felt that she had aged at least 20 years in that space of time, what with the passing of Esther, the disappearance of both David and Tom, time had surely caught up with her mentally. She hesitated at the door as she watched Grace and Milton, not knowing exactly what kind of a reaction was awaiting her and Tom, speaking of which she wondered where Tom had gotten to as he wasn't anywhere to be seen in the large room. It was then that she felt the familiar arm around her shoulder as he whispered into her ear.
"Ready?"
They had but a few weeks in isolated bliss together before they were pushed to this day.

"Tom! There you are son, and Elsbeth. It seems like an age since we saw you both."
Milton took the lead as was his way, with Grace quietly standing behind.
"Mr. Billoughby, Mrs. Billoughby, thank you for coming. The children have been quite giddy waiting for your arrival. Sit, please. Are we still expecting Adam and Cate?"
Elsbeth could hear the rattle of nervousness in her voice, she shuddered to think what Tom's parents' must have thought.
"Now, now. Don't stand on ceremony for us, it's Milton and Grace, was before and is now." Continued Milton as he gave Tom and Elsbeth a hug. Grace took a seat on the plush settee and was promptly joined by Ruby. She eyed their host from across the room, the woman that she had befriended that now held the heart of her beloved son.
"Adam and Cate will be along shortly, we passed them on our way. Well now, this all looks very nice, doesn't it Gracie?"

Saving Grace | D M Roberts

Milton was carrying far too much of the conversation and he knew it.

"Shall I fetch you some cake Mr. Billoughby? I think the pink one looks the best or you could have the one with cherries, I like the pink one."

David was clearly less interested in the coolness of the adult air and more in the cakes that teased him from the stand.

"Pink one you say? Well then, let's give them a try shall we?"

Elsbeth poured the tea for the grown-ups and Sally poured fruit juice for the children.

Tom was quite relieved when he heard the familiar tone of his brother's voice in the hall, this felt like a strange kind of torture, and these were all people that he loved dearly.

"Hey there, come in. Oh, let me look at you little one, aren't you growing quickly. You'll be as tall as your dad soon."

Tom took the baby Maisy from his brother's arms and was very quickly surrounded by the children, all wanting to get a peek at this infant who had apparently grown so much.

"She's tiny!"

declared William after studying Maisy for a moment.

"But she'll grow, she'll grow as big as you and one day, and as tall as her dad."

Laughed Tom.

"If the amount she eats is to go by she'll be bigger than her daddy in no time! Hello everyone. Oh, that spread looks good enough to eat Elsbeth."

Cate sensed the tension which was now becoming obvious even to the children.

"Mrs. Billoughby, do you have a bad throat?"

asked Ruby.

"No dear, what makes you think that?"

Ruby stared up at the woman sitting beside her.

"Because you aren't speaking, you always speak lots."
Milton tried to cover his chuckle with a cough, he failed miserably. Elsbeth could bear the atmosphere no more, it was not what she wanted, and she knew that it wasn't what Grace cared for.

"Grace, could you come and give me your opinion on something in the kitchen garden, please." Grace nodded and the 2 women left the room.

"Great, now we can have cake."
cheered David.

"Yes, now we can have cake." Laughed Milton.

Sally kept close to the kitchen door as the 2 women walked around the kitchen garden in the sunshine.

"Come away will you, they'll not thank you for snooping."
hissed cook as she put more pies in the hot oven.

"I'm not snooping, I was getting myself a touch of fresh air, ain't my fault if they happen to be out there. What do you think they're saying to each other? I'm guessing the Inspectors missus is none too pleased with this how d'ya do."

Cook shook her head, the exasperated look on her face told Sally that she wasn't going to get any words of gossip from her.

"Rhubarb, that's my guess. The Mrs. was saying to me only this past week that she needed to ask someone with a good knowing about her rhubarb."

Sally scowled at the cook; it was no fun if the woman didn't take her seriously. Rhubarb indeed!

"Grace, I know this is as difficult for you as it is for Tom and I, and I know if it could be any other way you would have it that other way…what I am trying to say, quite badly in fact, is that I love Tom and I believe he loves me. No, that is wrong. I know he loves me and whilst we aren't asking for your blessing, it would be good to have."

Grace continued to walk along the paths between the beds of vegetables as she listened to Elsbeth try to plead her case.

"I tried to break it off, you have to believe that. It was the reason Tom was here at the Hall, when David first went missing. Tom went too, it was more than I could bear. If he had gone on that ship, I can't even imagine."

Elsbeth had said all she could, and she waited, for something, anything.

"He came back for you, not his father, not me. He came back for you and I am grateful for that but it's a difficult thing as a mother and you will come to see this as your charges grow older, they will do things that you don't understand and they will do things that people will not like and as their mother you will stand by them. It does not for a minute mean that you accept it. My Tom will never have children with you, nor will he be taken seriously by folks around here and at some point, somewhere down the road, that will tear his heart out. If you can live with *that,* you have my blessing and my prayers because mark my words, you will need them."

Grace did not wait for a response as she swept past Sally and took her seat in the parlour next to her husband.

The afternoon went slightly better and while those in the parlour now assumed the matter was resolved, the 2 women knew it was anything but as they put on their best smiles if only for the rest of their respective families. The group was joined by Mary and Robert and the afternoon remained pleasant on the surface. David got to eat his cake, and that of Milton's and Ruby played a wonderful round of duets on the piano with Cate. The small crowd, adequately fed and watered, sat in awe of the young child who Mary said on more than one occasion had been blessed by God himself.

"How is the new help working out, Elsbeth? I hear she comes all the way from the other edge of the country."

"She does, and she is a huge help with the children. Not as cheery as poor Esther was and sometimes a little difficult to understand but on the whole she's doing well, and the children listen to her which is a blessing."
"That's good. Yes, they must miss Esther terribly, you too I imagine. I hear the woman married a chap here and he passed with the influenza bug. Dreadful sickness that it took so many." continued Mary.
"Yes, having a purpose is what has kept her going. She has a day off today, otherwise you would have been able to meet her, but you must come over and say hello when you have time."
"I will. Is she a younger woman or is she older?"
"I would say early 30's but I could be wrong. I think you will get along very well with her, her name is Jennifer Williams."

Milton sat up in the bed; he never corrected Grace in her opinions or ideas but this! This conversation she had retold to him not 10 minutes ago was spinning around in his head and would not let him sleep.
"Are you awake, Gracie?"
Grace closed her eyes tighter, not that he could see her in the darkness of their bedroom, but she did it all the same. Milton continued.
"Gracie, I know you are. I haven't been your husband all these years to not know your awake breathing from your asleep breathing. This thing with Tom and Elsbeth, well it's his life my love and if he chooses to spend it with this woman and her family then who are we to tell them different?"
Grace sighed; she sat up next to her husband.
"I only spoke my mind, you have never had a problem with that in the past so what's changed?" Milton was trying to figure this particular question out himself, he couldn't. The room was pitch

black which was as well, had it been light the man would be able to see the irritation in his wife's eye's.

"He doesn't know what he's doing, he's too young to understand love and all that goes with it, and she should know better, what with 2 husbands in the ground already and I don't want my Tom to make it 3."

"Do you know, we were younger than Tom is now when we met and fell in love. Did we know what we were doing, was that not real love and one that has stood the test on many occasions?" Grace threw back the covers and leapt from the bed.

"I'm going to the kitchen, and you are not to compare this, this, thing between them and our life together. I won't hear it, I won't!"

The kettle boiled almost as much as Grace's blood, her heart racing at the words her husband had dared to say in his defence of this unholy mess. For it was unholy in her mind, the boy she had raised to be shacked up with a middle aged woman for all of the village to see, to point at and gossip about. It wouldn't stop there either, no, there were the children to consider. Grace could well imagine a scandal such as this would be at the top of the Parish meeting. What were they thinking!

"Are you more upset that he didn't come back for us, that it was Elsbeth who made him stay?" Grace was furious, more so because a large part of her upset was for exactly that reason.

"I don't want to discuss it any more. If that's why you came downstairs then I suggest you take yourself back up there."

Well, Milton had never heard his wife speak to him in such a way. Many a husband would have given her what for, but not this man, he sighed as he walked back up to their bedroom alone. Grace sat at the table with her cup in hand, the sound of footsteps told her that Milton was coming back into the room.

"You don't have to like it, or approve but you won't stop it, Ma. I didn't only come back for Elsbeth, I came back because I missed my family, I missed you. I thought that the people here had turned against me and there was nothing I could do to prove to them that I had done nothing wrong, that's why I left. I thought Elsbeth had met somebody else in my absence and I couldn't bear to be here day after day knowing how I felt about her. I do know what love is, Ma, and I have no intention of giving it up."

"But you're so much younger than she is, Tom. How is that going to work, how will you both handle the gossip, because there will be gossip. Will you run away again, taking all of the children and the household with you?"

Tom smiled, he was tired, but he was happy.

"It's a number, Ma. There are so many young women forced to marry men so much older than Elsbeth is, and nobody says a thing, why should this be any different. I know she may pass before I do but, Ma, I don't want to look back on my life and say I could have been happy, but I listened to the gossip instead. You were friends before this, can't you try to be happy for us, for me?"

Grace buried her head in her hands, she wanted both of her children to be as happy and settled as they could be, but this was not what she had envisaged. It had been the longest day, and she would be glad when it was over. Tom put his hand on her shoulder, and she took it, squeezing it hard.

"I'll try, get yourself back to bed or I'll have Robert around complaining you've been falling asleep on the job tomorrow."

She smiled wearily and Tom went back to bed, content that she would at least try.

Mary and David brushed down the young foal in the yard.

"He's a handsome boy, don't you think Miss Mary?"

"He most certainly is. When he's a little older maybe you would like to ride him?"

David's eyes lit up.

"Can I? Are you teasing me Miss Mary?"

Mary laughed; she lit up around the youngster.

"Would I? First we have to give him a name. We can't keep calling him boy now can we."

"Chestnut Miss Mary, I think we should call him Chestnut on account he is the same colour as a chestnut."

"Good choice, and yes he is the same colour. Now, run along into the kitchen and fetch us both a nice mug of lemonade, I think we earned it."

Mary watched as the young lad skipped off to get the drinks.

"You look even more beautiful when that lads around, so you do."

Robert was standing across the yard at the stable door.

"Oh, get away with you. How long have you been there?"

"A while. Have you spoken to Elsbeth yet about young David coming here for a while?"

Mary scowled; she had wanted to have a talk about David but hadn't seemed to find the right time what with all the goings on.

"No, I thought it might be too soon with her just getting him back and now with the other developments over there. What do you make of it all?"

Robert grinned back at his wife.

"You know me, my love. I am not one for poking my nose where it doesn't fit. I will say this, I wish them the best of everything, not often a person is lucky enough to find that special one so good luck to them and that's all I'll say on the matter. This other matter, about the lad. Speak with her, you know it's a good idea for him and for us."

"What's a good idea Mr. Robert?"

David returned with the drinks and his inquisitive mind couldn't help but want to know what the grown-ups were discussing.

"I was saying to Miss Mary, do you reckon that young nipper David would enjoy mucking out this here stable, it's a might overpowering for my nose on such a warm day."

Mary laughed, knowing full well what reaction they would get from the lad.
"Oh, I would but I have to get back and do my maths lesson with Miss Williams."
"Never thought I'd live to see the day!"
laughed the man as he strolled back into the stable block chuckling to himself.

Mrs. Jennifer Williams was in the now converted 2nd parlour on the other side of the hall. Elsbeth had turned it into a schoolroom as the nursery was now a little overcrowded for all of the children. She stood and surveyed the large room with its chalkboard and desk at the far end and the row of polished wooden writing desks and chairs. Yes, this would do just fine, she thought. Far enough away and not a soul to recognise her in this quiet out of the way part of England.
"Are you Mrs. Williams?"
Mary asked as she walked into the airy room.
"I am, and you are?"
Mary sensed the hostility in her voice and had to bite her lip from taking this helper down a notch.
"I am Mary. I've returned young David for his lessons."
Mrs. Williams looked the woman up and down then proceeded to walk briskly to the front of the room. She turned and stared at Mary for a while before she spoke again.
"Was there something else?"
Mary didn't care for her tone one bit.
"Not really, I simply wanted to introduce myself."
"Thank you, then you may leave. Cook might give you a bite to eat if you go to the kitchen, tell her the governess said so."
Mary left, the smirk on her face quite evident to Sally.
"Ah Sally, can you kindly inform the children that they should be here and not playing in the nursery."
"I see you met Miss Mary. Lovely woman don't you think?"

Mrs. Williams shrugged.

"I barely noticed, but then I'm not engaged here to make small talk with the help."

Sally, who would normally have a heap of things to say, simply chuckled at the woman.

"Do you find something amusing?"

"Me? Oh no, nothing at all. I'll fetch the children. Oh, I would forget my head I would, Mrs. Stanhope asked me to remind you that she will be having her sister-in-law over this afternoon for tea, and you will be required to serve as the kitchen girl has gone home sick."

"Very well."

replied Mrs. Williams.

Milton was headed over to Canterbury for the day, he had so much paperwork to catch up on and truth be told he was secretly relieved to get a break from home with the mood his Gracie was in. Daisy met the Inspector at the vicarage as they were to travel over together.

"Morning, Sir."

"Morning Miss It's a warm one and no mistake, have you got everything?"

Daisy nodded as she climbed onto the cart.

"All in here."

She patted the large bag that she had set on her knees. The Inspector liked his young companion, her conversation was as easy going as the calm ripples on the shore at Dungeness on a Summer's Day.

"Have you heard from Mr. Richardson lately?"

Daisy grinned; it seemed odd hearing her Julian's name so formally.

"Mr. Richardson is well, thank you for asking. He will be coming here in a week's time, we thought it might be nice to have a small dinner party, you know so he can get acquainted with everyone, I do hope you and Mrs. Billoughby will join us."

Billoughby nodded, it would be nice to chat with the fella for longer than a couple of minutes.

"You just tell us where and when we'll be there."
The rest of the journey was a nice enough one, they caught a train and were soon deep in administrative catch up.

Reverend Tobias Moore took the letter from the young man, he waved him goodbye and returned to his breakfast. The Reverend had slept in today, his week had been a busy one and the man felt he deserved a restful morning. Placing the letter to one side he began to eat only to hear yet another knock at the door.
"Can't a man enjoy his breakfast in peace."
He grumbled to himself as once again he left his food and made his way to the door.
"Mr. Nash, good morning. I clean forgot you were making a delivery today, please come in."
"Have I interrupted you Reverend? I smell sausages."
"It isn't the first time I've been interrupted today Mr. Nash and I'm quite sure it won't be the last."
Mr. Nash frowned, he didn't like to think he had disturbed the man and his meal, but it was a nice morning and he wanted to get a head start on his deliveries as he had promised Mrs. Nash a drive out to the beach later that day.
"Sorry Reverend, I won't keep you."
He set the box down on the sideboard, the breakfast smell making his stomach grumble having missed his this morning.
"Sit down man, have a bite to eat with me, it sounds like you could do with something in your belly. There's plenty."
Mr. Nash didn't hesitate as he pulled up a chair and took a plate from Tobias.
"Very kind of you Reverend, I didn't want to wake the missus up just because I got up early."
"No problem. Is Mrs. Nash in the shop today?"
"No, not today, one of the boys is looking after things while I do my rounds."

Saving Grace | D M Roberts

The 2 men ate without further chatter, both sitting back satisfied once their plates were emptied. Mr. Nash swallowed down the cup of tea poured for him, he stretched out his legs and patted his stomach.
"That was a wonderful treat Reverend, thank you. I'm going to knock a few coins off your bill for that act of neighbourly kindness."
Reverend Moore shook his head.
"Wouldn't hear of it, I was never going to eat all of this, and I had quite forgotten young Miss Harvey was to have an early start today."
"What do you make of this business with Mrs. Stanhope and the lad Tom? I say good luck but there's many will have a sharp word or 2 to say about it."
Tobias' eyebrows rose on his forehead.
"Not for us to get involved I should think. The church may take a dim view on it I'm sure, as for me, well I have seen enough hardship for those 2 people in the past years to say grab your bit of happiness where you can. I do hope this comment stays between us Mr. Nash."
"It will indeed. Right-o, I best be off and thanks again for the breakfast. He-he, now that I know what a good cook you are I might be tempted to call another time. See you soon Reverend."
Mr. Nash let himself out leaving Tobias wondering why on earth he had said what he did. It was sure to come back to bite him, he could be sure of that.

The headquarters in Canterbury was full to the rafters when the pair arrived. There were people in every available space and the Inspector wondered whether this had been the best idea to have come all this way for a task he could quite easily have carried out at home.
"Oh, look. Over there, there's a desk in that corner."
Daisy nodded to the tiny desk that stood in the back of the large bustling room. She walked quickly over and as though claiming a piece of land triumphantly placed her bag onto the surface.

Saving Grace | D M Roberts

"Oi! I was going to sit there, Miss"
The tall man with a face as red as tomatoes stomped over to where Daisy now sat.
"I'm sorry Sir, but it was vacant when I spotted it therefore I believe it was up for grabs."
The man grumbled to himself as he glared at the smiling woman who was now setting out her things on the desk.
"Afternoon."
Billoughby nodded to the man that was still standing beside Daisy.
"I was telling the girl, I had my eye on this empty desk."
"And I was telling the gentleman that I got to it first."
replied Daisy with a look of annoyance at this persistent man who refused to leave.
"Are you from the area, your accent wouldn't suggest so."
Billoughby enquired as he set down his coat and hat on the chair behind him.
"No, I'm here investigating a missing person from the South West, and once I have finished my enquiries I'll be heading back to Redruth."
"I'm not familiar with it, I must say. Bad luck about the desk. I'm Inspector Billoughby and this is Constable Harvey, pleased to meet you."
The man shook Billoughby's hand as he continued to scour the room for a space to sit.
"You're not a secretary?"
He levelled the question at Daisy.
"No, Sir."
"I don't think I've known a female Constable. I'm Andrew Hirst, I work with various departments when it comes to persons of interest."
"There's a first time for everything. Oh, there, a desk has just become vacant."
Daisy pointed behind the man.

"Well spotted Constable Harvey, nice to meet you both."
The man left the pair to secure his space.

Chapter Two

Elsbeth sat in the parlour as she waited for Mary to arrive, the children were now busy amusing themselves in various parts of the house. Ruby's melodic piano chords drifted softly through the rooms.

"Ah, Mrs. Williams. Please set the tray down over here, my guest should be arriving any time." Jennifer Williams did as she was asked, and Elsbeth noticed that the woman seemed slightly out of sorts. There was a tap on the door and Elsbeth shook the thought from her mind.

"Miss Mary, ma'am."

Sally stepped back and much to the dismay of Jennifer Williams, the woman she had insulted earlier in the day, stepped into the room.

"Mary, it's so good to see you, do come and sit. Are you well?" Mary hugged her sister-in-law, shooting a look over her shoulder at the 'governess' who stood with her eyes firmly fixed on the floor.

"I'm very well, thank you. The children are positively thriving, I had a quick talk with William and Jacob in the courtyard and they tell me they have settled in well."

"They have, all of the children seem to be happier than they were when they first arrived."

The 2 women talked about the children and their particular personalities for a short time until Elsbeth beckoned Mrs. Williams to pour for them.

"You haven't met our new housemaid, have you Mary?" Mary smiled.

"I did as it happens, this morning."

Mrs. Williams poured the tea and said nothing, however, she thought plenty, A housemaid! How dare she.

Saving Grace | D M Roberts

"Thank you, Mrs. Williams, you may leave us for the moment. I shall ring should I need you."

In the kitchen Sally could not contain her laughter, she would have loved to be a fly on the wall in the parlour but the look on Mrs. Williams face told her all she needed to know.
"All okay with the Madame and her guest?"
The laughter, still evident in her voice.
"I am to wait for the bell."
Replied Mrs. Williams, she had no intention of entering into any kind of conversation with this hag of a woman.
"That's the job of a housemaid, dearie."
said the cook as she put the top crust on the pie she was making. Mrs. Williams poured herself a cup of tea and went to stand at the open kitchen door. She watched the clouds roll across the sky toward the coast and wondered how long she would remain here.
"What are you looking at up there, Miss?"
It was Martha, one of the children with a more curious nature.
"The clouds, see how they move toward the sea, which means we are in for a cold spell." Martha shrugged, in her mind, clouds were clouds and what did that have to do with hot or cold.
"Why?"
Continued the young girl.
"Because it is coming from the North, the north wind is a cold one."
"But it's warm."
replied Martha as she made herself dizzy with the watching of clouds.
"It will change, make sure you wrap a little warmer tomorrow."
The bell rang from inside the kitchen, tossing the remainder of the tea into a bush, Mrs. Williams left the child to return indoors.

"Can you fetch another pot, thank you."

Elsbeth didn't look up as she gave her instruction, which vexed the woman no end. Taking the tray, Mrs. Williams once again left the room. This was not the type of working relationship she was used to, and she did not care for it. She swiftly returned with the pot and poured. Mary smiled at her all the time, a smile that didn't reflect friendliness, it was more a smirk.

"You may leave."

Mrs. Williams left the room, and the women continued their talking.

"Elsbeth, dear. I wanted to talk with you about young David. Robert and I have discussed it at length, and we would dearly love to have him stay with us for a while. He has so taken to helping on the farm and we believe it would be good for him, and us if I'm honest."

Elsbeth sat back, she knew that the pair had become very fond of the boy, more so than the other children. It may not be a bad thing for David, he did get along so well with Mary and Robert. On the other hand, Elsbeth felt that she had only just got him back and what kind of a message would she be sending to David if she let him go from the house he now called home?

"Don't you think it's a little soon, you know, after the upset?"

Mary had imagined this would come up and was ready with her answer.

"We thought, because David had stayed a few times before he was away, that this would be a simple method of getting the boy back to some sort of normal."

Elsbeth nodded, it made sense to her but how would David react?

"I will have a talk with David, I feel we must go gently with this. Can you leave it with me for a few days at least?"

"Of course, it is merely a suggestion, dear. So, how is your new housemaid working out?"

"She seems to be good with the children although, today I feel a strangeness about her that I haven't noticed before. It may be me. What did you make of her on your first meeting?"

Mary laughed.

"She thought I was your maid; I imagine she is now feeling very embarrassed."

Elsbeth's mouth dropped open.

"NO! Whatever did she say to you?"

"Oh, I wouldn't worry about it too much, easy mistake to make."

"But I do worry about it, she can't be disrespectful to my family, or my guests."

"I was still wearing my working clothes, and she did offer me a bite to eat."

Mary laughed as she said this, she had been spoken to much worse in her life.

"It's no excuse, Mary. I am tempted to have words with the woman."

"Please don't, not on my account. So, how are you feeling after tea with the Billoughby's? Grace is going to take a lot of work if you want my opinion."

Elsbeth sighed, she knew this would come up and as yet she had no coherent answer to this situation or question.

"Tom and I are glad that we no longer have to hide our feelings, it has never been my way nor his. Grace; there will be the issue, which is a shame because we got on so well. In the yard she told me in not so many words that I was denying her son the chance to have children of his own and a long relationship, she mentioned the backlash we will likely face from the people in the village. Am I such a terrible person to want happiness with a person half my age?" Elsbeth asked.

"We know more than most that time doesn't wait, we have no idea what tomorrow may throw at us and they may talk behind your back but in time they will be talking about somebody else. It is wonderful to see you smiling again, dear, don't allow anyone to take that from you."

"And Grace, what do I do about Grace?"

"You continue to live your life, she will come around when she sees how committed you and Tom are to each other."
"Thank you, Mary. I will be sure to let you know the outcome of my talk with David and keep you informed of how everything is going in other areas. Shall I walk you out?"
Mary stood, straightened down her skirts and opened the door of the parlour.

Daisy put the final sheet of paper into the tray, sat back and yawned. There was nothing quite so tiring as paperwork, she liked her job; no, she loved her job. Daisy loved the adventure and the piecing together of a case, what she didn't enjoy so much was the writing up of the case. Billoughby chuckled, he knew how boring his constable found all of this, as he did himself.
"That's that, shall we make a move for home, or would you like me to find you some more to do?"
Daisy screwed up her face and shook her head.
"Did anyone ever tell you how funny you are, Inspector?"
"Not lately."
"I wonder why."
Laughed Daisy as she pulled on her coat. They started to make their way out of the room to be stopped by the man Andrew Hirst.
"You 2 are off now?"
"We are, it was nice to meet you and sorry about the desk earlier." replied Daisy.
"I don't suppose I could trouble you for a ride to the station?"
He asked as he too put on his overcoat.
"I don't see why not. Are you headed out of Canterbury back to home?"
Asked the Inspector.
"Not home, no. I'm going to a place called…hang on, oh, there it is. Dover."

"Oh, not too far from us. Come on then, if we're all set we'll get moving."
Billoughby bid farewell to the men in the office and the 3 of them made their way to the waiting cart.
 The journey was a mixed bag of chatter and long silences with Daisy catching the odd nap here and there. Billoughby listened to the man's story about his missing person with vague interest. It transpired that a prominent businessman and his elderly parents had been found dead in their quiet rural village home; bringing the investigator here in the hope of tracking down the culprit. Billoughby nodded and shook his head where appropriate but in truth he had other things going on in his mind and as this was not an investigation that involved him he didn't feel too bad in his half-hearted attempt to listen.

 The train pulled into the station and the 3 parted ways. Billoughby went off home to the village, Daisy went into Ashford to meet some friends and Mr. Hirst, well Mr. Hirst went his own separate way.

 Grace was busy in the kitchen when Milton returned.
 "In here, love."
Well, she certainly sounded chirpier than she did this morning, he thought as he changed from his shoes to his slippers. Kissing Grace on her cheek he slumped down into the kitchen chair.
 "Long day, I don't know if it's my getting older or the hustle of the headquarters makes me so tired. How has your day been, my love?"
Grace placed her husband's dinner in front of him and then poured him a drink.
 "Get away, you're not that old. It's been a nice and quiet day of baking and gardening. Cate called by for a minute but other than that I haven't set eyes on anyone. How was your trip?" Billoughby looked down at his dinner, his mouth watered at the prospect of Grace's speciality stew but judging by the steam coming from it he

had a minute or 2 to quickly re-tell Grace about his odd encounter with Mr. Hirst. Grace listened attentively; adding the occasional comment here and there. Milton finally tackled his dinner and he sat there, fully restored by the meal. He wondered if he should broach the subject of Tom and decided he wouldn't spoil the tranquil moment. Instead, they washed up together and talked of lighter things including their granddaughter.
 "She is going to be a real heartbreaker, such a bonny child." cooed Grace.
 "Takes after her grandmother."
He smiled as they sat together on the sofa.

Mr Andrew Hirst unpacked his small bag of personal items and placed them neatly on the dresser. He had a clean shirt and undergarments, a few toiletry items and several notebooks. The room was nothing too grand considering its position in the building but for the paltry sum it cost he wasn't complaining, all he needed was somewhere to lay his head. He could put up with the noise from the Hotel below, he had stayed in rooms for the past month now and was quickly getting accustomed to them. Breakfast was not included in the charge, but dinner was; he was glad of this as his day had not afforded him the time to eat. After a small rest he went downstairs to collect his meal, he ordered a mug of ale and sat down in the corner of the restaurant to eat.

The Lord Warden Hotel was busy that night, there was a lot of chatter and excitement about a previous guest being the first woman to have flown across the channel, but Mr. Hirst had had his fill of the workings of women so did not engage in the conversation from the waiting staff. The meal was satisfactory and well received by the man with the strange accent. He tossed a coin to the server and ventured outside for a walk in the cooling sea air that brushed against his face.

Saving Grace | D M Roberts

His thoughts were that of where he would next concentrate his search, for he was sure that the person he sought would intend to leave by ship and when they did he would be waiting.

"Nice evening for it."

The voice startled him as he turned to face the stranger. The stranger was an older gentleman, dressed in expensive looking clothing and sporting a cap. His stature was short and robust, Mr. Hirst could hear the wheeze in the other man's chest.

"It is. Do you live in these parts?"

asked Mr. Hirst; he neither cared nor wanted the conversation from a stranger but his polite nature pressed him to ask.

"Not far, I have been to dinner with acquaintances and felt the need to walk it off as it were. You, I assume, are not from the area."

"You would be correct in your assumption, Sir. A break, I'm having a small break."

"Ah, a man should strive to rest when the opportunity presents itself. Are you staying at the Warden?"

"Indeed. Yes, only for a short time and then I imagine I shall move on to a different place. Do you have a chest complaint? Excuse my forthright question, Sir, my mother had a similar sounding ailment."

The older man smiled as he nodded.

"Sadly, I do. I find the sea air helps along with regular walks. How did your mother fare?"

"Quite so. Mother managed it well, much like yourself she kept on her feet and refused to let it beat her."

"Good for her, it is the sitting about with no will that does it to many. That is not my way at all."

"I shall leave you to your walk, good evening, Sir."

"Thank you, and if you find yourself in the area of Hythe, please feel free to call on me. Here is my card. Have a pleasant evening."

The man tipped his cap and continued on his stroll along the walkway. Mr. Hirst looked at the card in the now dimming light, he slipped it into his breast pocket for it may come in handy.

Cate did not feel good, and as much as she protested, Adam sent her back off to bed.

"What about the little one, how are you supposed to go to work and look after the little one with me in here?"

"Don't you worry about that, get back into bed and leave it to me." He ordered.

"But Adam."

She wailed, her voice sounding weary.

"Shush, try to get some rest. I will fetch the bowl and some fresh water. Now sleep!"

Cate was rarely ill; she didn't like it but on this occasion she gave in and did what was asked. Adam returned with the water and bowl then closed the door quietly.

In the kitchen he began making breakfast, he was fortunate that during his time away he had learned to fend for himself if he had to. Maisy was still sleeping in her crib, that was a blessing for the moment. Grace was calling this morning, that made Adam feel better to have a possible extra pair of hands, he knew his mother would take charge whether he asked her or not. The sound of a visitor at the door, followed by Maisy's gurgling brought Adam's thoughts back to breakfast, going to fetch the little one and answer the knock at the door.

"Good morning, son, and good morning to you my bonny girl." Billoughby took the child from her father as he entered the home.

"Morning, Pa. It's early for a call, is everything alright at home?" Billoughby was busy cooing and laughing with his granddaughter.

"Everything is fine, lad. Your dadda worries far too much, little miss, yes he does."

"Why so early? Is Ma calling later, she said she would, only Cate isn't feeling all that good today and I might need a hand with young Maisy."

Saving Grace | D M Roberts

Billoughby frowned, settling Maisy into her chair he put his hand on Adam's shoulder.

"What's the matter with Cate? Is there anything I can do, do you want me to fetch the doctor?"

"We think it's something she's eaten Pa, she'll be fine after a bit of rest."

"You're sure? It's no bother for me to go and bring the doctor back."

"We'll see how it goes, if she's still no better later today then we'll call for the doctor. Terrible sick she was last night. Small wonder there was anything left in her belly for the amounts that kept coming up."

"Thanks, son. I don't care to hear about the contents of your wife's' stomach, not at this time of the day, or any other for that matter. Do you want me to take young Maisy back with me, your Ma has been up for a while now. Which brings me to the reason for calling; do you have any of those nice beans you've been growing? They were so tasty."

Adam laughed, his father could handle many things and more but when it came to the sickness he had never been one to revel in description.

"I pulled a fresh clump only last night. I'll wrap a bundle for you. Yes, if Ma doesn't mind it would be a help."

Adam began separating the beans from the large mound sitting on the sideboard, he wrapped a piece of twine around a large bunch and handed it to his father.

"Great stuff, thanks Adam. Here, have you seen anything of your brother since last week? I've barely set eyes on him, mind you I have been out a few days."

"No, I can't say that I have. Is Ma any better on the whole thing yet? I know she isn't pleased about it, but he's never looked happier to me."

"It'll take time, it isn't how things were done in our day, and we take a while longer to come around to new ways."
"But you're okay with it, aren't you?"
Billoughby shrugged, nobody had asked him what he thought about the situation.
"It makes no difference to me, son. I'd rather the lad had someone his own age but who's to say he would be truly happy, who's to say a younger woman would actually provide him with children. I say life is short, get what happiness you can, while you can."
The pair were interrupted by the sounds of Cate being sick from up the stairs.
"I'd best go and check on her, won't be a minute."
Adam left Billoughby and Maisy as he ran up to his wife.

Grace was concerned about her daughter-in-law and why Adam had not wanted to call the doctor over.
"It's down to them, love. I offered to fetch him, but Adam was of the mind that they would wait and see."
"What if it's the same thing that poor Esther had. I would never forgive myself if we could have done something, it isn't right, this wait and see nonsense."
Grace could be stubborn when she wanted to but as Billoughby knew, so could Adam.
"It didn't sound much like coughing to me, that thing Esther had was a lot of coughing. No, reckon it's as the lad said and she's eaten a thing that hasn't agreed with her."
"Did you see Tom this morning? He was gone before I woke, no breakfast either, that won't do him any good."
"He will most likely get breakfast at the farm, Mary usually makes it up for the farm hands. I didn't see him, he was gone when I came downstairs. Busy time again, for the farm."
Grace nodded, busy time plus he was avoiding her.

"Come along young Maisy, let's get you ready and we can go for a nice walk."
"Are you going anywhere special love, or just a walk?"
Grace continued putting the little ones' outdoor clothes on her.
"I thought I might call over to see Reverend Moore, we still have things to sort out with Daisy's wedding coming up. Oh, and the parish committee has some other items that need going over. What about you, do you have plans for the day?"
Billoughby nodded, he always had something to do.
"Yes, a few local issues and a couple of not so local issues I've been asked to cast an eye over. Give my best to Tobias, will you?"
"I will, hot tea in the pot. See you later, say bye-bye to Grandpa."

Reverend Moore read his letter again; he had read it several times over the days in which he had it. In his mind he imagined it had many possibilities, one of which he could hear joyfully singing away to herself as she dusted the large wooden cabinets in the sitting room. He assumed at some point that there would be a backlash of sorts regarding the courtship of Miss Daisy Harvey and Mr. Richardson, but what to do about it, that was the thing. The reverend often pondered what great achievements might be made if the church would only put its efforts in places other than that of the gossiping of those small minded village few that had nothing better to do with their time. Ah, well. There was little he could do until he knew what *it* was.
"All spotless and ready for inspection, Sir."
Laughed Daisy as she tidied away the cleaning things.
"I daresay it is, you seldom leave a speck of dust. You are too good to me young lady."
"It's the least I can do, you have always been so kind to me, besides I need the practice for when I become Mrs. Julian Richardson."
"I can hardly imagine that a man of such stature would have his wife doing the cleaning chores." Laughed Tobias.

"I can't say I will put up too much of an argument with that. What time are you expecting Mrs. Billoughby, I could put a few sandwiches out if you like?"

"That's very kind, but no, you have things to do, and I've kept you long enough. Mrs. Billoughby will be happy with a slice of cake and a pot of tea, I'm sure."

Daisy turned to leave; she paused as she spied the letter on the table. Over the past few days, she had noticed the reverend pick it up and put it down several times.

"Is that causing you a worry, Reverend?"

She nodded toward the folded piece of paper.

"Oh, a little but nothing I'm sure that can't be dealt with."

"If you want to talk about anything, you know I will listen and be discreet?"

"I do and thank you dear girl. Now, off you go."

Daisy waved; she knew that the reverend was not the type of person to burden others.

"David, David would you come into the parlour for a moment?" Called Elsbeth as the young boy went tearing through the large hall. Coming to a swift, if ungraceful halt, David peeped around the doorframe.

"Am I in trouble, Miss?"

Elsbeth chuckled out loud, shaking her head as she stretched out her hand to the boy.

"Do you think you are?"

"I don't think so, I ain't, haven't, done nothing today yet. Have I?"

"No, dearest boy. I wanted to have a quiet talk with you. Miss Mary, and Mr. Robert have asked if you would like to pay them a visit."

"I visit all the time, Miss"

"You do, that is true. They would like to know how you might feel about spending a whole week with them, like a holiday. Now, I told Miss Mary that you might not want to do this because you have been away for such a long time, and you might think it is because we have the other children here now; Miss Mary said that you were far too clever to think such nonsense."

"Miss Mary said I was clever? Well, blow me. I like it here Miss, but I reckon a nice holiday would be fun. I can come back when I have had my holiday?"

David asked, his little face stared in earnest at Elsbeth.

"You need to understand David, this is your home and no matter how many times you may go on a holiday or anywhere else, you will always come home to me. I'm like your extra mother, you have one looking over you, and you have me looking after you."

David was a tough young man, the glint now appearing in his eyes did not betray him as he stood up straight, hugged Elsbeth and replied.

"Well Miss, as long as you can manage without me for a week but if you need me back for anything send the stable hand."

"I will make a note of that. Now off you go to play with the others."

She smiled as she watched the lad walk from the room. Her thoughts turned to the day when she first saw the trio of underfed and dirty street urchins, a small tear escaped her and rolled quietly down her face as thoughts of 'what if' filled her mind. Shaking her head she went back to her correspondence. The first lot of letters were the usual invitations to social gatherings that Elsbeth didn't much care for, nor have the time. It was the letter with almost the scrawl of an uneducated person that caught her attention. It simply read *God will punish your wicked ways…*

Cate had been in bed for most of the day, Adam checking frequently as pottered around in the now quiet house. Grace tapped at the kitchen door and pushed it open, not waiting for a reply.

"How is she?"

Grace asked as she put the sleeping child into her crib.

"I don't know Ma, she doesn't have a fever and she isn't coughing but still she has sickness. I tried giving her some broth, but it came back up. She looks so tired; would you go up and see what you think?"

Grace didn't wait to be asked again and was halfway up the stairs before Adam had finished speaking.

Cate looked pale, her skin wasn't hot, but it looked whiter than normal. She flickered her eyelids as Grace entered the room.

"Ma, hello. How is little Maisy?"

"Maisy is just fine my love, how are you feeling?"

"I have felt better, but not today."

Grace sat on the bed.

"Can you remember what you ate yesterday?"

Cate shook her head.

"Nothing out of the ordinary, it's the smell, I keep catching the smell of a thing and my belly just turns in such a way."

Grace sniffed; she could smell something although it wasn't an unpleasant odour.

"Is it your flowers, there in the vase?"

Grace stood up and brought the vase from the windowsill forward and within seconds Cate was reaching for her bowl.

"Yes, yes, take it away, please."

Grace nodded and left the room.

"Adam, have you more of these?"

She held up the vase.

"We have, they're so pretty I thought Cate would like them around the house. Why?"

"Collect them up for me, there's a dear. Cate will be fine, I think I know what is going on here." A puzzled Adam retrieved 4 vases of the offending blooms and placed them on the kitchen table. Grace swiftly took the hoard outside and walked down to the far end of the garden where she tossed them over the fence.

"What are you doing Ma, have you lost your mind?"
Grace laughed as she washed her hands.
"Can I be the first?" Said Grace as she winked, kissed her son and left.
Adam wondered if he should go and find his father, for his mother had surely now lost her faculties!

Chapter Three

David could not contain his excitement much to the annoyance of Mrs. Williams; who had told the boy off several times during breakfast and again during lessons.
"If you cannot listen and comply then you will most certainly NOT be going to stay at the farm. Do I make myself clear, child?"
David wasn't very fond of this one, he missed Miss Esther a lot, he even preferred Sally to this one and that said it all.
"Miss Elsbeth said I AM going to stay with Miss Mary, and Mr. Robert and you can't stop me. Miss Elsbeth is in charge, not you."
The exasperated woman threw her hands up into the air. How was she supposed to control such an unruly child, a child that by all accounts was nothing more than a beggar on the streets. It wasn't right!

Sally came into the schoolroom with a tray of drinks and shortbread.
"Time for a break, Miss Elsbeth said to bring the children some refreshment."
Placing the large tray down Sally took a bite from the sweet biscuit, they were still warm and whatever words went between her and Cook, Sally knew that nobody baked better than Cook.
"Do you have to do that? You would be best served taking your food in the servants area and not in my schoolroom."
Barked Mrs. Williams to the disinterested Sally.
"Is she going to be staying forever?"
whispered Ruby as Sally handed the youngster a cup.
"I hope not."
Chuckled Sally as quietly as she could with Mrs. Williams glaring at the pair intently. In turn, Ruby, Martha, William, Jacob, David and

Doris chose a shortbread shape from the tray. They liked that Cook put small pieces of fruit from the garden into them, and that she took the time to make shapes.

"Would you like one, Mrs. Williams?"

asked Doris as she chewed on her piece.

"No manners! That is one of your many flaws, you have no manners. We do not speak with food rumbling around in our mouths."

Doris shrunk back into the skirts of Sally.

"They're children, time for manners will come and they have them when they're needed!"

Sally felt her voice raise, as much as she had protested the extra work at the off-set, Sally had become very fond of the strange little group in her way.

"You may leave, take the tray."

Was the only reply from Mrs. Williams.

"She thinks she is something, I must say. The way she talks to those little ones, the missus wouldn't like it and then there's the way she talks to us, like she's better than we are."

Cook turned around; her hands still doughy from the batch of pastry that she was busy preparing.

"Who are you talking about?"

"That woman, calls herself a governess, my back teeth she's a governess, more like a prison warden if you ask me. Made our little Doris upset she did, I tell you Cook, she should mind her step and no mistake."

Sally could tell by the changing look on Cook's face that they were no longer alone in the kitchen.

"What exactly did she do to upset Doris?"

Mary demanded. Sally turned around to see the anger on Mary's face.

"I'm sorry, Miss Mary. I shouldn't have spoken out of turn."

Mary tapped her foot on the tiled floor, she had no patience most of the time with Sally.

"Sally, what did she do to Doris?"

Sally retold the incident as Mary's face grew redder.

"I know it's not my place to be telling tales, Miss Mary but I have a bad feeling about this one." Mary could hardly berate the woman standing in front of her, after all, she had that same sense in the pit of her stomach.

"Leave it to me, I will deal with this. Sally, listen to what I say, it is your place. You too, Cook. Keep your ears open and your eyes on the watch. If there are further incidents please come to see me." Sally, and cook nodded. It wasn't often that Mary got into household politics with the staff, but she would if it concerned the family that she loved.

"Do we tell the missus Miss Mary?"
asked Cook.

"I wouldn't bother Mrs. Stanhope with this just yet, she has many things on her mind at present. Sally, has young David got everything he needs for his stay?"

Cook nodded and went back to her pastry as Sally and Mary left the room.

"Yes, Miss I'll go up and fetch it, he's been that excited this morning, he's hardly been able to sit still."

"I'm glad he's excited, he does so love the farm and we love having him there. Is Mrs. Stanhope in her study?"

"She is, Miss I'll get the things."

Sally went off to get David's overnight bag as Mary ventured to Elsbeth's study. Mary stopped at the schoolroom door, she wasn't in the habit of listening in but she felt compelled to. The voice of Mrs. Williams was loud, louder than it needed to be. Mary could hear what sounded like sobs coming from inside the room, she opened the door to see Doris standing at the front of the room, her little face red and wet with tears. Mrs. Williams stopped shouting and turned to see Mary walking quickly toward her.

"What is the meaning of this? Doris, dear, come to me."

Mary put her arms out and the child leapt into them.

"The child is upset because she doesn't know her numbers, she is too timid that she gets upset so easily. You mustn't cry every time you get a sum wrong, girl."

The word, girl, stuck in Mary's throat. She knew the woman was goading her.

"The child has a name. Doris, in case you didn't know, and Doris along with the other children in this room have had a bad start to life, therefore we do not expect them to be spoken to in the way that you are speaking to them now. Should I hear of this happening again I will leave you in little doubt that Mrs. Stanhope will be told."

Mary slammed the door as she left.

Elsbeth stared at the piece of paper in her hand, hearing the knock on her door she thrust it into her side drawer.

"Come in. Hello Mary, my goodness is that the time already?"

"Has it been a very busy morning for you, my dear?"

Elsbeth yawned, her arms stretching up above her head showing Mary just how thin her sister-in-law was becoming.

"A little. Shall I call for some tea?"

"That's very kind but I have had one. It is still set that David will come to stay for a few days? I sent Sally to collect his overnight things."

Elsbeth nodded, she would miss him terribly but even she knew that it would be a nice change for the youngster.

"Sally tells me that he has been awake since sun-up, if not before! I mustn't have heard him, although I did have the company of sweet Doris in the night. I do so worry about her dreams, they make her so fearful, Mary. It is not the best for the child to sleep with me but what else can I do to make her less afraid?"

"I think if the little one is fretting she needs a mother's comfort. You do the right thing by all of these children Elsbeth, there are many that say it. Have you had any luck finding a more suitable helper for them?"
Elsbeth could not hide the surprise at Mary's question.
"You don't think Mrs. Williams is a good fit?"
Mary shrugged. It wasn't for her to say anything about the running of the household, but she knew she would not be able to hold her tongue for too long.
"I only say this lightly my dear, I feel the children would be better suited with a, let's say, a happier disposition?"
"I too have given it some thought, I am making enquiries albeit discreetly. There is a young lady I am set to meet at the end of the week, she comes highly recommended, and I believe to be a very lively soul. I have not as yet spoken to Mrs. Williams about this as I may feel inclined to keep her on in the role of housemaid."
Mary couldn't stop the chuckle that sprang from her lips.
"Please can I be here when you impart this news?"
Elsbeth gave a tut and smiled, what a funny one her once rigid sister-in-law had become.

Cate stared at Adam, Adam in turn sat at the table and nodded.
"Whatever did she mean?"
She asked her husband as she bounced little Maisy on her lap.
"I don't know. I worry about Ma; do you think she is suffering from a brain fever?"
Cate grinned.
"Your Ma is as sharp as a pup's new tooth. Funny how she knew straight off what was causing my sickness, don't you think?"
"Yes, no more evening primrose flowers for you!"
"Do you think I should see the doctor, just to make sure it wasn't anything else?"
Adam scratched his head, maybe it would do no harm.

"You said you were going for a walk in the village today, you might as well ask while you're there."

Adam had stayed home with Cate and Maisy the day after to see for certain that his wife was well enough.

"If you need any help, or feel sick again, send the young lad out to the farm to fetch me. Promise me now."

Cate kissed her husband as she handed him a packet with his lunch.

"Away with you, we'll be fine, won't we little one?"

Maisy gurgled; her bright green eyes fixed on her mother's face. Adam stroked his daughters head and headed out the door to work. Cate sat and thought about what Grace had said, it couldn't be…could it?

"Hello, are you in here dear?"

The familiar voice of Inspector Billoughby rang out in the room.

"In here, come in, pa. Maisy, it's Grandpa, look."

Billoughby ruffled the little one's hair as he sat down. Cate poured out a cup of tea.

"What brings you down here? You just missed Adam, I made him go to work today, he's such a fuss-pot."

"I came to see you, to see how you're doing. Gracie tells me it was evening primrose flowers, a strange one that. Did Gracie ever tell you about her dealings with them?"

Cate shook her head.

"No, I can't imagine what sort of dealings a person would have with a flower."

Billoughby laughed, he laughed loud and heartily, making Maisy jump.

"Did Grandpa scare you? I'm sorry my precious girl. Ask her, ask Gracie about it. I hear young David has gone for a stay at Mary and Robert's, Tom tells me the lad is at home there."

"Can't you tell me? About the flowers I mean? Yes, Adam said he's so inquisitive about everything there, make a great farmer one day so I hear. Mary, she loves the bones of that boy, so she does."

Billoughby was shaking his head, a wry smile on his face.
"Women talk, I'll leave that to Gracie. He will be a fine young man, no doubt about it. Right then, I'll be on my way unless you need anything?"
Cate was still as baffled as she was when he arrived.
"No, thank you pa. Give my best to Grace and we'll call in later this afternoon."
Billoughby drank down his tea and went on his way.

David sat on the fence watching Tom and Adam wrestle the lame ram to the ground, he thought this was cruel as it had a sore leg, and they didn't. The young boy watched as the 2 men rolled him onto his back.
"I reckon that's him done for a bit."
Said Tom, eventually as he got to his feet. David only heard the words 'done for' he came bouncing off the fence toward the startled pair, waving his arms and shouting as he ran.
"NO, NO. You can't."
his face sweaty, anger raging from his young eyes. Tom held out his arm and swept David up as he passed, the young boy kicking and wriggling with Tom wondering what the devil had gotten into him.
"Whoa, there youngster. Calm yourself down, tell us what it is."
Adam stood back from David's reach as the child continued to kick.
"PUT ME DOWN."
His shouting soon brought Mary running from the house.
"Whatever is going on out here? David, what has upset you?"
"They're going to kill it, Miss Mary, I heard them, said it's done for they did, heard it with my own ears."
Mary stared at Tom, he shook his head and put David back on the ground.
"Tom? Adam, is this true?"

Mary knew that on a farm, these things are often a necessary occurrence but to say it in front of a child, well that was not the best of ideas.

"You daft bugger, we didn't say we were going to kill him! He's a good old fella this one, I said that's him done for a bit. He needs rest is all, same as if you hurt your foot."

Tom chuckled as he explained to David, Adam dug his elbow into his brother's side, he could see that Miss Mary did not find this a chuckling matter.

"You're not going to eat him?"

David asked, his face hopeful.

"Heavens, no lad. Besides, he'd be tough as my Pa's old boots and I don't know about you, but I like my meat nice and soft."

"Come with me, David."

Mary took his hand, and they left the 2 men to deal with the ram.

"Are you taking me back to the Hall? I'm sorry I made a fuss, Miss Mary."

She laughed.

"No, silly. Why would I do that? We all make mistakes. No, what I thought is that we should have a talk about the ways of the farm and what is done here."

David looked up at Mary, he was confused as he thought he knew a lot about the farm. Mr. Robert had told him all kinds of things.

"Because I was shouting, you told Mrs. Williams off for shouting. I don't like shouting, Miss but I thought they were going to do him in."

"Ah, I see. No, dear I don't like shouting but sometimes we may need to raise our voice and sometimes, we do not. Do you see the chickens over there, David?"

He nodded, he liked the chickens, and he liked that Mr. Robert let him feed them; they would rush over when he came to them with the big bowl of grains. Mary continued.

"The chickens lay eggs and we collect them up to sell or to eat. That nice breakfast we have in the morning has eggs from these very chickens. Sometimes we have chicken on Sunday with our dinner, you said how much you enjoyed it do you remember?"

"Yes, it was lovely, Miss Mary with your gravy all covering it."

"That was one of our chickens David. You see, on a farm we grow things for people to eat, and we rear animals that people also eat. Do you understand, dear?"

David was still fighting the idea that he had eaten one of his friends, and what's more, he enjoyed it! His frown was evident to Mary as she tried to explain.

"That is what farmers do my dear, they provide food for the people in the villages and yes, sometimes we eat the animals, it is the reason you never hear Mr. Robert giving them a name. It would make him too sad.

"But not the ram?
Tom said."

"No, not the ram. The ram has a very different role on the farm, but we will talk about that particular thing a different day. Now, are you ready for some lunch?"

"Yes, but no chicken."

He laughed. David wasn't sure if he wanted to be a farmer anymore, he would decide after lunch.

Cate sat there with her mouth open, baby Maisy perched on her lap.

"Are you quite alright, dear girl?"

Asked the doctor, peering at her through his small spectacles.

"I don't know, I need time to think about this. Are you certain?"

The doctor let out a small chortle, it wasn't the first time somebody had sat in that chair with that very same surprised look.

"As sure as I've ever been in my 40 years of practising medicine. Is it a problem?"

"I just can't believe it, us only just settling in the house and all. I don't know what my Adam will say."
The doctor gave a sympathetic smile.
"He will be delighted, of that I am sure. It does take 2 people my dear, it is not solely down to you."
Cate knew this, of course she did but could they afford another mouth at the moment? Was the small cottage even big enough? They would grow, children do, and then what? They would have to move to a bigger house and poor Adam would have to work even harder and longer to support them. Oh, what were they to do?
"Thank you doctor. I'll not take up any more of your time."
Still stunned, Cate made her way to the door carrying her daughter in her arms.
"I will call and check on you in a couple of weeks but if you have any problems in the meantime, please come and see me or send for me. Oh, and Mrs. Billoughby, please don't worry. It isn't good for either of you."
Cate nodded and mumbled her thanks.

"Cate, Cate dear. Wait up, I'll walk with you."
turning around Cate got the second surprise of the day.
"Well as I live and breathe! Miss Geraldine."
Geraldine rushed forward, her arms wrapping around Cate and Maisy both.
"It is so good to see you, and you little one, haven't you gotten big?"
"Are you expected? Nobody told me you were coming."
Cate said excitedly, forgetting for a moment her own news.
"No, it was a last minute decision. How is Tobias, excuse me, Reverend Moore?"
"He is well, I saw him only this morning on my way down to the doctor."
Geraldine's brow furrowed.

"Are you unwell dear, or is it the little one?"
Cate smiled, she couldn't tell her news, not until you had spoken to Adam.
"I had a small bug, but I am much better now, thank you. Will you be staying at the Hall? I'm sure it would please Mrs. Stanhope, expect she'll be glad of the company."
Geraldine hadn't thought that far ahead and was on her way to speak to Elsbeth about this very thing.
"I am hoping to, I know it is an imposition, but I had no chance to write and ask. Do you think she will be able to accommodate me?"
"She will be thrilled to see you, so she will. We all are. What have you been doing with your time away?"
"All in good time my dear, for it is a long and not so interesting story that is best left to another day."
This intrigued Cate, but she didn't press the matter.
"Is it a secret that you're here? I do love a little mystery."
Chuckled Cate.
"Oh. no, nothing at all so melodramatic as a mystery. How have things been since I was last here?"
Enquired Geraldine, for she had been lapse in her correspondence due to other matters.
"Oh, you know village life, small problems that work themselves out and bigger problems that people spend a whole lot of time gossiping about but never say it out loud. You heard about poor young Esther?"
Cate stopped walking, shifting Maisy over to her other arm.
"The young girl from the hall?"
"Yes, the fever took her not long after you left. Poor thing, Mrs. Stanhope said it was mercifully quick."
Geraldine was the one to stop now.
"What a terrible thing to happen, it must have been a shock to everyone, especially the children. They were very fond of her as I recall."

Cate nodded.

"They were too, they have a new helper now. Mrs. Williams and from some accounts she's a one and others say she's fine. I suppose it takes all kinds."

"Hm, I shall draw my own conclusion. I often find that to be the best way. Well, I shall say goodbye for now, you will see me soon I am sure. Dear, please don't be offended but try to rest a little, you look positively pale."

Geraldine waved and turned down the lane toward the hall.

"Pale, is it Maisy? I think my complexion is the least of my problems, wouldn't you say bonny girl?"

"Sally, can you please answer that door. I have heard it 3 times now."

Elsbeth was busy settling Dolly and Lily in the nursery for their afternoon nap. Elsbeth stared at the pair, it was remarkable that the 2 were as alike as peas in a pod.

"Just going down there now, Miss I was changing young master Jacob on account he had fallen over and cut his knee."

Elsbeth silently berated herself for her impatient nature, and where was Mrs. Williams?

"I'm sorry, Sally. When you have a minute. Is Jacob alright?"

Sally stood at the nursery door now.

"He's a brave little man, Miss There was a fair amount of blood, but we sorted it out. I don't know where the woman has gotten to, I really don't. I'll go to the door now, Miss"

"Thank you, Sally."

Elsbeth had noticed a marked improvement in Sally, she had thought it previously and wondered if it was a rare occasion but now she wasn't so sure.

"Did you not hear the door? You are steps away from it and you have left someone outside waiting! The missus will not have that!"

Sally barked at Mrs. Williams who sat in the parlour not far from the front door.

"I don't know if you had noticed, I am neither a footman nor a butler."

"And I don't know if you had noticed but you are not the lady of the house neither, so get off the missus' seat!"

Sally stomped off to answer the waiting visitor.

"Well, bless me. Come in, come in. Oh, excuse me Miss Geraldine, it is so good to see you again, it is that. Mrs. Stanhope will be that happy."

Geraldine smiled; it was nice to get such a welcome.

"Hello Sally, it is good to be back. Mrs. Stanhope is home?"

"She is that, Miss Geraldine. I'll fetch her right now."

Sally had her foot on the first step when Elsbeth appeared at the sweeping rail above.

"Oh, my goodness! It is you, I thought I recognised your voice. How long have you been here? Come in, come in and let me look at you."

Elsbeth practically skipped down the stairs with the 2 women sharing a warm embrace. Sally looked on, her smile as genuine as her thoughts, for she liked Miss Geraldine and her down to earth way.

"Is it too much of an imposition to beg a cup of tea? I feel parched after my walk."

"I will bring it through, Miss. Cook has only 5 minutes since made a large pot. Would Miss like something to eat, you must be hungry I should think?"

"Oh, you read my thoughts, thank you Sally, that would be most welcome."

"I'll get straight to it, Miss Mrs. Williams, can you take Miss Geraldine's bags to the guest room at the top of the stairs. You'll be staying, will you, Miss?"

Geraldine looked at Elsbeth, she had hoped to put it more graciously.
"Of course you must stay. A good idea Sally. Mrs. Williams, the bags please."
Mrs. Williams snatched the 2 bags up from the polished floor, beginning her ascent up the stairs she shot Sally a look that brought a chill to the woman and she did not know why.

Upstairs, Mrs. Jennifer Williams was grumbling to herself as she tossed the bags onto the day seat next to the window. Furious at being given orders from the low-life Sally and in front of both Mrs. Stanhope and her prissy guest.
"What are you doing, Miss?"
asked Martha as she paused at the door.
"I highly doubt it's any business of yours girl. Go away."
Martha, sturdier in mind than Ruby, stuck out her tongue and continued downstairs.
These children were sorely lacking discipline, that was for certain, she thought. Jennifer watched the rest of the older children as they ran around in the gardens at the rear of the house from the window. She would whip them into shape, she would show the mistress of the house that a child is better behaved with moral values instilled in them at the earliest possible convenience. It worked for her as a child, her mother would never have stood for such rude behaviour and bad manners, and neither would she! Of course, she would have to tread a little lighter with the eyes of everyone, including that insufferable Miss Mary, watching her. Yes, she would have to curb her impatient tongue if she was to remain in the employ of Mrs. Elsbeth Stanhope. Jennifer straightened the bags on the day seat, opened the window and pulled back the bed covers.

"I wonder why she has come back in such a hurry. Cate said she had not made so much as a plan as to where she was going to stay. I'm

sure they will put her up at the hall, they have more than enough room and those 2 have always gotten on like a house on fire."
said Grace as she placed Milton's dinner on the table.
"No Tom tonight? I don't know, love. It's news to me, but she will probably stay up there. It would be nice to see her again, I have a lot of time for that woman."
Grace chewed her food as she watched her husband.
"No, Tom is having dinner with Robert and Mary tonight, they want to make David's stay as fun as they can and thought it might help having a younger person around. Me too, she is a very nice person, not an ounce of bad in that one."
"Maybe we can go over there, to see her while she's in the village. Be a shame to miss her" Billoughby didn't dare look up as he made his suggestion to Grace.
"She will call, I'm sure of it."
Grace refilled her teacup and said no more on the subject. This was going to be a tough one to crack.

"How was your day, my beautiful wife?"
Adam kissed Cate on the top of her head and went to the kitchen sink to wash his hands.
"It was a strange day. I bumped into someone in the village, Geraldine. Can you believe it? She's staying up at the hall with Elsbeth and the children, I don't know for how long, but it was a nice surprise and no mistake. Oh, then I called to see your Ma, just to let her know I was grateful for her help the other day and that I was alright now. Then Maisy and I had a little doze and I made dinner. How was your day?"
Adam dried his hands and sat down to eat.
"It was a busy one, young David had a bit of a to-do, he thought Tom and I were going to kill one of the rams, ever so upset he was. Mary put him straight and then we had...Did you go to see the doctor? In all the to-ings and fro-ings of the day I forgot to ask."

Cate stood up and knelt beside her husband as he shovelled potatoes into his mouth.

"I did."

Adams' expression was that of a worried man, he placed his fork back onto his plate and turned from the table.

"Are you sick, my love? Please don't say you're sick, I couldn't bear it. Did he give you some medicine?"

Cate smiled sweetly, gazing into the eyes of this wonderful man she had felt destined to love.

"I may yet be sick again. Adam, I don't know how you will feel about this, and I promise you that I had no idea, we are going to have another child. Are you very angry?"

"What? We're having a baby? That is wonderful. Why would I be angry? Do you think we can get a boy this time?"

His grin was as big as the large sky outside.

"You don't mind?"

Adam pulled her up onto his lap, his arms hugging Cate so tight that she thought she might pop.

"Do I mind? Do you know how long I have wanted for us to have another baby? I told you once that I would have 10 or so of the little you and me running around. Have you told Ma?"

Cate shook her head.

"I thought it was right and proper that you hear it first."

"I wouldn't be shocked if Ma already knows, all that babbling about flowers and the like, and the way she winked and congratulated me. That was all very odd."

"We shall tell them together, for now we can keep it to ourselves."

Cate leaned in and kissed her husband tenderly, still with the taste of gravy on his lips.

The old gentleman rose to his feet as the man was presented by the butler.

"Mr. Andrew Hirst, Sir. The gentleman says you may have been expecting him?"

It took the man a few seconds, his eyes staring as he searched for some familiarity to kick in, and then his face eased of its furrows.

"The Lord Warden! Well, I must say I was not expecting your visit so soon, but you are most welcome. Please do come and sit."

Mr. Hirst handed his coat and hat to the butler and took a seat in the parlour that had a smell of age and money.

"I do hope I have not caught you at an inappropriate time. As I mentioned, I had planned to be in the area, and you kindly gave me your card. I felt it would be remiss of me not to call and say hello. If it is not a suitable time I am happy to leave."

"Good heavens man, I wouldn't hear of it. You are, in point of fact, just in time for supper. Do you have a place to stay the night? I imagine you do, silly question."

"That would be very hospitable of you, Sir. I passed an Inn on my walk over here, I imagine they have suitable rooms."

"Nonsense, you will stay with me. Now, what would you like to drink? We have a mix of port, sherry, whisky and wine."

"Port will do me fine, Sir."

Mr. Hirst got the impression that the old gentleman was a lonely soul; not that he meant to take advantage of that fact, but it would be handy to have a comfortable place to stay for a couple of nights.

The 2 men chatted late into the evening. They discussed everything from the political rousing of one Mrs. Emmeline Pankhurst to the tragedy of the liner Titanic.

The conversation was easy enough and Mr. Hirst learned a great deal about his new found friend. Mr. Mitchell Gregory had been born in the house they sat in, a mother and father that had worked hard to provide a good and decent education for himself and his brother. The father had been a magistrate and his mother a couturier to the wealthy women of London. Mitchell spoke openly about his struggles as a younger man, to keep up with the rising successes of his older brother, a brother that eventually settled in London with his wife and children, whereas Mitchell had never had a wife, or children. He impressed on his guest that these things did not matter to him, although Mr. Hirst could see in the old man's face that they did.

"I will get my man to show you to a room, I hope you find it congenial. Myself, well I must sleep. It has been an agreeable evening. Good night dear chap."

"It has been a very enjoyable time, my thanks to you as I don't often get to spend time in such engaging company. Good night, Sir."

The room was indeed a comfortable one, as was the house. Mr. Hirst had noted this the moment he had set foot into it. It was a grand place in comparison to many he had been in and yet it had a homely feel, a home that had known and encouraged love. The decor was not extravagant although it was of an expensive taste. The polished wooden floors with their woven coverings of deep reds and golds complimented the furniture of oak. Yes, this would do him well for a time he thought as he settled down in the large bed to sleep.

Mr. Hirst bid the old man farewell with the promise he would return by early evening. He was going to check out a lead that may or may not prove useful and an early start was needed if he was to reach the small village by mid-morning. He was an experienced horseman, and the gelding was a fast beast. The pathways were mostly steady as they made their way through the English countryside, stopping only to refresh. The church spire soon came into view as did signs of people going about their morning chores. He paused to speak with a farmhand.

"Morning. Am I right in thinking this is the village where I can find a Reverend Moore?"

Tom swallowed the piece of apple he had been chewing on.

"You are, Sir. If you follow the lane down into the village you will see the church. I imagine the Reverend will be up and about at this time. If he isn't in the church he might be in the rectory. Good day." Mr. Hirst nodded his thanks as his horse trotted on. Tom continued to eat his apple as he watched the stranger disappear down the lane.

Chapter Four

Grace was delighted when Cate and Adam broke their exciting news. She didn't know who to hug first as she jumped from the seat.
"This is wonderful! I thought when you had your sickness it might be, but I didn't want to say. Isn't this wonderful Milton?"
Billoughby patted Adam on the back.
"I expect a grandson this time, you know that don't you?"
He laughed.
"You're going to have a little brother or sister to play with Maisy, isn't that going to be fun?" Maisy merely babbled her happy sounds to her grandma as she continued to chew on the toasted bread that Grace had given her.
"Speaking of which, does your brother know yet?"
asked Billoughby.
"No, I, or that is we thought we would tell you first."
replied Adam. Grace scowled.
"I doubt we will be getting the same news from your brother anytime soon!"
"Now, love. Let's not spoil the moment. Cate, Adam, I am that happy for you."
Billoughby smiled but not before shooting a disapproving look toward his wife. Grace was not that easily silenced.
"I am not spoiling the moment, why would you say that? I am pointing out a fact as well you know. Cate, what do you make of it, you're close as anyone to Tom and you have dealings with… well you go to the Hall to do your piano lessons with young Ruby. Do you think it's natural?"
Cate put her hand onto Grace's, she knew she had to tread a very fine line here.

"You know, Ma, I have been that wrapped up these past weeks that I hadn't given it much thought. I will say one thing, Tom looks happy, I have never seen him so happy, and you know, it might run its course? I find the more you draw attention to a thing the longer a stubborn streak hangs on."

Grace shook her head at the woman, how could people not see what was happening here?

"But for how long, how long will he be happy when he sees all of his friends having children of their own, going to dances and such like, how long will he be happy then?"

Adam stepped in, sensing the topic was making his wife uncomfortable for she had no wish to have words with her mother-in-law.

"Ma, he's a grown man and he's older in the head than many twice his age. It's not for any of us to say what he's doing is right or wrong because to our Tom, it is right. You have always said that the happiness of your family is everything to you, let him have his happiness, Ma."

Adam could see that his mother was torn as she scooped up her basket and she left the house without saying another word.

Grace walked slowly along the lane, taking in the smells, sounds and sights of the countryside. A part of her knew that Adam had spoken sense but that other and more protective part of her felt that this whole situation would at some time, maybe down the line, bring her son a grief he simply wasn't equipped to deal with, and that was what tore at her. Her thoughts were interrupted as she stared across the field of newly grazing lambs and their watchful mothers.

"Good morning, lovely day for a stroll."

Grace turned to see the stranger as he dismounted his horse. How had she not heard the hooves coming up behind her?

"Good morning, yes it is. A nice day for some quiet thinking. Are you passing through?"

The man took off his hat as he tied the rope to a hitching post.

"I do apologise, I didn't intend to disturb your contemplation. Passing through, yes, in a way. I have a little business to do in the area and thought I would take advantage of a look around."

"You didn't disturb me. Your accent tells me you're not from these parts, I've heard it before, but I can't put my finger on where."

The man's eyes widened at this snippet of information although he didn't push the comment.

"I am to visit a Reverend Moore; I believe he is to be found at the rectory?"

Grace nodded as she sat down on the stone wall, resting her basket beside her.

"Yes, the reverend is most often found there or the church itself."

Grace was not one for being inquisitive, a man's business was his own. Mr. Hirst sat down on the wall beside her, the basket between them. It hadn't gone unnoticed by him that she was a most attractive woman, her face was soft although he could pick up on the fact that she had burdens.

"I hope you don't mind?"

He asked as he unfolded a sandwich from its waxed paper wrapping. Grace smiled, shaking her head she knew she should be on her way but stayed sitting there as the stranger ate all the same. It was oddly pleasant to be in the company of a person that wasn't disagreeing with you, she thought.

The grocer Mr. Nash slowed his cart as he approached, the peculiar look across his face told Grace that she should not be sitting with a man that was not Mr. Billoughby but there were a lot of people doing things that they should not be doing at the moment, so Grace stayed where she was.

"Mrs. Billoughby, out for a stroll are we?"

"Mr. Nash, it would appear so."

"Mr. Billoughby not with you then?"

Grace turned and looked over the wall.

"It would appear not."
The man beside her chuckled under his breath, Mr. Nash shook his head in disapproval and continued on his way.
"You will be the talk of the village!"
He laughed.
"Better me than other folk."
Replied Grace.

Reverend Moore could hear the tapping at the door, but blast it, could he find his other slipper? Exasperated, he pulled on his sandals instead. Making his way to the door the tapping stopped.
"Heavens above! Have people no patience anymore."
He opened the large wooden door and peered both ways, there did not seem to be a soul in sight. He called out several times and was about to give up and close the door again when he heard a voice coming from around the corner of the building.
"Hello there, are you the Reverend Moore by chance?"
The tall man strode toward Tobias.
"I am indeed, and you are?"
Mr. Hirst held out a hand.
"My name is Andrew Hirst, I have travelled from Redruth in search of a person that I believe may be in the area, a person that I have on good authority you introduced to recent employment in the village."
Tobias scratched his thinning hair; he had put many a lost soul in touch with various employment opportunities in the area over the past few months.
"You might have to be a little more specific, you see as my post requires. I find many people work in the area, surrounding areas too. Some as far out as Canterbury and Folkestone and right down to Hastings in fact. Where are my manners, please come in. Can I offer you a cup of tea?" Mr. Hirst walked through, Tobias standing to the side to let the man pass.
"Tea would be most welcome, thank you."

Saving Grace | D M Roberts

The 2 men went through to the kitchen and Tobias set about refilling the pot.

"The trouble is, you must understand that some people do not wish to be found, some are merely looking for an escape from an abusive situation and so on. Have you tried the constabulary? They are usually quite helpful with this kind of thing. Honey, milk?"

The man shook his head.

"I haven't as yet, I was hoping to settle this without involving all manner of other people. Yes please."

Tobias placed the mug onto the table and sat down.

"Well, I would say that would be the first thing I would do. Man or woman? The person in question."

"Woman, my sister to be honest. She has had a difficult time with the passing of her husband and as with these things she walked out of her house one morning and simply didn't return. So, you can understand it is most important that I find her, if only for my peace of mind and that of our family."

Tobias stirred his tea; he had heard all manner of tales in his time, and he was shrewd enough not to fall for the first line that came out of a stranger's mouth.

"Sad state of affairs, the loss of one's spouse. It can stir up all sorts of emotions in a person. There was a woman…"

The man leant forward in eager anticipation.

"Yes."

"Yes, she said she had travelled a fair way and was looking for gainful employment within a family. I pointed her in the direction of a household in Tunbridge, a large and decent family offering room and pay. She arranged an appointment, that being the last I saw of her."

Mr Hirst nursed his mug as Tobias spoke, in his mind he was certain that a man of the cloth would have no reasons to lie.

"You recall her particulars?"

He asked quietly.

Saving Grace | D M Roberts

"Hm, I'm not as young as I once was. The problem, you see, is I encounter so many in my day to day duties. Of course it could be any of the others. I have placed perhaps 4 or 5 women since January. 2 went to Whitstable, the 1 in Tunbridge and a few in Canterbury, well they would, wouldn't they, Canterbury being as wealthy as it is."

"Any with an accent like mine?"
He asked.

"My dear man, they all have accents. They are looking for a new life and they are hardly going to do that in their own back garden, as it were."

The reverend had a point, thought Mr. Hirst and no reason to mislead him and so Mr. Hirst took the information in the nature it was given.

"You have been most helpful, not to mention hospitable. I'll trouble you no more, thank you." Tobias let the man out and made a quick note of his enquiries and looks. He would speak to the Inspector maybe.

"Tom?"

Tom was laying in the grass, his hand entwined with his beloved Elsbeth's.

"What are we going to do about your mother? It bothers me that she has taken such a view of our love, but it is also understandable."

Tom sat up; he too had been having many a thought in regard to his mother's complete refusal to even listen to him.

"I tried to talk with her again, did I tell you? She wouldn't listen, she won't listen to Pa either. I had hoped she might come round but it seems the more people talk about it, the more she digs her heels in."

Elsbeth sighed, for she loved this man more than she ever thought possible.

"She said you would come to regret it, us, because you would never have children of your own. Will you, my love?"

"Now you hear me good, I will never regret a single second with you and if children are not to be, then we shall make do with the ones we already have. Besides, can you imagine having another little one with the bunch we have at the Hall?"

Tom chuckled at the thought of more children in the now bustling house.

"I like that you call them ours, it's nice. If you ever do change your mind…"

"Hush now, I will never change my mind about you, and they will be our children once we are wed."

Elsbeth's mouth dropped open.

"Is that a proposal young Mr. Billoughby?"

"Not as yet, but there will be, make no mistake."

He leaned in, taking her face in his hands and kissed the woman he had only ever dared dream about with a tenderness and passion she had never felt before.

"How do, is that permitted at this time of the morning, and in full daylight?"

laughed Robert as he walked through the field toward the love-struck couple. Elsbeth's face turned a crimson red as she hastily jumped to her feet.

"Good morning, we weren't expecting anyone this way."

She stammered at the smiling man.

"Rest easy Miss, I'm on the lookout for a stray calf, buggered if I know where he's gone to. Tom."

"Robert, I haven't seen him, is it the dark one again?"

"I doubt you'd notice a combine pass you lad. Yes, little so and so that he is."

"We'll keep a look out for him. How is your morning? It's not often any of us get a bit of time to ourselves."

"Mary all but threw me out while her and young David try their hand at some baking, what the lad wants with baking is beyond me! Still, it keeps him occupied while the hands get on with their jobs.

It's been a real treat for Mary to have the lad, me too and what an enquiring little mind he has on him. You must miss him up at the Hall, Miss?"

Elsbeth smiled, she was pleased to hear that David was engaging in more than mucking out.

"We do miss him, but I feel that he enjoys having that singular attention especially after his time away. They can be a noisy bunch at times, and I'm not too certain he enjoys our new helps company."

Robert nodded, his face taking on a grave expression now.

"That's true, I asked him about it but all he would say was she gave him the odd feeling. In truth Miss, I can't say that I'm overly keen and I've met the woman but once."

"Yes, I'm afraid I will be keeping a close eye on things and if that means finding a replacement, then so be it. Did you hear that Miss Geraldine is staying with me for a time? I am hoping to convince her to stay permanently and that would solve the issue as she is so good with the children."

Replied Elsbeth.

"Now that would be a good swap, Mary would be delighted for one, she gets on well with Miss Geraldine. Did she say what brought her back?"

Elsbeth shook her head, although she knew why, it was not for her to say.

"Whatever it is, it has to be good for us."

added Tom.

Back at the Hall voices were once again raised. Sally blustered into the kitchen for the umpteenth time that morning, her face as red as the apples sitting on the table.

"You have to keep out of her way, Sally. I tell you, no good will come of the pair of you arguing like you do and in front of those little ones too."

Saving Grace | D M Roberts

"Ain't right Cook, the way she talks to them when the missus ain't about. I won't have it and I told her I won't. Those 2 babby's not even old enough to chatter and she's shouting at them like they're grown men. It's small wonder they fret so much when she's about them."

Geraldine came into the kitchen. Sally flushed even more than before, for she was sure to get what for now and no mistake.

"Cook, Sally, can I have a word if you're not too busy."

Closing the door Geraldine beckoned the 2 to sit down.

"Listen, Miss I'm sorry, I lost my tongue, I did, it won't happen again."

Geraldine was shaking her head at the woman now.

"Is that pot still hot? I could do with a cup. Sally, I did not come in here to chastise or argue, it isn't a good example to set around the children. They pick up on these things as do we all. Has this been a regular way since Mrs. Williams began working at the hall?"

"She is not a pleasant woman."

Sally and Geraldine stared at Cook, who up until now had kept her thoughts on Mrs. Williams to herself.

"In what way, cook?"

said Geraldine softly.

"They're children, Miss They don't mean no harm when they play, it's what this house is meant for to have children laughing and playing in it, not her shouting and screaming with their every move."

Sally was nodding in agreement.

"Does Mrs. Stanhope know of this?"

"Not much, Miss, we try to keep things smooth you see. Miss Mary, now she knows, not happy either if you want the truth and told me to keep my eyes and ears peeled. Her, up there, well she doesn't do it much when the missus is around, does she Cook?"

Cook shook her head.

Saving Grace | D M Roberts

"I see. Well, I think I will have to keep a watch, Sally, try to keep your tongue civil around the youngsters and come to me if you have any problems."
"Yes, Miss. Are you going to be staying a while, Miss?"
"I might be, we shall see."
Geraldine left the 2 women and returned to the schoolroom, dismissing the children for the rest of the day from their lessons much to the fury of Mrs. Williams.

Daisy and Julian sat in the drawing room as Tobias went through the lessons, Daisy looked bored, and Tobias had noticed.
"Dear girl, it is a necessary part of the nuptials, and you cannot have a wedding without all that goes with it."
"I know Reverend, but does it have to be so laborious? I go to church every Sunday, so too does Julian. We only want a simple ceremony so why do we have to do all of this?"
Daisy waved her hands toward all the books that lay open on the table in front of her.
"My dear, please let the Reverend get on with it, and then we can enjoy the rest of the day together."
Pleaded Julian to his normally patient intended.
"It is not merely a ceremony, Daisy. There must be absolute certainty in what you are both intending to undertake. Marriage is a serious and lengthy commitment. Now, where were we?" They sat in the drawing room for 2 more hours until Tobias relented and waved them off at the door.
"Everybody is in such a rush."
He mumbled to himself.

Daisy and Julian had arranged to visit Billoughby in the afternoon. The ride over was a nice if not slightly bumpy one with Julian telling tales of his new automobile back in London. Daisy was excited to see it, even have a ride in it when she visited next. They arrived at the cottage to find Billoughby in the front garden pulling up weeds.

"How good to see you again, Julian. Give me a minute and I'll be in, Grace is in the kitchen I should imagine. Take yourselves in then."

The pair went inside and Billoughby could hear the chatter of the 2 women begin.

"Sorry about that, I had to do them, or they would take a hold. How are you both? Have you set a date yet?"

Asked the Inspector as he washed his hands.

"We were thinking June, not as hot as July but that doesn't give us a huge amount of time to prepare. Reverend Moore thinks we should say September, it's something we will have to work out quickly." Said Daisy as she hugged Grace and Billoughby.

"September sounds better, if you want to have a dress made that is or are you wearing one that needs alterations?" asked Grace.

"I will have Julian's mother's dress, she has insisted on it, although it needs a little alteration."

"Oh, that sounds nice dear. Do you have much family Mr. Richardson?"

"I have one sister who will also make use of the dress, it's a family tradition, and 2 brothers that are already married, they are older than I am, but my mother has hopes that my sister will marry soon."

He laughed as he pictured his mother and her desperate attempts to marry the out-spoken woman that was his sister, off, to a man bold enough to take her on.

"Bit of a handful is she?"

Chuckled Billoughby.

"And some, she has a way that scares off most prospects. That said, she is a kind and generous soul. There has been a suitor over the last 6 months, we feel that she has now met her match."

"There's someone for everyone."

Smiled Grace as she set the table for afternoon tea. Billoughby fought back the temptation to ask his wife to think about that sentence.

"There is indeed, and I consider myself a lucky man to have found my someone. I am erring on June, the sooner the better for me" Julian added as he looked at Daisy.

"Oh, I meant to tell you. There was a visitor at the rectory today, the Reverend said he was looking for someone that might be in the area, a woman he said. The reverend suggested speaking with the constabulary about it but he said he would rather not."

Daisy had been asked to pass on the information as she was going to the Billoughby's anyway.

"Hm, it's not often we get strangers around here, but I imagine the Reverend will have sorted the chap out?"
replied Billoughby.

"I'm not so sure, the Reverend said he wasn't too keen on sharing information, so he wasn't exactly forthcoming with what he knows."

"For what reason?"
asked a puzzled Billoughby.

"He said, some women leave home for many reasons including beatings and it's not for him to be giving out ways for a man to find such a woman."

Billoughby nodded in agreement, he was wise was Tobias.

"Did the man say where he came from?"

"He did, but I can't remember. Ruth, something or other."

"Okay, enough talk of work. Daisy, have you chosen a seamstress?" asked Grace as she changed the subject from that of the encounter she had that same morning.

"Oo, I know what I want but I haven't had time to engage a seamstress as yet. I was hoping you might help me with this, Mrs. Billoughby."

The 2 women went into the parlour to talk about dresses leaving Billoughby and Julian in the kitchen to talk about other matters.

Saving Grace | D M Roberts

Mr. Hirst was stumped. The areas mentioned by the Reverend would take him off in many different directions that he felt would only be a waste of his time. He wasn't overly convinced that the man had gotten his facts right, he did seem a man with too much going on in his head. Heading back toward Hythe he had time to think things through carefully before he decided on a solid plan. He was grateful for the room and board with the old gentleman; it gave him a chance to save on lodgings and be close to the place that he knew to be a last sighting of the woman.

"How was your day? I wondered if you might like to join me at my club for dinner this evening." Offered Mr. Gregory as he sat reading the news sheet in his armchair.
"It was not as productive a day as I had hoped and a little tiring, Sir. Yes, that would be a nice distraction as long as you don't mind the company?"
"Not at all. So, you did not make any headway in your inquiries?"
"Not as much as I would have liked, there is always tomorrow. What time shall we be leaving, I may have a quiet rest."
"Oh, not for a good hour. Would you like me to call the boy to fetch you some refreshment?" Mr. Hirst shook his head, he could wait for dinner.
"Thank you, that is kind but no, I feel a rest is more pressing."
In his room, Mr. Hirst laid out his jacket and hat on the chair, he placed his shoes underneath and lay on the bed. He woke only when he heard the knock on his door.
"Yes."
The houseboy pushed the door open.
"Sir said to tell you he will be leaving shortly."
"Thank you."
The boy closed the door and went back to his duties.
"Ready when you are."

he said as he entered the parlour. The 2 men departed for the club.

"Mrs. Williams, can you come through please?"
Elsbeth called quietly as she settled the youngest child into her crib.
"Yes, Miss"
"Tomorrow we will be taking the children on an outing to the seaside. I would like you to accompany myself, Sally and Miss Geraldine. Please be ready after breakfast, Miss Geraldine and I will deal with the children's dressing and breakfast."
Mrs. Williams nodded; she disliked the sea for many reasons but she would go because it was part of her employment.
"Yes, Ma'am. And you're sure the weather won't cause any issues, I had heard it may rain." Mrs. Williams had heard no such thing.
"The weather will be fine, I have it on good authority."
"If you say so, Ma'am."
"I do. Besides, a little rain never hurt anyone. You may retire for the evening, good night." Well! That told me, thought Mrs. Williams as she made her way back to her room.

Jennifer Williams pulled the case from under the bed. In it she had several personal possessions including a long wrapped up bundle that she hadn't dared open, until now. She smiled to herself as she caressed the item, her thoughts turned to that fateful day when she had left the place that she once called home. She had to be quick in her escape, the alarm would be given the minute they didn't turn up to church. They always attended the church, and she despised it, with all its hypocrisy and preachings. She thought with a smile how satisfied she had felt after each deed had been carried out with precision. The horse and buggy had to be disposed of, fortunately the beggar she had met along the way must have thought that the Lord himself had blessed him on that very day when she handed it to him as a gift 'for the needy' and as he didn't ask any questions of the strange woman, she was free to board her train to her new life. She was upset that the man she had hoped would return her feelings had wanted no part of her; still, he would pay dearly for that now, wouldn't he.

"Have anything you like, my treat."
Said Mr. Gregory as he handed his guest the menu.
"I couldn't, please let me pay. It is the least I can do considering your hospitality."
Replied Mr. Hirst as he glanced down the list of meals. True, they were pricey, but he had saved so much thanks to his host that he felt it only right and proper that he should be the one to foot the bill.
"No, I insist. I asked you to join me, therefore I should pay. I enjoyed our talk last night, it was good to have normal conversation again and it reminded me how fortunate I have been in this life. Do you have children, Mr. Hirst?"
The question took him by surprise, it wasn't an unreasonable thing to ask of a person.
"I did, I had a son and a wife. Sadly, the strains of my work took me away from home so much that I came back one day to find they had gone. I would hope to have more but the time passes so quickly now that I can't ever see a point where it will happen. I still have my work, which keeps me from thinking about what once was, even though it was the cause of my loss."
"Mm, quite right. A man needs a thing to do, otherwise he simply fades away. Damn bad luck for you, it must have been a dreadful time, so many marriages end that way of late."
"He will be 10 this Summer, I wish I had spent more time with them, alas, you never assume it will happen to you."
The 2 men sat in silence a while, each lost in thoughts of what could be.
"Are we ready to order, Sir?"
The waiter seemed to appear from nowhere, his stark white and navy-blue uniform as fresh as the day it was made.

"I do believe we are. I shall have the beef with potatoes and vegetable selection, a bottle of your finest red too."
replied Mr. Gregory.
"And you, Sir?"
"I shall have the same, thank you."
The meal was excellent, the men talked well into the evening as they had the previous night. Mr. Gregory became a little unsteady on his feet as they made their way out to the waiting buggy. He was in exceptionally jolly spirits, recounting tales of his younger more virile days which brought the laughter pouring from his guests mouth.
"You seem to be much more relaxed, dear boy. It is a good thing to see."
Mr. Hirst smiled, he felt relaxed, and it had been some time since he had laughed.
"Although it is a working trip I have felt more at ease these past few days. It helps to have open space and sea air, everybody should try it. I thought tomorrow I would take a day off to explore the coastline, you are welcome to join me if you haven't any plans?"
Mr. Gregory handed his coat and hat to the butler and made for the sitting room.
"Do you know, I just might do that. Can I pour you a nightcap?"
"That would be excellent on both counts."

The morning was a warm and bright one, and much to the irritation of Mrs. Williams, there wasn't a cloud in the sky.
"Do we have everyone and everything?"
Called Elsbeth as the children piled into the cart.
"All children counted and loaded, picnics stacked and secured Mrs. Stanhope."
Called back Sally taking her seat with Lily, one of the infants, tucked safely in her arms. Geraldine was charged with Dolly, the infant sister of David and Doris. The remainder of the children bounced

around excitedly, with Mrs. Williams hardly able to contain her glares.

"Don't fret too much, the little darlings are happy to be going to the seaside, they do love it." Geraldine whispered to Mrs. Williams.

"I am not fretting, if they fall and hurt themselves they will have nobody to blame but themselves."

Geraldine could hear the tone in the woman's voice and wasn't sure whether she was being serious or trying to be humorous.

"We'll stop to pick up Mary and David on the way."

Added Elsbeth as the carts began to move. Wonderful, thought Mrs. Williams, another lah-di-dah to add to an already surely dreadful day!

Chapter Five

"Come quick Miss Mary, David has found a crab and it's a real live one too. Quick Miss Mary."

Mary followed Martha to where David sat on the sand with the small creature trying to escape from the hole he had dug in the sand.

"David, what are you doing with that? Why don't you let it go back to the sea."

David shrugged, he had found it fair and square.

"But I found it, Miss Mary. I want to take it home, we could keep it on the farm. Plus, he has a bad leg, look."

Pointing to the claw that had clearly seen better days.

"You want to look after it, I can see that, but he is better off staying here on the beach with his family. Come along now, let's get him out of that hole and back to his family."

David reluctantly piled sand into the hole for the crab to crawl out. It hadn't gone too far when Mrs. Williams, after hearing the conversation, walked toward them crushing the creature under her sturdy shoe.

"Oh dear, that is unfortunate."

She muttered walking away.

David let out a screech that brought Elsbeth running.

"Whatever is the matter, what has happened?"

"She killed it!"

He wailed, as he pointed at the woman.

"I'm sure she didn't mean to, dear. You didn't mean to, did you Mrs. Williams?"

Mrs. Williams shook her head, the smirk evident.

"Of course I didn't, it's only a crab boy. Why are you getting so upset?"

Mary had to hold David who was desperately trying to get to the woman now.

"Stay with me dear, it was an accident. Come on now, let us go for a walk."

Under protest, David left the scene with Mary.

Sally was not so forgiving.

"You did that on purpose, even if they don't know it. You're a wicked woman, that's what you are."

Mrs. Williams shrugged; she cared nothing for what this lowly servant thought.

Mr. Hirst and Mr. Gregory strolled leisurely along the front, they watched from a distance as a family enjoyed the warm breeze and a picnic on this gloriously sunny day. They talked about the past as children and the lure of the seaside.

"Many a time my mother would bring us to this very spot. Precious memories."

Mr. Gregory' warm smile made his eyes twinkle as he thought about his childhood.

"It was a favourite of my son and wife. We holidayed in Wales when I could get time away from work. They were happy days."

The wistful look was evident to the older man, what a sadness it must be to carry the loss of one's child he thought. The closer they got to the large family on the sand, the more Mr. Hirst had the strangest feeling he recognised that silhouette, but it couldn't be, could it? He watched the woman as she sat amongst the group.

"Are you alright dear boy?"

"Oh, yes. I was a little taken watching the group down there. They look like they're enjoying themselves."

"Indeed. I might head back now, don't feel you have to return with me. It's about that time of the day I have a doze."

Mr. Hirst nodded.

"I might walk some more, if you are alright with that? Can you manage the walk back?"
Mr. Gregory chuckled, shaking his stick playfully.
"Of course I can, there's many a time I wander along here. It has been a much more pleasant experience with your company. I shall see you later for dinner?"
Mr. Hirst nodded and waved the older man goodbye.

He sat quietly, he knew for sure that this was the person he had been searching for. The sound of the children as they enjoyed their day rang out with an echo carried on the sea breeze. That she was installed amongst a family sent chills through his blood and yet if he was to achieve his goal he dared not approach them for fear she would vanish again, and he could not risk that.
"Hello Mister."
The voice startled him. The young boy that stood beside him was similar in age to the child he had lost.
"Hello there, are you enjoying the sand?"
"I was, but that missus down there killed my crab. Miss Mary said best we take a walk."
Mary caught up, out of breath having quickened her pace in a bid to keep David in sight.
"David! You shouldn't run off, you know what can happen. I'm sorry if my youngster disturbed you Sir."
Mr. Hirst smiled and shook his head.
"Not at all, Miss He tells me he's had a bereavement of the crab sort."
Mary nodded.
"Sadly, yes. An accident I'm sure."
"Are you local?"
"Not too local, a way up through the marshes."
David had taken a seat next to the man.

"Do you think Reverend Moore would say a special prayer for my crab at church, Miss Mary?" asked David.
"I am sure if we ask him he may well do that for you. Well, it was nice to make your acquaintance, enjoy the rest of your day Sir."
Mr. Hirst tipped his hat to the pair. Having learned all he needed and not having to ask them a single thing as it was freely presented.
Quite the result he mused as he began the walk back to Mr. Gregory house.

Sally could not wait to get back to the hall and tell Cook all about the wicked deed of Mrs. Williams. Cook gasped as the woman retold how she had made the young Master David cry and how the missus thought it must have been some sort of accident.
"Accident my teeth! She's a bad one, no good will come of her being here with these nippers."
"You have to speak with Miss Mary again, has she gone home yet?" Sally was busy rubbing her sandy, aching foot.
"No, in the parlour. They'll be having a pot of tea before she leaves."
Cook set to making the tray up while Sally put her day shoes on.
"I reckon you should have a quiet word with her before she goes, it can't be allowed to go on and the missus none the wiser. Here, take this in, there's a dear."
The steps outside the kitchen were light as they made their way to the staircase.
"You snooping at keyholes?"
Asked Sally as Mrs. Williams made her way up.
"Should I be?"
She laughed as she disappeared around the landing.
"Miss Mary. Can I have a moment before you go?"
Sally whispered as she handed Mary the cup and saucer. Mary nodded, not wanting to draw attention.

Saving Grace | D M Roberts

The 2 women stood in the courtyard as Sally voiced her growing concerns about the new help.

"Ain't good, Miss. I've had my moments as you know but I would never be cruel to those little ones, no right-minded person would. I thought about saying something to the missus but that one up there would deny it and we all know I don't have the best record if you know what I mean?" Mary could well understand Sally's reluctance to go to Elsbeth with this and promised to have words with her sister-in-law at a more appropriate time.

"Do be careful Sally, like you, I have a bad feeling about this one." She bid the woman goodnight and set off for home.

Grace lay in her bed, and she was wide awake. It was a dark night, and she didn't want to disturb her husband by getting up especially as it had taken him so long to fall asleep with that cough of his, but she couldn't just lie here thinking, not when she had so much going on in her head. Tip-toeing out of the room she made her way down the stairs being careful not to stand on the ones that creaked. There was a light that shone from the kitchen and Grace wondered if she should turn around and go back to bed. This is ridiculous, she thought, I live here. Pushing open the door she saw Tom sitting at the table. It was too early for him to be up for work.

"Tom?"

Grace waited for a response but there was none. She gently shook his shoulder and Tom looked up.

"I must have dozed off. I hope I didn't scare you."

"No son, why aren't you in bed? You're going to be that tired in the morning."

Tom shrugged. He watched as Grace put fresh water in the tea urn and cut herself a slice of bread.

"You're hungry at the most peculiar times, ma."

He laughed quietly.

"Aye, I always am when I have things on my mind. Why are you still up?"

Tom sighed, stretching his arms out he yawned. He certainly didn't want to get into a debate about his relationship at this time of the night.

"I don't know, I sat down and fell asleep. No real reason."

Grace took a bite from the slice, she knew her son better than he thought, they were always so similar. Adam was like his father but Tom, well Tom was like her in so many ways.

"Listen Tom, you're my boy and I only ever think of what is best for you. I know you think you're in love with this woman, but son, think of your future that's all I ask."

Tom counted in his head; he knew what he wanted to say but he also knew where that would lead.

"I don't think now is the time to talk about this, ma."

"Hear me out, please. It is tearing me apart that you cannot see sense. Where will it go? Nowhere, that's where. She's near on my age than yours and you won't ever have little ones like your brother."

Tom stood up; he couldn't listen to this anymore.

"I am not my brother."

"No, at least he had the good sense to find a wife his own age!"

As soon as the words left her mouth Grace knew that she could never take them back and as much as she meant them she also knew that she should have kept them to herself.

"What is going on down here?"

Billoughby stood at the doorway, his brows raised as he stared at his wife. Tom pushed past his father and left through the front door.

"He'll be back."

Said Grace quietly.

"Oh, my love. What have you done?"

Pulling his coat from the rack, Billoughby ran into the dark lane after his son.

"Did you catch up with him?"
Grace asked, she had sat at the table until it was light not knowing what to do.
"No, I couldn't find him anywhere. What did you have to go and do that for, Gracie. Wasn't it bad enough when he went the last time? I can't go through this again, now you can have your thoughts on the matter of course you can but you best make your peace with that lad or…"
"Or what, Milton? You think I didn't miss him when he left?"
"You have a funny way of showing it woman that you make him leave all over again."
Grace was on her feet now. The rage that never showed itself poured from her eyes.
"Don't dare say that I don't care about that boy."
Billoughby shook his head and his fist slammed down hard onto the tabletop.
"That's the thing, Gracie, he is not your little boy, he's a grown man with thoughts and feelings and a damn good mind of his own."
Grace wanted to cry, but she didn't, her anger wouldn't let her. How dare he talk to her in this way after all the years of marriage they had shared and all of the times she had gone along with his work and his ideas, no, she would not have it.
"He is still my child."
Grace walked quietly from the kitchen, Billoughby heard the front door close. He sat down and put his head in his hands as he tried to make sense of what had just happened.

Grace didn't know where she was going, all she knew was that she needed time to think, time that she would never get with Milton shouting at her. She wondered if she deserved it, she could have said nothing after all. It seemed that she had walked for miles when she spotted the bench, there wasn't a soul in sight as she sat down and began to cry, and pretty soon that cry turned into a sob.

"Grace, Grace is that you? Oh, my dear woman, whatever is the matter?"

Hastily Grace dried her face with the hem of her dress as best she could. Robert sat next to her, his brotherly arm swept across her shoulder and Grace buried her sobbing head into his chest. Robert stayed quiet, he thought it best to let the woman get it all out before he would attempt to ask what 'it' was. He thought all manner of things as he sat there patting the woman's back until finally Grace lifted her head. Her face red and tear stained she once again attempted to dry it.

"Here, have this."

Robert said as he handed her his handkerchief.

"Thank you, you must think I've lost my wits."

She mumbled.

"No such thing, you have your reasons I'm sure, and if you want to talk it out I'm in no rush."

"I've made a terrible mistake, Robert, and I don't know if I can ever fix it."

"That doesn't sound like you, Grace. You're not one to make a mistake, least not one that would have you this upset."

Grace blew her nose again, her head shaking from side to side.

"Oh, but I have. Milton is furious with me, Tom has gone again and I don't know where to turn."

"Come back to the farm with me Grace, Mary will cook you up some breakfast and we can sort this out. Come on love, up you get."

Grace wanted to argue, she didn't want to intrude on Mary or Robert's morning, but she didn't want to be sat out here on her own any longer.

She walked next to the tall man as they talked about her thoughts on Tom and Elsbeth. It was the first time that anyone had listened to her on the subject without telling her that she was wrong to think that way. Robert gave no opinion either way, which, although Grace was grateful for, seemed odd. Grace talked about how much she had missed Elsbeth as a friend and her worries that they would never get that back, of her fear at losing her son because she could not at present come to terms with his relationship, and of the words she and Milton had exchanged for the first time in all of their years together. Robert nodded and uttered the occasional 'Hm' and before she knew it they were close to the farm. They did not pay much attention either as Mr. Nash went by in his cart.

Mary and Robert spoke in hushed voices as Grace sat by the warm fire. It had been a chilly night, but it was only now that she began to realise how cold she was. Her dress felt damp with the morning dew and the light shower that followed.
"Grace, let me get you some warmer clothes, come with me. Robert has gone out to start work and won't be back for a while, well until he smells breakfast at least."
Mary offered a smile as she took her friend through to the back room. Mary sifted through some clothes that hung in the cupboard. She handed a couple of them to Grace.
"Thank you, Mary. I'm not sure I deserve your kindness, but I am grateful for it."
Mary sat down in the armchair, she felt at a loss as to what she should say to her friend.
"You are always worthy of everyone's kindness Grace. I'll leave you to change while I go and make a start on breakfast, take your time dear."
Grace appeared in the dining hall a few moments later. Having washed her face, straightened her hair and changed, she began to feel much better.
"There you are, sit yourself down and pour yourself a drink."

Said Mary cheerily. Mary could see that the woman was struggling, it was strange she realised that she had never before seen Grace looking as vulnerable in all the time they had known each other.

"How are things with you Mary?"

Grace didn't want to talk about her own problems again this morning.

"Oh, you know. The farm is having a better year up to now, we had young David to stay for a week. Oh Grace, he is such a delightful breath of fresh air. I would take that boy on tomorrow if I could."

Grace sipped her tea.

"Is there no possibility that you could?"

"I don't know, I have thought about it, but I haven't said it aloud until now. He's had such a time of it, I wouldn't want to unsettle him by even asking such a thing."

Mary paused as she went into the kitchen to fetch the plates. Putting one in front of Grace and one at the head of the table for Robert, she then fetched her own and rang the outside bell.

"I haven't even spoken of it with Robert."

She added as she sat down to eat. Grace began to eat, she felt famished and was glad of the meal. She wondered if Milton had managed to make himself something but then shook the thought from her mind in silent defiance.

"Maybe you should. There are many children placed with, over at, well there are. I am sure it would be good for David, he adores both you and Robert."

"It saddens me when I think of the lives they have had at such a young age, mind you, that one working over there is going to feel my wrath if she keeps on the way she does."

"What do you mean, which one?"

Grace had heard nothing of the goings on at the hall for some time.

"Mrs. Jennifer Williams no less, the one that replaced young Esther. It must be bad when Sally is begging me to do something about her, says she gives her the creepiest feeling and is often heard shouting at the little ones."

"Her employer lets her behave like this?"

"It isn't a thing she does when Elsbeth is around, which is the reason that Sally came to me. I said I would speak with Elsbeth when the woman isn't around."

Grace sighed; she knew Sally's ways, but she also knew that Sally doted on the children in her way.

"Sooner rather than later would be good, I imagine. And how is little Dolly now after her illness, is she getting stronger?"

Mary grinned from ear to ear.

"She is so much better, such a pretty child as is Lily, they could be sisters, twins even."

"I do miss them, the children. They are such a happy bunch when you consider how it was."

The door opened and Robert came in for his breakfast, the footsteps behind him told the 2 women he was not alone.

"Is there a spare plate going my love?"

He asked as Billoughby came into view.

"Of course."

Mary gave her husband a quizzical glance as Billoughby sat down at the table.

Billoughby leaned over to Grace, he looked at her face that still had signs of her distress.

"Are you alright Gracie?"

Grace nodded, she wanted to jump up and hug the man until she could hug him no more, but she couldn't. Instead, she quietly whispered that she was and carried on eating.

"There you are tuck in."

Mary said as she handed the Inspector a plate.

"Not often do we have company for breakfast, well apart from the lads. I like it."

Exclaimed Robert as he tried to make the time light.
"There's an idea, we could sell breakfast to passing trade."
laughed Mary.
"Speaking of passing trade, have any of you caught sight of the fella that's been around and about these past few days?"
asked Robert. Grace looked up, not sure if she should mention the man that had sat with her on the wall.
"Reverend Moore had a visitor the other day, said he was in search of someone. The Reverend said he had an accent that he's heard before, but he couldn't put his finger on where."
Added Mary. She put the fork into her mouth and stopped.
"Come to think of it, David and I spoke to a man at the seaside, and I too thought the accent sounded like one I had recently heard."
"Was it like Cate's?"
Robert asked his wife.
"No, I know the accent of the Irish, this was something else."
Grace looked around the table, not sure if she should say anything.
"Grace, have you spoken with someone similar?"
asked Robert.
"Yes, yes I have. I had forgotten about it until now. It was on the lane 2 days ago, he said he was going to the rectory, stopped for a bite to eat and went on his way. Mr. Nash saw him too."
"You didn't mention this to me."
Billoughby said as he looked at Grace.
"I didn't think it was that important, and it probably isn't. People are permitted to come to the village are they not?"
Grace replied.
"They are, of course they are. Where was this?"
Billoughby didn't like the thought of his wife sitting out by herself in the lanes with a strange man.
"Halfway between home and the village, look, does it matter? He seemed harmless enough to me."

Billoughby shook his head, she should know that not everyone that looked harmless was harmless more than most.

"Grace, more tea?"

Mary could feel that this conversation was beginning to go down a troublesome path.

"That's very kind dear but I think I ought to be making a move. I have many things to do today. Can I help you with the washing up?"

"No, I wouldn't hear of it. Drop by anytime, our door is always open."

replied Mary. Grace nodded her thanks again and picked up her bundle of wet clothes from the sideboard.

"I'll bring your things back in the next couple of days, see you soon."

Grace let herself out, leaving her husband sitting in the kitchen, his face again perplexed.

"She'll settle down, it's a difficult thing for a mother when her youngest flies the coup."

offered Robert.

"Gracie, wait up."

Billoughby walked quickly in an attempt to catch his wife up, he could feel the tightness in his chest worsening. He wasn't certain if she could hear him or whether she was choosing to ignore him. All the same he chose to believe it was the prior. He walked beside her now, his chest wheezing as he tried to keep in step with her brisk pace. Grace could hear the wheeze as it grew louder, the last time it had this sound had been after a bad bout of influenza.

"Stop Milton, sit down before you do yourself an injury. How long has your cough been causing you trouble?"

Milton was grateful for the break as he perched himself on the rickety wall.

"It's fine, it's the dew in the air I should think."

Grace wasn't so sure, and she berated herself silently for being too wrapped up in her annoyance to have noticed it.

"How long!"

She demanded as she rested her hand on his upper back to feel the rattle for herself, his coat felt damp, but it had rained.

"A few days or so, it's fine. Walking will do it good."

"So will a visit to the doctor. Stay here and I'll fetch the cart, you hear me Milton?"

He nodded; he was far too out of breath to argue with the woman.

"I won't be long, it's not far."

Grace made quick her walk down the lane to the cottage leaving Milton at the side of the road.

Milton sat alone as he waited, he knew that he should have made an effort to see the doctor when he first felt the rattling but as was his way he didn't want to cause alarm to his family, especially at a time when things were so strained.

"Pa?"

"Hello son, where did you get to?"

Tom stood behind the wall; he didn't like the look of his father's colour at all.

"Never mind that. What are you doing sitting out here, you aren't looking too good. Are you feeling alright?"

Milton shook his head followed by a very long bout of coughing. Tom knelt by his father's legs. Eventually Milton stopped coughing, his voice raspy he replied.

"You Ma has gone to fetch the cart for me. I'll be fine, son."

Again, he breathed in a large gulp and began the terrible coughing fit as Grace jumped down from the cart.

"Help me get him up Tom."

She said, as the 2 of them helped the now breathless man into the back of the cart.

"I'll come with you."

Tom leapt into the back leaving Grace to handle the ride into the village. She could hear her son's soothing voice as he spoke to his father, telling him that he was going to be just fine and that they would be there soon. Grace was frightened, she was angry with herself, and she knew that should anything happen to her beloved Milton she would never forgive herself.

"I am going to have Milton admitted for a stay in the Royal Victoria, he has contracted an infection and needs care that we cannot give him at home. It would be better if Tom went with him and you went home to get some rest, you will be no use to Milton without it."

Grace felt the colour drain from her face. What was happening? Everything seemed to be falling apart and she was powerless to do anything. Tom put his arms around her.

"He's a strong man, Ma. He will get through this, come on now, best smile when you go in." Grace ran to him, he looked suddenly so frail and she wanted nothing more than to whisk him up and take him home.

The doctor made the arrangements and handed Tom a letter.

"Give this to the Matron when you arrive, please inform them that I will be by this evening to speak with them. Don't fret Master Billoughby, he will be in good hands, lucky you got him here when you did. The buggy is waiting outside, I will have my man help you settle Mr. Billoughby into it comfortably."

Grace watched as the men carefully positioned her husband into the buggy.

"What's happening? Grace, whatever has happened, is Mr. Billoughby alright?"

"I don't know, they are taking him to the hospital in Folkestone. How is this happening, what have I done?"

Grace sobbed as the buggy pulled away, taking her husband and son. Elsbeth pulled the distraught woman to her.
"What can I do? You cannot be alone at this time, come on. I'm going to get you over to Adam and Cate's."
Grace nodded, unable to speak.

Sally stood open-mouthed as Elsbeth quietly explained the situation to her and cook.
"I don't want the children hearing of this, I must go and inform Mary so I would be very grateful if you could keep a watch on things here until I return."
The women nodded. Mrs. Williams entered the room.
"Is there a problem, Ma'am?"
She asked, sure that Sally had been telling tales about her.
"I have to go out. Sally and Cook will be in charge during my absence. Miss Geraldine will be back shortly and will take charge. Can you make a start on cleaning the nursery and the schoolroom, I feel you have been a little lapse on your housework of late. That is all, I will return as soon as I can."
"But surely that is better suited to…"
Began the indignant Mrs. Williams.
"I have given you instructions, please do not test me today of all days. If you feel these tasks are beneath you I can find a housemaid that will be happy to replace you."
Elsbeth did not raise her voice and yet the tone was stern and decisive.

Mr Hirst sat in his room and tried to devise his plan. He was well aware that his presence in the small village would soon draw attention if the village was anything like his own. Small communities were rife with gossip as he well knew to his cost. The now familiar knock on the door came to alert him to dinner.
"I will be down shortly."

Saving Grace | D M Roberts

He called. The footsteps could be heard walking away from his door and he continued to scribble in his notepad. There! With small satisfaction he closed the pad and placed it back into his bag.

"Ah, there you are Sir. I have poured you a port, I noted that you are not overly keen on the claret."
Mr. Hirst sat at the table and nodded.
"I have never gotten used to the taste, it is true. Port will do just fine. I hope your day has been a good one, Sir?"
The older man smiled as he carved his meat.
"I have. A very dear friend had lunch with me. I haven't seen him in some time, and it was jolly decent of him to make the trip over for my birthday."
Mr. Hirst raised his glass.
"Happy birthday, Sir. Many more ahead of you too."
The older man nodded his appreciation.
"And what of your day, Sir. Did you manage to entertain yourself in my absence?"
"I did. I visited the church, sat and had lunch at the inn in the high street and then I came back to do a little work."
"Excellent. Your work is coming along well?"
"It is. I am so grateful for your kindness, but I feel I should be moving on, I would hate for you to feel that I was taking advantage of your good nature."
Mr. Gregory frowned. He had been enjoying the company of this fellow, it wasn't often that he had guests and he realised he had missed that.
"Poppycock, I am a self-indulgent man and I enjoy our talks. It is of no bother to me however long you wish to stay, but I would rather you did if you still have business in the area."
Mr. Hirst felt for the man, in his large and splendid home with nobody to talk to but the birds that occupied the trees in the garden.
"I too enjoy our talks. If you are sure that I am not imposing?"

"I am sure. Now eat up, my cook has made the most delicious blackberry pudding."

Chapter Six

Jennifer paced up and down in the nursery. She was furious at being reprimanded but that paled into insignificance at being referred to as a housemaid! How dare these people treat her in such a way. If they knew what she was capable of they wouldn't dare.
"What you doing, Miss?"
Jacob wondered if the woman was practising marching like the people he had seen in the towns, they had bells and tambourines, but Miss didn't.
"Come here boy. Close the door."
Jacob did as he was asked, he thought Miss would let him march too. That would be fun.
"Can I march too, Miss?"
He asked, his smile bright and his eyes wide.
"You are a very bad boy to come into this room when I am busy. Did you not have any manners taught to you boy? Do you know what happens to nosey boys that have no manners? They are punished. Do you know what happens to boys that come into a lady's room without knocking? They are punished again, until they learn to use their manners and mind their business."
Jacob's smile vanished from his face, he had been punished before, he had been punished before he came to Miss Elsbeths, and he didn't like it. Jennifer's hand shot out sending the young boy hurtling across the room. She walked slowly to where he lay on the rug clutching his stomach, the harrowing expression on his face gave the woman an elated buzz that she revelled in. She crouched down next to Jacob as he cowered away from her hand that was now beginning to rise again. Pressing her finger to her lips she let out a sound.

"Shhh. It will be our little secret. You don't want me to punish you again, now do you?"
Jacob shook his head frantically as he scrambled to his knees and bolted for the door. The echoes of Mrs. Jennifer Williams' delirious laughter followed him down the landing to the closet that he flung himself into and pushed the door shut.

Mr. Nash was in jovial spirits when he delivered the groceries to the hall. He laughed and joked with the children as he had become accustomed to doing over the time since they had lived there. He was a kind man that had always had time for the youngsters of the village. He came from a large family himself and secretly felt in awe of the way Mrs. Stanhope had opened her home to such unfortunate souls as these.
"I have a special treat today. Can anyone guess what it is? There's a sweet in it for the one that does the guessing."
The children huddled around, their excited faces calling out all manner of things including a pony, a dolly, and a toy soldier.
"We give up, Mr."
said David as they had exhausted all their answers.
"Well, the missus has made you a trifle, have any of you tasted a trifle?"
Their little faces puzzled, and they shook their heads.
"Do you mean a rifle, Mr.?" asked William.
"No lad, a trifle. Wait there and I'll fetch it, cook can keep it cool until you have your tea."
Mr. Nash returned with the bowl and the children peered at the enormous cream covered dessert with wonderment.
"Do we eat it?"
Asked Martha.
"Course we do. It's got cream in it. We do eat it, don't we, Mr.?" asked Ruby.

"Aye, you do an all. You'll have to let me know next time what you make to it. Missus says you'll love it."

Mr. Nash took it to the kitchen and presented it to Cook.

"Well I never, that looks good enough to eat. You mind that you thank Mrs. Nash for me."

Mr. Nash nodded, pleased at the response he had gotten with his surprise gift.

"Where's the little fella today? He's usually the first to the door when I get here."

Cook shrugged.

"Up the stairs I shouldn't wonder. I reckon the little man is sickening for something, barely touched his supper last night, or his breakfast."

"Mind if I pop along up and say hello?"

Cook shook her head.

"If you can get a word off him I'll be happy. Here, did you hear about the Inspector? Right poorly he is by all accounts, at the hospital in Folkestone I hear."

"Aye, I did. Robert told me all about it this morning. Happen there'll be a fair few prayers said for the man these next few days. Right, I'm off to see the little one and I'll be on my way, I've got a big cart of deliveries today. I don't know where they put it, I don't."

Mr. Nash tapped quietly on the door of the upstairs library. It had been mostly stocked with children's books and soft toys. He spied Jacob sitting on the window seat staring through the window. Jacob had his knees pulled up to his chest, his arms wrapped around them.

"Hey lad, I missed you this morning when you didn't come down to see me. Are you feeling poorly? Cook said you didn't finish your food today."

Jacob shook his head and said nothing, he continued to stare out to the fields beyond the gardens.

Saving Grace | D M Roberts

Mr. Nash sat down at the other end of the seat. He watched the little boy and wondered what was going through his mind.

"Are you watching rabbits lad?"

Again, Jacob shook his head.

"Has somebody made you sad? You can tell me if they have. Be between you and me?"

Jacob looked over to Mr. Nash and the grocer knew there was something.

"Tell you what lad, you tell me what it is, and Mr. Nash will see what he can do to go about making it right, eh?"

The man put his hand forward for Jacob to shake, he was shocked when the child recoiled from it with a look of fear that stabbed deep into the grocers heart.

"Alright lad, I'm not going to hurt you. You know me, don't you lad?"

Jacob nodded, a tear rolled down his face and he quickly rubbed it away.

"I have to get back to work now, young Jacob. Do you think if we ask the missus she might let you come and help me with my deliveries? I tell you, my back has been paining me something terrible this past week and I could do with a strong pair of hands today and no mistake. Would you like that?"

Jacob was up and down the stairs in no time, standing at Mr. Nash's cart before the man had even reached the library door.

Mr. Nash squared it with Elsbeth and went back to the cart outside.

"Here, let me help you up."

Offering his hand to the child he was again surprised when the child refused it and scrambled up himself, albeit in a most awkward fashion. They made several stops on their way down to the village with Jacob saying little, if anything to the man.

"I think we deserve a break, what do you think lad?"

Jacob merely nodded as Mr. Nash pulled the cart to a stop. He took out a small hamper that contained a couple of pieces of fruit, some crusty bread and a chunk of cheese. Handing a piece of each to Jacob he watched the boy carefully, there was something not right, but what he didn't know. They ate as they admired the view across the marsh, on days like this one it was a beautiful sight to see.
"Right then lad, on we go."

The cart set off again and in no time at all the deliveries were finished and they were back at the shop belonging to the Nash family.
"See if you can get anything out of him, can you love?"
Mr. Nash asked his wife.
"I'll give it a go, but I won't force the boy."
She replied. Jacob sat in the back room now, he had a number of toys on the floor that Mrs. Nash had given him to play with. His small hands spun the wooden objects around as he looked at them from all angles.
"You like that one?"
Mr. Nash asked as he stood at the door. Jacob nodded.
"That was our lads, he would play with that for hours he would. Mrs. Nash wants to know if you can help her with the potatoes, they're a bit muddy mind you."
Jacob stood up leaving the toy on the floor.
"You here to help me wash the tatties?"
Said the woman as she pulled a box across the floor for Jacob to stand on. Standing on the box the boy began to wash off the mud and dirt then placed them in the next bowl as Mrs. Nash had shown him. He liked this, it was fun. It was better than being at home with the mean lady, he thought. The potatoes were finally finished, and Jacob dried his hands, as he tried to lift the bowl with the muddy water it tipped, sending dirty water all down his front.
"Oh dear, it isn't bath time is it?"

Laughed Mrs. Nash as she approached Jacob. Jacob shrank back away and sobbed loudly.

"I'm sorry, I'm sorry please don't punish me, please don't."

Mrs. Nash put her hand to her mouth, the chill that ran through her body at seeing such a response was not a pleasant one.

"Oh, my little lamb, come here, come to me. I am not going to punish you dear, why ever would you think such a thing? Let's get you something dry to wear, reckon I got one of my lots old things in the back. Come with me, it's alright."

Jacob walked against the wall to the room, keeping clear of the woman as he went.

Mrs. Nash rummaged in some crates until she found an article of clothing small enough.

"Here you are dear, try this one."

She passed it to the boy, watching as he struggled to remove his sodden top. Jacob eventually tugged his shirt over his head revealing a large area of bruising over his ribs.

"I'm just going to find a bag for your wet things, back in a minute."

She smiled, she wanted to shout and scream at whatever the animal was that had done this to a baby.

"Husband!"

She hissed as Mr. Nash finished serving his customer.

"Wife?"

He grinned back.

"Lock up that door, don't ask me the why's just lock it."

Mr. Nash did as he was asked, his expression one of bewilderment.

"What's going on?"

She pointed him in the direction of the back room, Jacob was about to pull the garment over his head.

"What in the name of…"

Mrs. Nash poked her husband.

"Don't raise your voice dear, we don't want to have the child even more in a flutter than he is."
"Wait until I go to that hall, there will be hell to pay."
Jacob popped his head through the long shirt. He stared at the 2 older people who were staring at him. Mrs. Nash leant down.
"Dear, did you hurt yourself?"
Jacob shook his head.
"I didn't, I was bad, and I was punished."
He whispered as he looked around the room.
"By who, you can tell me lad, who punished you?"
Demanded Mr. Nash. Jacob didn't reply, he remembered his warning and was saying not another word.

Tom sat at his father's bedside for 2 days solid. After Billoughby had been admitted he fell into a long and deep sleep, rousing only to cough up the darkest of phlegm into a bucket. The doctor had assured Tom that the medicine would mostly make him sleepy, and the rest was his body needing to sleep to repair itself. Every hour or so a nurse would come in and check various things, pat Tom on the shoulder and leave.
Elsbeth had visited late the night before, she brought with her some food stuff for Tom, and they had talked in the quiet corridor at length. Elsbeth had wanted to let Tom know that she was praying for them, all of them but that she would keep her distance until his father was on the mend. Tom had taken this news as a sign that Elsbeth was letting him go at first, the woman reassured him it wasn't the case, but his family must come first.
"I will always be here for you, come and find me when you come home. You need to be strong now my love, your mother and your father need you."
She kissed him tenderly, a young night nurse raised her eyebrows as she passed, they giggled for a moment forgetting themselves.
"I love you more than life, don't forget that."

Saving Grace | D M Roberts

replied Tom as they parted ways.

Grace cleaned the cottage with a relentless fervour until it shone brighter than the sun in the sky, and then she cleaned it again. It was the middle of the night but regardless of the doctor's instructions to rest the woman could not. Time and again she stopped and scalded herself for not seeing what was right under her nose. Has it come to this? That the person she had spent her life with played a bad second to her own selfish brooding. Grace knew that she had to pull herself together and accept what was with her son if they were ever going to get back to the way they had been. Exhausted, Grace lay down on the sofa and fell asleep. Adam placed a rug over his mother and decided it was not the time to wake her.

Tom felt a prodding on his shoulder. He had fallen asleep with his head resting on the edge of the bed.
"Son, Tom. You're crushing my hand, son."
Tom didn't know if he was dreaming as he looked at his father. Billoughby pulled his hand from under and tried to sit up.
"Let me help you Pa, I'll fetch the nurse."
Helping his father to get more comfortable, Tom noticed that as well as looking better in his colour, Billoughby was not rattling as he had done the past week. This had to be a good sign.
"How long have I been here, son? Is your Ma here?"
"You've been here 5 days, Pa. They wouldn't let Ma stay or even visit but she has been sending her love."
Billoughby was shocked, he felt as though he had gone to sleep not a day since.
"5 days you say, are you sure?"
Tom nodded as he left the cubicle to find the nurse.

The nurse was pleased with Billoughby's rate of recovery as was the doctor, and it was decided that Billoughby could now receive some

visitors under strict instructions that they were not to tire him out. The first persons to call were Daisy and the Reverend Moore. They had been asked to keep the conversation light, and it was, until the Reverend mentioned his strange visitor. Daisy had wondered if it could be the same man they had encountered in Canterbury, Billoughby listened intently to the pair and their thoughts. Next to visit was Robert and Mary, they too eventually got around to the mystery man in the village.
Cate and Adam arrived and spent time cheering up the now bored Billoughby, he wanted to go home that much was evident. Cate and Adam left the room and Billoughby rested against his pillows while the nurse administered his medicine.
 Grace stood at the curtain, she watched the man as he argued with the nurse quietly about how he was taking up precious space that could be used by a sick person. Grace smiled, trust him, she thought.
"Oh, there she is. Nurse, this is my Gracie. I have missed you my love."
Grace walked quietly to the bedside and taking his hand she sat down on the edge.
"How are you feeling, love?"
Her voice was low.
"I reckon I'm fit enough to come home…"
The nurse laughed.
"And I reckon you need to do as you're told and stay put! For a few more days at least. It's nice to meet you Mrs. Billoughby, if you like I can bring you a cup of tea?"
"That would be nice, thank you."

 The nurse hurried off, her starched uniform rustled as she walked down the ward.
"How are you, love? I worry about you over at the cottage on your own."
Grace smiled.

"I'm doing okay, lots of people calling to ask after you. Molly and her lot from the Inn send their best. I wanted to say that I'm sorry Milton, I got that wrapped up and I should have noticed you were unwell. Can you ever forgive me?"

Grace wept quietly as she kissed her husband's hand that she had kept clasped in her own.

"Now, Gracie. It wasn't for you to keep a check on me, I could feel it myself and did nothing. It was silly of me. Love, you can't help the way things have turned out and you can no more help the way you feel about the other stuff."

"I feel foolish, all this nonsense and it's not that important is it? I want our boy to be happy and I miss my friend, I will come round in my way I promise."

Milton shook his head; he knew this had taken a toll on Grace much greater than anyone realised.

"It will sort itself out. Now, I want you to go home and get some rest. No point in both of us being ill. I love you Gracie, always have and that will never change."

"I love you too Milton."

Geraldine entered the rectory, it was quiet and she couldn't see Tobias or Daisy anywhere. Calling out she stood in the hall and waited. How very odd that neither of them was around when they had made arrangements to meet her here this morning. Turning around she shrugged and made her way outside. Mr. Nash was walking through the churchyard toward her.

"Is the reverend about, Miss?"

He asked as he stood with his cap clutched to him.

"It would appear not, he should be, but I can't find him, or Miss Harvey and we were set to meet this morning. It's quite a nuisance, but Tobias is often forgetful."

She replied with a light laugh.

"Oh, I see. I wanted to speak to him, it's important. Maybe I'll wait."

Mr. Nash sat on the low wall that surrounded the garden.

"Is everything alright Mr. Nash? I don't want to pry but you look rather like you might burst with worry."

Mr. Nash looked down at the gravelly floor and wondered if he should speak to the woman, she was staying at the hall.

"I don't know Miss, I don't think everything is alright but I don't know who to have a word with and I thought maybe the reverend because he knows about these kinds of things. I don't know if that's the right thing to do, it must be, mustn't it, Miss? Him a man of God and all."

Geraldine was utterly confused. Mr. Nash, in her experience with the man, always struck her as a sharp and decent man so to see him looking so uncertain was strange to say the least.

"Would you like to talk with me, Mr. Nash? The rectory is open, we could go in and wait for Tobias and perhaps you could tell me what troubles you? I might be able to help."

Geraldine gestured for the man to come back into the building. Still unsure, Mr. Nash lingered on the wall.

"If nothing I could at least make a pot while we wait? Tobias won't mind."

Mr. Nash stood up and gave the matter a little thought, he nodded, and they went into the rectory. Geraldine placed the kettle onto the burner and Mr. Nash stood awkwardly in the corner of the room.

"I can come back, I don't want to be keeping you, Miss."

He said.

"Nonsense, I have no place that I have to be except for here. Sit yourself down."

Geraldine said as she offered the seat.

Mr. Nash was very quiet as he sipped the freshly brewed drink and Geraldine couldn't help but wonder what he was thinking or what it was that he was keeping to himself.

"I would have gone to speak with the Inspector you know, but he's still away in the hospital and I'm not sure that I should bother him when he comes back either if he needs to be resting."

He finally spoke.

"Mr. Nash, you must forgive me, but I can tell that something is deeply troubling you. I understand that you would rather speak with Tobias, I do, but I feel that in his absence you should tell me what it is. You have my word that it will stay between us unless you say otherwise."

Mr. Nash sighed heavy sigh as he placed the cup onto the table.

"The missus you see, Miss. The missus says we can't keep a thing to ourselves, ain't right." Geraldine nodded and prepared herself for a marital problem, she had done a lot of work with people regarding marital problems and her thoughts relaxed knowing that she could handle this.

"Your wife is right, Mr. Nash. A problem shared and all of that."

"It's the young lad, came back with me as he was feeling out of sorts."

"Oh, do you mean Jacob?"

"Aye, good little chappie he is."

Geraldine nodded and wondered where this was going as it was obviously not a marital problem as she had thought.

"Did he break something? Oh, he didn't steal anything from the shop did he? He's had a rough life Mr. Nash, if he has done something please remember that he needs time to learn proper ways."

Mr. Nash shook his head, he wasn't sure now that he should tell her any more what with her talking about learning proper ways.

"I'll wait if it's all the same, Miss."

Mr. Nash picked up his cup and continued to drink his tea.

Saving Grace | D M Roberts

"I can't help you if you won't tell me, most importantly I can't help Jacob."
"He's took a beating. There, and I'm hoping and praying you know nothing of this. Ain't right, he's a babby and not only that he's had a warning that he's to say nothing to no-one else he gets another one."
Geraldine gasped in horror.
"You know this for certain?"
"Aye, I saw the bruising with my own eyes when he got his shirt soggy and the missus fetched him a clean one. The missus is that angry, I had to stop her going to the hall and fighting anyone that might have done this."
"Did he say who it was, was it one of the children?"
Mr. Nash shook his head.
"By my reckoning it were no child that did this. He is terrible scared, I didn't want to take him back there and that's the truth"
"You leave this to me Mr. Nash. I will find out who did this, and the good Lord help them when I do."
Geraldine was furious, leaving Mr. Nash sitting at the reverend's table she stormed from the room and out to her cart. Mr. Nash turned to see a confused Reverend Moore and Daisy standing behind him.

Elsbeth picked up the familiar looking envelope as she closed the front door. There was that same writing, it was the same as the 3 she now had locked in her drawer.
"Mr. Tom is in the parlour; Miss. Would you want me to fetch tea?" Asked Sally upon hearing her Mistress return.
"Thank you Sally. Sally, is there anything I should be aware of in the household?"
Sally didn't know what to say as Miss Mary had said she would deal with the issue.
"I don't know Ma'am, there's a feeling lately. I'll fetch the tea."
Sally left as quickly as she could, she wanted to avoid the difficulties that would surely follow after such a remark. Elsbeth puzzled over

the comments as she placed the letter into her cuff and entered the parlour.

"Tom, is your father alright? I must say I was surprised when Sally said you were waiting for me."
Tom stood, he felt strange in his working clothes amongst all the splendour of the lavish room.
"Pa is doing well. The nurse sent me home until the end of the week when we can bring Pa home. I have come to bring a message from Ma, she would like to have you call over to see her." Elsbeth was shocked, was she in for another talking to she wondered.
"Do you know why?"
He shook his head, for he had no idea why.
"Only that, she called to the farm this morning."
The pair sat and talked a while, Sally knocked on the door to bring in the tray. She was setting it on the table when they heard a pounding on the front door.
"It's all go today, Ma'am. I will see who it is, everyone except Cook is out or upstairs."
Elsbeth nodded as the knocking got louder and more impatient.

Geraldine stormed past Sally and into the parlour, she slammed the door shut behind her so hard that Sally had to jump back to avoid it hitting her in the face.
"Elsbeth, I need to speak with you this instance. Alone!"
"What on earth is going on?"
"Mr. Billoughby, could you leave us."
This was not a question as Geraldine meant for the young man to go.
"Geraldine, you can't speak to Tom that way. Sit down and tell me what is wrong. Tom, sit down, I would like you to stay."
Said Elsbeth trying to retain her authority in the room. Tom was bewildered, he didn't know what to do.

"Very well, if you would have an outsider hear this then so be it. I spoke with Mr. Nash this morning and I am furious. Mr. Nash has informed me after much cajoling on my part, that he has witnessed bruising on young Jacob, bruising that has occurred after a beating that took place in this very house! I am assured it was not one of the children. What do you know about this?" Elsbeth sank to the chair. There had to be some kind of mistake, she would know if such a thing had happened under her roof.
"He must have misheard?"
Stammered Elsbeth.
"He saw the bruises and spoke to the child, there is no mistake." Raged Geraldine.
"You're not accusing Elsbeth, surely?"
Asked Tom, his voice strained but hushed to almost a whisper as he stared at Geraldine.
"That is not what I said Mr. Billoughby but someone in this house has caused that young child harm and if you don't find out who it is and have it dealt with immediately then I shall be forced to report this matter to whatever authority I see fit."
Elsbeth felt sick, a person in her home had seen fit to do this kind of thing and she was unaware. Jacob had been acting out of character of late, but they had put it down to some type of bug. Elsbeth stared at the 2 people in the room now, she wanted answers. The door opened and Mrs. Williams entered.
"Did I ask you to come in? Get out, get out this instance."
Elsbeth screamed at the woman. Tom and Geraldine sat in silence as Mrs. Williams backed out of the room.

Chapter Seven

Elsbeth and Geraldine told Cook to assemble all of the children, they were to bring their coats as they were going for a walk. The babies were taken by Tom and Geraldine, and they made their way out of the hall. The door opened behind them, and Jacob turned to see Mrs. Williams walking quickly to catch them up. He squeezed William's hand so tight that William squealed.
"Too tight Jacob, you're hurting me."
he wailed. Elsbeth stopped.
"It's alright dear. Mrs. Williams, where are you going?"
"With the children, Ma'am. You'll never manage them with only the 3 of you."
"Go back to the house, we can manage just fine."
Mrs. Williams continued to follow.
"I think it's better if I come with you, they can be a handful you know."
Tom handed the child to Elsbeth and approached the woman.
"Mrs. Stanhope asked you to go back to the house, please do so. We don't need help with the children, we looked after them well enough before you got here."
Mrs. Williams shrugged, her face taking on a smirk. She kept her voice low as she leaned toward Tom.
"You set a bad example for their innocent minds, wicked the pair of you."
She walked back to the house leaving Tom speechless.

They walked down the lane toward the village.
"Where are we going?"
Asked the children, who found their trip mostly exciting.

"It's a nice day, I thought we might go to visit the ducks on the pond."
replied Elsbeth.
"We don't have any bread for them, Miss."
Ruby answered as she skipped along.
"We can call and ask Mr. Nash if he has any spare crusts. My brother Adam and I used to do that when we were young lads, " said Tom.
"You have a brother?"
Said Martha with surprise in her voice.
"Of course, you know them don't you? Adam and Cate and baby Maisy. Cate comes to do the piano playing and she is wed to my brother."
Martha now looked confused.
"I like Cate."
Offered Ruby.
"I like Cate too, she's a good sister-in-law."
Laughed Tom.

Behind the group Geraldine and Elsbeth were talking quietly.
"I am sorry for my outburst, dear. You can understand my upset?"
Elsbeth nodded.
"I do, but who could do such a thing and for me to be unaware? It sends chills through me. Am I to dismiss all of the staff until we find out what happened?"
"And how would you manage? I will be here to help for some time, with your permission of course, I think we are safe with Cook, and I would like to think that for all her odd ways, Sally dotes on the little ones. That makes 4 of us to start with. I can't offer my opinion on the younger girls that help out or the stable hands and gardeners." Geraldine paused as she looked over to the children, Jacob walked on his own a few steps behind the others with his head low.

"And, I also cannot comment on Mrs. Williams although I am not overly taken with her."
"I will have to speak with Jacob, but where do I start? I don't want to startle the child or have him become more guarded than he has already become. The repercussions of this could be disastrous for the children. They might take them from me, Geraldine."
"It is unfortunate that Inspector Billoughby is away for the time being, he would know what to do."
replied Geraldine.

They reached the village and Tom took the older children over to the shop. He had asked them to mind their manners while he begged a few crusts from the grocer.
"Good day young 'uns, what can we get for you?"
Smiled Mr. Nash as the youngsters crowded around the small counter.
"We are looking for a few spare crusts to give to the ducks, Mr. Nash."
Replied Tom.
"Well then, happen you've come to the right place as well you will remember, young Tom."
Mr. Nash sifted through a basket behind him. Lowering his voice, he asked Tom if all was well.
"It's in hand, Mr. Nash. We thought we would come out on a little adventure, didn't we you lot?"
The children nodded.
"Did you see your Ma on the way down the lane? She was headed up to the hall."
"No, maybe she called to see Cate and the baby on her way."
"Aye, growing into the bonniest child she is that one."
Mr. Nash handed the paper bag to Martha to hold on to and he gave another bag to William with instruction not to get the 2 mixed up. They thanked him and made their way outside.

"I'll pop in and say a quick hello."
Said Elsbeth as they emerged.

"Shocking Mrs. Stanhope, and I hope you pardon me that I didn't know who to talk to about the whole thing. Is the lad going to be alright? He's awful quiet."
Elsbeth rocked Lily in her arms and shrugged.
"You did the right thing, Mr. Nash and we will get to know the culprit. I wanted them out of the house today so that I could think and know that they were safe. Jacob should be fine I hope, once we get to have a talk on our own and I can assure him that this is not acceptable, and it will never happen again."
Mr. Nash nodded, it was a tough road she had ahead of her and no mistake.
"You know where we are should you need any help."
"That is very kind, thank you."

Grace knocked again, there had to be someone in, there was always somebody around at the hall. Maybe they were in the back, she remembered that the children enjoyed playing out there when the weather was nice. Passing the stables Grace thought it strange that the young men who tended the horses were nowhere to be seen. She stopped on hearing a voice calling from the front.
"Oh, there you are. I knew there had to be someone home. It's ever so quiet here today."
"Mrs. Stanhope has given the staff a day off. She and Miss Geraldine have taken the children out for the day. Can I help you?"
"All of the children, just them 2?"
Asked Grace, that seemed a lot of children to take with only 2 of them.
"Yes, I offered my help, and it was declined."
"Mrs. Williams, isn't it?"
"That's right. You are?"

Saving Grace | D M Roberts

"I am Grace, Grace Billoughby, my husband is the police Inspector for the area."

Mrs. Williams smiled. What a convenient visitor she was turning out to be!

"You must come in; the mistress would insist I make you a pot of tea in her absence."

Grace was thirsty, it was a warm morning and the walk had seemed longer than usual.

"Thank you, that would be nice."

The 2 women entered the large house and Mrs. Williams locked the door behind them.

The cottage was quiet when Tom entered, a strange feeling crept over him as he made his way through to the kitchen. He had helped Elsbeth and Geraldine with the walk over to visit Mary and Robert at the farm in a bid to keep the children out of the house for as long as possible and taken the horse.

"Ma? Ma are you here?"

Tom called as he ran up the stairs. The bed was made up with no signs of Grace. Coming back down he searched through the cottage once again, but Grace was nowhere to be seen. He had called at Cate's to be told that his Ma hadn't stopped by as Mr. Nash had suggested. This was all very odd, he thought as he left the home. He untethered the mare now and walked it a while before mounting her and taking off down the lane. He was surprised to see Sally walking toward him.

"Morning Sally, what brings you out this way?"

Sally shielded her eyes as she looked up.

"The missus gave us the day off, I thought I might take a walk and see my sister over the marsh, Mr. Billoughby."

"When did she do this, Sally?"

Tom was puzzled.

"That woman said so, when she came back this morning. You know, after you left?"
"I don't know what you're talking about Sally."
"Mrs. Williams said the missus told her to tell the staff they could have the day off. Cook didn't want to at first, but I said if the missus says so we best do as she asks."
"Thanks Sally, say hello to your sister."
"Will do, Mr. Billoughby."
"Oh, have you seen my Ma up there this morning?"
"No, can't say I have. Cheerio then."
Sally continued down the lane. Tom sat still, this was all very strange, he didn't hear Elsbeth say anything of the sort to that wretched woman.

Reverend Moore opened the door, and the 2 clergymen came through, each nodding as they passed him and made their way into the sitting room. He did a last silent prayer and followed them through.
"Do sit down. I will bring the tea through; it is freshly brewed."
They sat on the leather high back chairs and waited for Tobias to return. They spoke in whispers as Tobias placed the tray on the table.
"Thank you, please sit down. You received the letter?"
Asked the older man.
"I did, and I am somewhat unhappy about your plans."
replied Tobias as he poured.
"Come now, you must have been expecting this at some point?"
"No, I was not. I have a good congregation and have gotten to know all of my parishioners personally over the years."
The men exchanged glances, the elder of the 2 opened his small case.
"We have concerns that we have to act upon."
He shuffled various pieces of paper in his hands.
"Concerns? Regarding what exactly?"

Demanded the Reverend.

"Conduct, we have concerns regarding the conduct of your guest. It has been brought to our attention that the young woman in question receives a male visitor on these premises. You understand that we cannot be seen to condone such carrying on?"

"The young woman in question has a fiancé, he is from a prominent family, and I can assure you that they are supervised by me personally. Who has made such vile accusations?"

Tobias was furious. He had known that this would come up at some point.

"You know that we cannot divulge the person or persons."
replied the younger of them.

"Perhaps your informant is unaware then, that the young woman is no longer residing here and as such no longer needs my approval or indeed a chaperone, and yet she still asks for both of these things."

"Is this true?"

"It is."

"That puts things in somewhat of a different light, although we still feel that a younger, fresher pair of eyes may be beneficial to the parish."

Tobias sighed, had it come to this? He had heard stories about acquaintances being retired off and replaced with much younger clergymen.

"I would ask you to reconsider. My parishioners are from old stock, their families have farmed this area for generations and they are not as adept to change as some of the younger towns." implored Tobias.

"We will take this information back and speak to you again. Now, are we going to stay for lunch?"

The older clergyman asked, his face softening. Tobias knew they were following orders and bore no ill will toward them.

"Of course, would you like to walk around the village and speak with some of the locals? It's a wonderful day for a stroll."

Grace sat in the parlour while Mrs. Williams went to fetch refreshments from the kitchen. It seemed strange to be in the house when it was so quiet, and Grace wasn't sure that she liked it.

"Here we are. I'm sure they won't be too long."

Jennifer sat down opposite Grace and began to pour. Grace wondered if Elsbeth would have something to say about the housemaid taking it upon herself to sit down in the parlour for tea with a visitor.

"Does the mistress of the house normally allow you to sit in the parlour? I wouldn't want you to get into any trouble on my account."

Jennifer's eyes flashed as Grace spoke, leaving Grace with a very uneasy feeling. Handing her the cup she eyed the woman carefully. She watched as Grace sipped the tea. Behind all of this warm countryside manner she was no different to the rest of them.

"It's your young boy that is tangled up with the missus here, isn't it? I imagine that can't sit too well with you. It's downright wicked behaviour if you ask me."

She sipped her tea not taking her gaze from Grace.

"I don't think that is any of your concern and if you don't mind me saying I would rather you did not discuss my family. You don't know us as we don't know you. I will call back at a more convenient time, if you let your mistress know that I was here I would be obliged."

Grace stood up and made for the door.

"I do hope I haven't offended you Mrs. I was only trying to have a conversation with you."

"It takes more than idle gossip to offend me."

Grace replied as she walked across the hall.

She felt hot, her skin was beginning to perspire but then it was a warm day, and she hadn't slept as well as she might have. The doorknob turned but when Grace came to pull it, nothing happened.

Saving Grace | D M Roberts

She tried again, becoming aware of her heart thumping loud and fast in her chest.

"Would you please…"

She stopped talking, she couldn't breathe. Jennifer stood by the parlour, she didn't speak as she watched the woman struggle for air. Grace felt for the wall as she lowered herself to the floor. Her mind was racing almost as fast as her heart, and she was vaguely aware of the person pulling her up.

Tom went back to the farm, he had looked everywhere he could with no signs of his mother. He was worried, especially with talk of a stranger in the village.

"I can't find her."

He said as he went into the kitchen.

"What do you mean, you can't find her? She can't have gone far, did you check in the village?" Asked Mary.

"Of course I did. I spoke to Sally too; she was on her way over to see her sister."

Elsbeth stared at him.

"Why on earth is she going to her sister? Has the woman taken leave of her senses?"

Tom shook his head; he gulped down some water then proceeded to tell Elsbeth what Sally had said.

"I heard no such thing."

Geraldine retorted.

"I did not say anything of the kind, well you were there Tom, and you too Geraldine. Did either of you hear me say this?"

The pair shook their heads.

"It's not my place dear, but I do think the woman is trouble." added Mary.

"She will be more than troubled when I speak with her, that she takes it upon herself to dismiss my staff as if she owns the place. I will not have it."

Saving Grace | D M Roberts

Said a furious Elsbeth.
"Will you make her leave?"
Whispered Jacob who had been standing at the door.
"Oh dear, I'm sorry Jacob, did we startle you with our loud voices?" cooed Elsbeth.
"Will you make her go?"
Jacob whispered again.
"You want her to leave?"
asked Tom as he knelt next to the boy.
"Yes, and I don't want to be punished no more."
The grown-ups in the kitchen turned to stare at the child as he stood with his back against the wall, he wasn't sure if he was going to be in trouble for what he had said, and his tears began to fall.
"Oh, my dear little one, come here, you will not be punished. We will make sure of that. Did Mrs. Williams punish you? You must tell me Jacob so that I can make sure it doesn't happen again."
Jacob nodded, still he would not go near the adults.
"William, Martha, come here."
The 2 older children came running into the kitchen.
"Yes Miss."
they said together.
"Can you take Jacob into the parlour to play? There are some blocks and some wooden soldiers in the chest, there's good children."
said Mary.
"Come on Jacob, let's build a castle and put the soldiers on the top."
The trio went off to play, leaving the adults to utter their disbelief at the revelation they had been witness to.

"She cannot stay, Elsbeth. We need to tell someone about this. Tom, do you think that as your father is still at the hospital it would be appropriate to speak with Constable Harvey?"
Tom nodded, for he too had realised that he could hardly burden his Pa with such a thing and then there was his Ma.

Saving Grace | D M Roberts

"Aye, Mary. I'll go over there now and ask her to come back with me. I'll need to have another look around for Ma. I won't be too long; I'll call on Adam to help me."
Mary patted him on the shoulder as he set off.
"She'll no doubt be having a cup of tea with one of the ladies in the village, Tom. Try not to worry, it's been a tough time for your Ma."
Tom nodded, Mary was probably right, his Ma never strayed very far from home he knew this.

Grace clutched her stomach, the pain was searing and the sweat was falling from her like rain in April. The cellar was dark, she knew it was a cellar by the smells and dampness. She wretched and the vomit flew from her mouth into the darkness. There wasn't a sound to be heard and she had no energy to call out, so she lay there, alone in the dark with her pain rising and her heart thumping. Grace wished that she had seen her husband and her family one more time before the good Lord took her. She wept tears of fear and remorse between bouts of sickness. Why had she been so harsh with Milton, he had never been anything other than kind to her, and Tom, all she ever wanted was for her boy to fall in love and be happy, and he had. She thought of Maisy and the expected grandchild that would arrive by Christmas, would she see them? She thought not as exhaustion overtook her and her eyes closed.

Mr. Hirst returned to the village, it seemed eerily quiet on a day when the weather was good and the breeze warm. He called into the grocers and bought some apples, a piece of cheese and a crust of bread. Mr. Nash eyed him suspiciously.
"You come far?"
He asked the man.
"Not really, Hythe. Do you know it?"
"Aye, I do that. Staying with family are you?"

Saving Grace | D M Roberts

"Friends, I have some business in the area and am fortunate to have a good friend that has put me up for a short time."
"I've seen you here the other day?"
said Mr. Nash as he recalled the man and Mrs. Billoughby on the lane.
"Maybe, although I can't say I remember you. Anyway, thank you for this. Good day, Sir."
Mr. Hirst waved the bag and left the shop. He stared up and down the lane, where to start! A tall young man passed him, he walked quickly as though in a great hurry. As he stood deciding which way to go the young man passed again but this time he was accompanied by a young woman, pretty thing too he thought.

Tom and Daisy got into the cart and made their way back to the farm, they made a few stops including Billoughby's cottage and the Hall but there wasn't a soul in either.
"We will find her, Tom. I have learned a lot from the Inspector and with everyone's help we are sure to have your mother back home in no time. Have you sent news to the Inspector about this or is it better to keep it quiet for now?"
Tom hadn't given it a thought, but now he had he didn't relish the idea of breaking this kind of news to his father.
"You don't think she's left, do you? She has been very irritable lately what with everything." Daisy knew what he was referring to, his relationship with Mrs. Stanhope, she chose not to go into it.
"Don't think such things, Tom. Likely she's gotten talking and forgotten the time. It can't be nice for your mother in the house alone."
"I suppose so, I never thought of it like that. I can't remember the last time Ma would have been there on her own."

The children were sitting at the table having tea when they arrived back. Mary quietly asked if they had found Mrs. Billoughby yet.

Tom shook his head, mindful of the little ears in the room and not wanting to worry them.

"Miss. Harvey, Elsbeth is in the back room if you want to go through she can fill you in on what's been happening."

Daisy wasted no time finding the room and soon, she and Elsbeth were deep in conversation as the young Constable took notes.

"Mrs. Williams is still at the Hall?"

Daisy asked.

"I presume so. Sally made no mention of her leaving to Mr. Billoughby, although when he called later there was no answer at the door."

Daisy nodded; she knew that an unanswered door did not always mean the house was unoccupied.

"Thank you Mrs. Stanhope. You will appreciate that it would be foolish of me to go there alone, therefore I will send word to Ashford for a couple of officers to come over tomorrow and assist me in this matter. I suggest you try to find a place to stay for yourself and the children tonight."

"Do you think it's that serious?"

Asked Elsbeth, her look turning to one of deep concern.

"I wouldn't like to guess, but I would rather be cautious."

Daisy made her way back to the kitchen where she whispered her thoughts to Mary.

"We have room, be a bit of a squeeze but we'll manage."

Mary reassured her.

"Thank you. I'm going to get back now and arrange things for tomorrow. I will call at some of the houses in the village to find out if anyone has spoken with or seen Mrs. Billoughby this afternoon. Oh, I do miss the Inspector."

She sighed as Mary walked her to the door.

"You're doing a great job, he will be proud of you. I am also glad that you aren't going to try to tackle that woman alone, there's something about her that I don't like. Take care, dear."

Daisy waved as she set off back to the village.

Mr. Nash had some very useful information for Daisy, who had made him her final call of the evening having come up with no further knowledge on Grace.

"That chap, the one that's been here in the last few days. He came in my store again mid-day, I saw him talking to Mrs. Billoughby only a few days ago, sitting on the wall up the lane he was, bold as brass and with her being a married woman."

Daisy frowned, this was how gossip started, and she wouldn't hear of it, not about the Inspectors wife.

"Did he say what he was doing here? Today, I mean."

Mr. Nash scratched his grey coarse hair.

"Business I think, said he was staying with a friend in Hythe for a while. Here, you don't think he's done anything to Mrs. Billoughby do you?"

Daisy shook her head.

"Now, Mr. Nash, we can't go jumping to conclusions."

Daisy replied, even though she had the exact same thought now running through her mind.

"It's a strange do that a man turns up and a woman disappears. When is the Inspector due back, do we know?"

"When he's better Mr. Nash. I'll say goodnight and if you hear anything you know where I am."

Jennifer sat at the head of the large table in the formal dining hall. She wore one of Elsbeth's satin evening gowns, it was a little tight in places, but the woman liked it all the same. She had to serve herself as the staff had all gone home. She made good use of the food that the cook had prepared earlier that morning. The house was silent, no more whining children tearing around the place with their dirty hands and feet and their ill-mannered ways. Yes, she liked it much better this way. The trunk sat across the room, it was a large trunk

that had taken her a while to move but the horses and cart would carry it with no troubles. Jennifer had decided that she would have supper first, to set her up for the long journey ahead as she did not intend to stop until she had reached her intended destination.
"The chicken is a little dry! Tell the cook that I am displeased and if she wishes to remain in my employ she must try harder."
The deranged woman said aloud as she pushed the half-eaten plate away.
"Let us see if she is better at the desert."
She plunged her spoon into the sticky pudding and cream and tasted it, she took spoon after spoon of the dish and when she was satisfied she pushed that too away from her. Swallowing down the large glass of wine she dabbed her lips and sat back in her chair. Jennifer sat for a while, occasionally making comments to herself then she stood up and took her large empty bag from the floor placing it on the table. Opening it up she began to fill it with various items of worth from around the room. She quickly moved through to the parlour and began the same procedure until the bag was full. Staring through the window she waited for the sun to set, motionless until finally, it was dusk.

The trunk was heavy, but she was a strong woman and it finally settled in the cart along with her bag of stolen items and her personal possessions. The horses let out snorts and whinnies, as though they sensed their occupants frightening behaviour. Jennifer flicked them hard with the crop which gave rise to louder snorts. Settling down at the head of the cart she laughed, they had no idea what she had done, and she cared not a fig as she began her journey.

Tom had been earlier to find out if she had any new information about his mother. She didn't, of course, and it saddened her to have to tell him this.

"I will have to tell Pa, I'm due to collect him this afternoon and he'll want to know why she isn't at home."
Tom had said.
"I'm sorry, Tom. I asked everyone that I could think of."
"I'm headed over to Adam's, we are going to start searching this morning. I can't think of what else to do."
The extra officers didn't arrive until after 11 and Daisy paced impatiently until that time.
"Do sit, dear. They will knock on the door when they arrive."
The reverend had insisted, but she couldn't.
"We don't know what this woman's background is, or how dangerous she could be. Ordinarily I would have gone on my own last night."
Remarked Daisy to the 2 constables.
"That wouldn't have been a good idea, Miss, sorry, constable. Not because you're a woman but as you say, you don't know what this person is capable of if she has no problem beating on a child like that."
Daisy nodded, she knew what he meant and that there was no insult intended.
"What of this other matter, constable. The missing wife of the Inspector and the stranger in the village?"
Reverend Moore was hearing this for the first time as he came downstairs.
"A stranger you say?"
"Yes, he came to see you I believe. He's been back a few times since, looking for something." Daisy turned as she spoke to Tobias.

"Oh dear, I thought he had left after I spoke with him. He was looking for a person he believed to be around here. A woman he said."
replied Tobias.
"Did he give you any idea where he came from?"

asked one of the constables.
"Hythe."
Interjected Daisy.
"His accent would suggest not."
added Tobias.
"Mr. Nash informed me that he was staying in Hythe, it would have been a help to know where, but we'll find him if he returns. It's a small village. Are we ready to go?"
Daisy ushered the constables outside, turning to Tobias, she added.
"Try not to worry and keep the door locked, Reverend. If the man comes back I would rather you didn't have him in here while you're alone."
Tobias nodded.

Cate swayed the baby in her arms as Tom tried to calm his brother down.
"If this man has done anything to Ma, I swear I will find him and kill him with my bare hands."
"We don't know as it's anything to do with this fella, Adam, and you'll do no good killing a person until we find out if he knows anything and even then there'll be no killing being done. You have a family to think of."
Adam grunted; he was not about to sit by doing nothing if some stranger had hurt his mother. Cate had only ever seen her husband like this once before, back in Ireland when a couple of lads had given her trouble as she walked home. He was a steady tempered man, until pushed.
"Tom's right, you need to keep a calm head until somebody can at least talk with your man."
"There's something not right going on, I'm telling you."
Adam stomped from the house returning after a moment to kiss his wife and daughter.
"It will be alright my love."

Whispered Cate as the 2 men left.

"When are we going home, Miss Mary?"
asked David as he threw chicken feed into the coup.
"You don't like the farm anymore?"
Laughed Mary.
"I do, I do Miss Mary, but I was rotten squashed in the cot last night."
"But wasn't it exciting to have a sleep out with the rest of the children?"
She asked as they walked back to the farmhouse.
"It was, but I like to have space in my bed, and William talks in his sleep."
Geraldine smiled as she listened to the pair talking.
"Not long now, David. Miss Mary will miss you when we go home, won't you dear?"
She said,
"I will indeed, we have the very best conversations, don't we young man?"
"We do that, Miss. I'm going to find William and Jacob; they can come with me to see the piglets."
David ran off in search of the younger boys.
"I wondered if I should go down to the village, find out what's going on. Will you be alright here with Elsbeth and the children?"
"Of course. It's a good idea, we can't just sit here waiting with no word."
Replied Mary.

Geraldine walked the distance down the lanes, she had refused the offer of Mary's buggy in case they might need it. The sun shone bright with the breeze, a warm one, and in no time at all Geraldine could see the cottages of the village in the short distance. The sound of hooves behind her made her turn. The man sat tall in the saddle as he said good morning.

"Good morning, lovely day."

His accent was similar to that of the dreadful woman, this must be the person that was being spoken about.

"You seem to like our small village, Sir."

"It is quaint, and I have business around here."

He dismounted and walked alongside the startled woman.

"You have been looking for a woman, or so I hear. Have you had any luck?"

"Not as yet, but I feel sure she has to be here somewhere."

"You are from the same place?"

Geraldine knew she was pushing her luck, but she needed more if they were ever going to get anywhere.

"Yes, a place called Redruth. It is most important that I trace this woman, she has problems."

"Do you have a name for her?"

"Not that it's important, her name is Nora Howard, but I suspect she will be using another name."

"You came a long way for this woman, is she your wife?"

Geraldine inwardly sighed as that certainly wasn't the name of the woman she knew.

"Heavens, No! It is purely work that brings me here to find her. Do you know of her?"

"Not by that name, although there is a woman who has taken up employment close by with an accent the same as yours, she has caused us quite a lot of upset and distress. You were talking with a woman not far from here 3 days ago, did you see her yesterday when you were in the village?"

Mr. Hirst looked surprised; it was a small place indeed that they knew his every move.

"If I recall she was a pleasant woman, but no, I haven't set eyes on her since that day. Is there a reason you ask?"

Geraldine did not see any reason to lie at this stage.

"She is the wife of our police Inspector, and she has gone missing." The man's mouth fell open, this felt too familiar, and he did not like it one bit.

"Where is the Inspector, I must speak with him immediately."

"Unfortunately, the Inspector is in the hospital, he is due to come home today. It is going to come as something of a shock to learn that his wife has vanished, and that a stranger has been in the village on the afternoon of her last being seen."

Mr. Hirst's face had turned pale, a fact that Geraldine was well aware of as she watched him.

"I need to speak with him."

He repeated.

"There is a constable in the village, I'm on my way there now if you would care to come along." He nodded, saying nothing more. His thoughts began to take a very dark path, he would surely swing, and nobody could save him.

Daisy stared at the man, why did she feel that she had seen him somewhere before?

"Geraldine, come in, oh and I see you have brought a guest."

Said Tobias as he stepped back to let them pass. Daisy and the 2 constables came into the rectory behind them.

"Good morning, Tobias. I hope you don't mind but we could not just sit there waiting, is there any news at all?"

She turned to Daisy now who was showing the constables into the sitting room.

"There wasn't a soul at the Hall, the horses and cart were gone, and the door was left open. We had a good look around, I'm afraid there are things missing. The woman had packed up her room and a lot of other items and fled. I remember you!"

Daisy turned from Geraldine and pointed at Mr. Hirst who was still standing by the door.

"Canterbury."
Mr. Hirst said, as he remembered the voice of the young woman that took the spare desk.
"You know this man, Daisy?"
asked Tobias who was now rather confused with the whole situation.
"I wouldn't go as far as to say that I know him, but we have met. So, you must be a member of the constabulary to have been using the office at headquarters?"
Asked Daisy.
"Yes, I told you I was here on business. The Inspector that was with you on that day, he is the husband of the missing woman from the village?"
continued Mr. Hirst.
"That's right. You spoke to her on the lane."
replied Daisy.
"I have not seen her since that day, I can assure you I had nothing to do with her disappearance, but I do believe we need to find Nora Howard as a matter of the utmost urgency."
Daisy sent the constables to assist Elsbeth and Geraldine in getting the children back to the Hall and to get a list of the items that had been stolen. She wanted them to be close to hand should she need their assistance again, sending them back to Ashford was not an option at this time. Tom and Adam continued to search through the fields and woodlands in the area but found nothing. Tom eventually had to leave for Folkestone to collect his father.
"What am I going to tell him?"
He said quietly to his brother.
"Tell him nothing until he gets back, Cate and I will go to the cottage so that he isn't on his own. We will wait for Miss Harvey."
Tom nodded and pulled his brother to him in a bear hug, it wasn't something he did often but today he felt he should for both their sakes.

Billoughby was perched on the edge of the hospital bed eager to get going when Tom walked through the ward.

"It's about time, son. I have all my things and the doctor said I can get out of here. Is your Ma not with you?"

Billoughby looked behind his son and down the ward.

"You come to take him home then? He's been up since before the birds this morning staring at that door, waiting. Medicine to take with you Inspector, please remember to take it and mind what the doctor told you about taking it easy."

Said the nurse as she gave the man a final once over.

"Come on then Pa, let's get out of here and get you home. You can sleep on the way if what the nurse said is true that you've been awake since dawn."

Billoughby patted Tom on the back, he was so happy to be going home at last to his Gracie.

Chapter Eight

"Where is your mother, Tom? Has she gone down to the village; we could have collected her on the way back."
Tom looked down at his feet, he knew he should have told his father sooner but secretly Tom had been hoping that she would be sitting here waiting when they arrived.
"That's the thing, Pa, nobody seems to know where she is."
Billoughby stared at his son now.
"Pa, it isn't Tom's fault. I told him to keep quiet until you were back. Ma hasn't been seen for a couple of days and Miss Harvey is doing everything to find her."
Adam pulled a chair out for his father.
"I don't want to sit, lad! I need to go out there and look for her. I can't believe that you both kept this to yourselves."
"You will do no good to Ma by wearing yourself out when you've only just got home. Miss Harvey has 2 constables over to help her and there's that Mr. Hirst, chap you met in Canterbury."
"What the devil has he got to do with anything?"
Billoughby felt hot, his heart was racing not with his ailment but fear for his Gracie.
"He came here to find someone, it turns out that someone is the new woman from up at the hall. She's disappeared too by all accounts."
Said Tom as he filled the kettle.
"Here, Tom, let me do that."
Offered Cate as the 3 men stood around wondering what to do next.
"I think somebody best go and fetch this Mr. Hirst over to me, if he knows what is going on then he is the man I need to be speaking with. Let Daisy know I am back and would like a word with her too."

Billoughby finally said as he sat at the table.
"I'll go over to the reverends now."
replied Adam. He placed a hand around his father's shoulder
"We will find her Pa, you'll see." and he was gone.

The reverend had suggested that Mr. Hirst stayed around the village as he was certain that Inspector Billoughby would want to speak with him. The sitting room was quiet considering that it held Reverend Moore, Daisy, 2 constables and Mr. Hirst. The knock on the door came as a welcome distraction to the small party.
"I'll get it."
Said Daisy as she got up from the desk.
"Hello Miss Harvey. Is that chap Hirst still here? Pa is home and he isn't best pleased that we kept him in the dark. He asked could you go over to see him and take Mr. Hirst with you."
Daisy nodded, she knew that the Inspector would have a great deal to say when he came home and was not looking forward to being the one that told him they had nothing.
"Come in, I'll grab my things and come back with you. We were in the midst of organising a search party."
Adam entered the sitting room to nods from the constables and an extended hand from Mr. Hirst.
"Pleased to meet you, I caught what you said at the door, and I am only too happy to come and speak with your father."
The tall man pulled on his overcoat while Adam spoke to the reverend.
"How is your father? I imagine all of this has him beside himself with worry. Is there anything that I can do to help?"
"Short of finding Ma, I'm not sure there is Reverend, but thank you for the offer. We'll be needing extra prayers this week and no mistake!"
Replied Adam.
"I am ready when you are."

Daisy appeared in the hallway followed by Mr. Hirst.
"Are we to stay here?"
enquired one of the constables.
"If you don't mind? The map of the area is on the desk, if you wouldn't mind taking it and following up on some of the areas we might have missed earlier that would be a great help."
Said Daisy.
"Right you are, Constable."
"I think we need to arrange another thorough search of the Hall in the morning."
She added.
"Makes sense to me."
Said Mr. Hirst.
The trio left for Billoughby's cottage, chatting about what ifs along the way. Adam remained the quieter of the trio, not wanting to think about his mother's possible fate.

Grace could shout no more, her throat hurt but at least she had stopped being sick. On her hands and knees, she searched around slowly in the dark. Her hands touched on what felt like an old blanket, it smelt musty, but it might keep her warm, so she pulled it over her shoulders. The pain in her chest and stomach nagged away at her endlessly but Grace knew that she had to keep moving around. Often she thought she heard voices but then silence resumed in this pitiful prison. Grace wondered if Milton was home yet, or if indeed he was still alive. She remembered how bad he had been and was well aware of how people can take a bad turn. Grace fought back the tears that inevitably came with this kind of thinking.
"Stop it! Do you hear me, Grace Billoughby. Stop that right now."
Her voice was hoarse and weak as she spoke into the silent damp air.

Jennifer Williams had a plan; Dover was not an option and so she decided that Liverpool was where she would take a ship to somewhere new. The journey would be a long and tiresome one but worth it. Of course, she could have found some small village out of the way, but did she really want to be looking over her shoulder for the rest of her life? The answer to that particular question was an emphatic no. The woman smiled to herself when she imagined the parishioners running around like headless chickens in their search for the Inspectors wife. She cared not that Grace might never be found, or that she would die an agonising death in the cellar she had dropped her into. It was a genius execution of hers and she began to laugh out loud in the misty evening air. The Inn came into view and Jennifer quieted herself as she dismounted the cart.

Mr. Hirst entered the cottage tentatively behind Adam and Daisy. He knew there would be harsh words from the Inspector, but he also knew that if the tables were turned he would have some damned harsh words to say too and so decided to give the Inspector his time to rant.
"Mr. Hirst, I take it. We've met previously."
Billoughby gestured for the man to sit.
"Inspector, I am sorry it has to be under such distressing circumstances. You have my most sincere thoughts and if there is anything that I can do."
"Would you all leave us for a moment? I need to speak with Mr. Hirst in private."
Billoughby asked of the others. Once the room had been cleared and only the 2 men remained, Billoughby handed the man a mug.
"There's tea in the pot or there's ale in the jug. Now, what I would like to know is why were you in the office in Canterbury? By my reckoning that makes you a member of the constabulary of some sort. What I would also like to know is how dangerous is Jennifer Williams, exactly?"
Mr. Hirst poured from the jug, this conversation was going to require more than a cup of tea, on his part at least.

"Her name is Nora Howard and in my opinion she is a very dangerous person. Can I be honest with you Inspector? I feel the time has passed for cloak and dagger antics."

"It will be the first time today from anyone."

Sighed Billoughby.

"I was able to enter the head office because I am, or I was, an Inspector of a place in Cornwall called Redruth. I know the woman Nora Howard because she lived in the same town as I did. She developed a strange liking for me, not one that was returned I can assure you, nevertheless she pursued me until I had to say something to her husband. Believe me when I tell you that I tried all other ways before I resorted to that action, but the woman was possessed. My lovely wife had put up with so much gossip on the matter that she took our son and left."

The man paused and Billoughby could sense the sadness on his face.

"That, as sad as it is, does not explain what the woman is doing here or why this makes her dangerous."

"She is trying to get herself overseas in the hope that she won't face the gallows. She planned it down to the smallest detail, what she did, leaving me to face the consequences. Well, I may be a lot of things but a cold hearted killer is not one of them. Nora Howard murdered her husband and his mother and father, she left enough stolen evidence in the house to lead my colleagues straight to my door. We have to find her, not only to clear my name but to have some chance of finding your wife."

Billoughby sat back in shock. He had little doubt that the man before him was anything other than what he had said. Thoughts of Grace and what this person might have done already to his beautiful wife overwhelmed him as his fists clenched and began to shake.

"You say she killed her family; how did she do this?"

He asked.

"Poison, she poisoned them. They were found when they failed to turn up to church, they never missed church. The medical examiner said it would have been quick with enough in the tea and cake to kill a herd of elephants by all accounts."

Mr. Hirst paused as the Inspector took in the gravity of what had been said.

"You have to believe me, Inspector Billoughby, I had nothing to do with this awful crime. I merely went in search of the woman to bring her to justice for what she has done not only to her own family, but to mine. I will give you as much or as little help as you ask for, but I have to ask that you keep my involvement in this to yourself as far as the constabulary is concerned. I will not hang for what was a misguided infatuation on her part. I may never get my family back, but I intend to do all that I can to give you back yours."

Billoughby nodded, he could see the man was in a desperate predicament and the law could be quite short-sighted when it wanted to be.

"I will do as you ask, on one condition."
replied Billoughby.

"That being?"
asked Mr. Hirst.

"We have to concentrate on finding my Gracie, I will be of no use to anyone if I don't give that my highest priority."

Mr. Hirst swallowed his ale and placed the mug on the table in the warm kitchen.

"I understand. First thing in the morning your constable has suggested that we do another search of the Hall. Clever lass that one. It is unclear if your wife ever went there but it is the last place that Nora Howard was seen and as she went no other place it stands to reason that Mrs. Billoughby must be either still concealed there or with Nora Howard."

Billoughby nodded, he too had thought this would be the first thing he would do.

"You will have to excuse me for a moment, I need to take this concoction from the hospital." Billoughby took the medicine from his pocket and took his specified amount, then placing it back where he had gotten it from he cleared his throat and called the others back into the kitchen.

Elsbeth finished putting the last of the children to bed and went downstairs to the parlour. Geraldine was already in there sipping a well-deserved glass of port.
"Would you like one, dear. It has been a difficult day one way or another."
"I would like 2, but I shall suffice with 1."
laughed Elsbeth as she sank into the large armchair in front of the fire.
"What do you think has happened to Grace?"
asked Geraldine as she handed Elsbeth her drink. Elsbeth sighed, she had thought of little else in the past few days.
"I am hoping that she has simply gone away for a few days to get her mind straight. Strange that Tom told me she was coming to see me, don't you think?"
"Very. Do you think she changed her mind?"
Elsbeth shook her head.
"That isn't like Grace at all. If she said she was going to do something, she usually does."
Sally knocked quietly on the door.
"Come in."
"I told my Harry that you might be needing me to stay over tonight Mrs. Stanhope, I don't mean to speak out of turn but you 2 look like you could do with a decent sleep, and I can be here for the little ones if they wake. It will make up for my day off."
Sally stayed at the doorway as she spoke to Elsbeth, not sure whether her offer would be taken in the manner it was meant.
"That is so very kind of you, Sally and would be greatly appreciated. Thank your husband for me, would you?"

Sally smiled and nodded, leaving the room and heading for the nursery.

"Drink up, I have an idea."

Said Geraldine suddenly.

"Oh, that sounds rather interesting. What are we doing?"

"We are going to check every room in this large house, just to be certain. I shall fetch some oil lamps if you want to fetch a throw for each of us. It is very cold in parts of this Hall."

The 2 women, lamps in hand, started at the far end of the house. Geraldine had picked up the spare set of keys for the rooms that they kept locked. Elsbeth had done this when the children came to live with her for their safety and there were many rooms that had not been entered since that time. There were rooms upstairs that led to the attics on one side of the house and the windows up there were old and fragile, this was definitely a place that the children were not permitted to enter, as were the cellars. The house had 6 cellars in total with only 2 in use. Elsbeth had looked in the others on her arrival but thought they were far too damp and vast to keep open, not even for storage purposes.

"Check in the large cupboards too, I don't want to worry you dear but one never knows."

added Geraldine as they walked into the first room. The air was cold and damp, it had once been a state dining room but had not been in use for over 20 years or so. They had become accustomed to using the breakfast room for meal times as it was closer to the kitchen. Elsbeth had often thought about re-opening it and having it freshly decorated, the cost had been far too extravagant after the children's rooms and the schoolroom were finished and so it was left.

Elsbeth could taste the musty scent of the large drapes that had not seen a clean in quite possibly 60 years and she had to cover her mouth and nose as she walked quietly around the large space. The furniture was beautifully preserved being of oak and as she ran her hand over the large table she could almost imagine the days when dinner would be served in the once brightly lit room. The centrepiece was undoubtedly the fireplace with its tall marbled surround and golden markings along the edges. Geraldine held her lamp higher as she stared up in admiration at the colossal chandelier that was perfectly placed above the table.

"What stories this room could tell."

Whispered Elsbeth as though she didn't want to disturb imagined guests at the table.

"From what Mary tells me, they were probably not very nice stories."

replied Geraldine in a hushed voice. The 2 women opened up the larger than normal wall cabinets that ran from floor to ceiling, stepping back as they did so. Geraldine hesitantly held her lamp to the opening, catching sight of a tiny mouse that scurried across the floor.

"I think we are possibly the first people he has seen."

Laughed Elsbeth as they looked at the masses of elaborate candlesticks and crockery that filled the shelves.

"There must be a fortune in silver in here! Have you never looked inside?"

Asked Geraldine.

"No, I don't know why. I imagined they would be full of old sheets and musty paper. Goodness, look at this!"

Elsbeth pulled out a vase that looked like it must be made of gold, it was certainly heavy enough, with jewels making up flower patterns all around, that shone brightly in the lamplight.

"It's as well that dreadful woman didn't think to come in here, you might never have known they were here, and she would have made off with them."

Said the companion as she closed the doors.

"Yes, I think we can safely say she hasn't been in this room. Let's get out of here, Geraldine, I fear my nose cannot take this unbearable smell much longer."

Grace could hear something, it sounded like faint footsteps and the first ones she had heard. Dragging herself to her feet she felt around for anything that she could find, her hands feeling against the walls. Tears fell rapidly as her frustration grew more desperate, and then she felt something. It must be a broom, or a shovel. Picking the object up she thrust with every bit of energy left in her as it pounded against the low ceiling, again and again she levelled pokes with force against it.

"Did you hear that?"
Geraldine stepped back into the room and waited.
"Maybe it's one of the children."
Whispered Elsbeth. The thuds came again.
"No, it's coming from underneath. Shh, listen."
They stood in silence as they tried to figure out where the noise was coming from. Geraldine walked slowly toward the end of the large table and stopped. Elsbeth joined the woman now and they both stood there, listening.
"Stamp your feet."
Said Elsbeth as she herself began to do just that. Geraldine banged her foot on the wooden floor, and they waited.
"There it is again. Where is the cellar?"
Geraldine was already searching around the edges of the room.
"I don't know, there must be a door somewhere."
They searched the room in every corner, but they could not find a door.
"It must be in another room. I think we might need some help, dear. Who knows what is making that noise and with the children in the house."
Elsbeth nodded, she didn't want to take any chances and she certainly didn't want to be crawling through dark cellars at this time of the night, not knowing what they might come across.

Grace could no longer hold the broom up, her stomach pain was agonising and she could feel the air drifting from her tight chest as she fell to the floor in a crumpled heap muttering the Lord's Prayer until she could feel the pain no more.

Sally was still awake when Geraldine tapped quietly on the nursery door.
"Everything alright, Miss?"
She asked as she pulled on her housecoat and slippers.
"We need to go out and fetch the constables. Do you think you will be able to manage until we return? The young housemaids are going to listen for the children if you could wait downstairs? We will be as quick as we can."
Sally nodded; this was all very strange.
"We're not in any danger are we, Miss?"
"No, I shouldn't think so and we would never leave you alone if we thought you were. Please do not go outside while we're gone and keep the doors locked."
"Yes, Miss."
Sally would as a rule ask a thousand and one questions but sensed that time was of the essence, so she simply followed Geraldine down the stairs.

Downstairs Elsbeth was putting on her boots and coat along with a hat. The air was cold tonight, and it wouldn't do any of them any favours to catch a chill. Geraldine proceeded to do the same and once ready the pair bid farewell to Sally and made their way out to get help. Elsbeth suggested they go to the rectory as the constables were to stay there for their time in the village.

On arrival they were met not only by Tobias but the constables, Mr. Hirst, Daisy and Adam.

"You seem to have a full house, Reverend, which is good for us. We need some assistance as soon as possible. We think there may be a person in one of our cellars, but we didn't want to open them up for fear it might be someone unsavoury."
Elsbeth spoke fast as the group began to pick up coats and hats.
"I will come too, if you don't mind?"
said Mr. Hirst as he walked to the open door.
"Of course, the more people the safer we should be, should we need it."
Replied Elsbeth.
"Should I fetch my father?"
Asked Adam.
"Not just yet, Adam. He has only just returned home, and I would feel dreadful to have him come out on a night as chilly as this with his ailment."
Elsbeth spoke softly, she knew that the family were still concerned for the Inspector and did not want to add to that if it turned out to be nothing.
"I'll stay here, if that's agreeable to everyone?"
Tobias had been through enough over the past few years.
"Yes, if you don't mind."
Offered Daisy.
They left the rectory and made their way back to the Hall. Nobody wanted to think about what they might find there so made small talk for the journey to pass the time.

Elsbeth called quietly through the door to Sally and the woman opened the door. They all went into the parlour and Elsbeth handed the spare keys and the main keys to Mr. Hirst and one of the constables. The women explained where the noise had been heard as Sally lit numerous lamps.
"I suggest, if nobody objects, that we start in small groups. If this Hall is anything like the ones in my home village the cellars may be

connected in parts. Where you heard the banging might not be exactly where the doors are located."

Said Mr. Hirst as he looked around at the group of people.

"I agree, Adam and you too constable, come with me. Mr. Hirst, if you take my other constable and Mrs. Stanhope with you. Geraldine and Sally, it would be a great help if you could go to the state room and make some noise on the floor, and we can figure out where we can hear it and where we cannot?"

replied Daisy. Once everyone knew what they were doing they set off to search out the cellar doors. Daisy and her group went through the kitchen and into the scullery as Sally knew there was a cellar in there, but she mentioned they had been in it that day and there wasn't anything out of the ordinary. Daisy still felt it prudent to check them all systematically. As Sally had said, the cellar was a working one and although the group searched they found nothing. There was a panelled wall that must have backed onto the state room, but it had been sealed many years since. The trio came out, locking the door behind them.

Mr. Hirst and his group took the next cellar, its door was located under the stairs and as they lit up the large space they could see another small set of steps that led to a second door far across the other side. The constable began walking toward it, the air was getting colder the further forward he went.

"This must be under the hallway; I've walked in a straight line and it's starting to feel bitter which might suggest the footings are coming to an end and the soil starts."

He called back across the room. Elsbeth turned out cupboards and pulled off dust sheets that revealed large trunks.

"Here, Miss. Let me open those."

said Mr. Hirst. Elsbeth stepped back and held the lamps high so that the man could see what he was doing. One by one, Mr. Hirst and the constable opened the trunks only to find endless amounts of household objects and clothing that had not fared too well in the damp conditions. After exhausting the entire space and not hearing anything from the upstairs room they made their way out, again they locked the door behind them.

Daisy and Adam had decided that the cellar door in the breakfast/dining room should be next and although it was on the other side of the house to the state room, it wouldn't hurt to check it. The constable now had 2 lamps in his hands and went down the steps first. He stopped and held his finger to his lips as he looked at Daisy and Adam standing at the top of the steps.
"What is it?"
Whispered Daisy as she made her way down.
"Listen, it's faint mind you, can you hear that?"
Daisy nodded, the thuds coming from upstairs could be heard in the distance.
"Hell's bell's, how big is this room? See, it seems to go on forever!" Exclaimed Adam as he started walking. Daisy and the constable followed, and the thuds began to get louder. The 3 of them split up with Daisy continuing to walk in a straight line, she stopped, and her hand clamped down over her mouth at the view her lamp was now shining upon. It took her a few moments to compose herself before she eventually called out.
"Adam, could you go and find the others as we know the noise is coming from in here now, I think it would be better considering the size of this space to have everyone helping."
She knew her voice was trembling as she spoke, Adam put it down to the musty air.
"Will do, makes sense. Back in a minute, be careful you 2."
"Come here, constable. Give me your jacket, quickly now."
The man placed his lamps down and soon realised the reason for Daisy's removal of the young fella.
"I'll keep him upstairs, Miss, sorry, constable. You'll be okay here on your own for a minute?" Daisy nodded in the light of the lamps.

Saving Grace | D M Roberts

She covered the body as best she could with the constables jacket and her own. The pulse was barely there, and she knew that they had to get the woman out of here as soon as they could.

"We'll need the doctor, as soon as you can. Send Adam over to fetch him but don't let on who it is."

The constable sprinted for the stairs as the sound of voices came into earshot. Daisy shifted herself from the fluids she had knelt in and prayed that it wasn't too late.

Chapter Nine

Adam was furious with the constable, but he had little time to argue his point with his mother clutching on for her life. The doctor had insisted that as soon as the woman was warmer and the morning light had come, she would be moved to the nearest hospital immediately. Elsbeth sat with Grace through the night. She held her hands as she prayed that God gave her the strength to pull through this. The doctor presumed a poison of sorts, but which one he wasn't sure. It was a good sign that the amount of vomit in the cellar meant that Grace had likely cleared most of it from her system and the rest? Well, that was in more expert hands than his, he had said to Adam.

"I should go over and tell Pa, and Tom. They must be wondering what is going on with me not going back there."
Adam said quietly to Daisy. His voice was shaking, as was the rest of him.
"Here, you're likely feeling a state of shock, you need to be strong for your mother and father." Said Geraldine softly as she pulled a cup from the sideboard. Pouring from the teapot and adding plenty of sugar she handed Adam the cup.
"Why would someone do this? I don't understand it. Ma has never done anything bad to anyone."
Adam asked as he stared at the people in the room. Geraldine patted him on his shoulder, she had no answer.
"This woman cares nothing for others, she cares only for herself, and it makes little odds to her that she causes suffering."
Mr. Hirst had been silent until now. In his mind he could think of nothing but catching this person and having her face the consequences of her odious crimes.

Saving Grace | D M Roberts

"Can you catch her?"
Adam replied, his eyes piercing now as he stared at Mr. Hirst.
"I will, you can bet on that. If it takes me the rest of my time I will make sure this woman pays for all that she has done."
Mr. Hirst replied, he then left the room. He felt sick. How many more lives would she destroy?
"Would you like me to come with you, to tell the Inspector I mean?"
Daisy knew that it had to be the next thing they did, she couldn't keep this sort of news from Billoughby any longer. Adam nodded and stood up.
"Let's go now and then we can get back before they take Ma to the hospital."

The Inspector shook his head. This couldn't be, no, his Gracie was likely staying over somewhere. She had been at sorts with things lately and would come home when she had thought things through.
"Are you sure?"
Tom stood by his father's chair; he too found the news hard to take in. Adam sat down at the table in the kitchen, he felt tired and useless. His forehead rested on the tabletop as he tried to stop his tears.
"Oh, there now son. It will be alright."
Billoughby got up from his seat and went to his boy, his arms encompassing the man and holding him tight. Daisy had never felt as sad as she did right at this moment. Here were 3 of the strongest men she knew, and one person had reduced them to this. She was not going to stand for this.
"I have to get back to the Hall, Inspector, would you do something for me?"
She asked.
"If I can."
Billoughby looked over at her, not letting go of his son.

Saving Grace | D M Roberts

"Would you stay here tonight, get some sleep and I will come and fetch you myself in the morning. I know you need to be with Mrs. Billoughby, but we really need you to get well too, and you won't do that if you don't sleep and definitely not if you go out at this hour of the night in the cold air."

"She is right, Pa. You can't afford to risk going back in the hospital, not when Ma needs you to be there for her. I will go back with Miss. Harvey and as she says we'll collect you in the morning. Adam looks beat, he needs to sleep, it's been a rough night."

Billoughby reluctantly agreed, not before he gathered a few things for Tom to take to Grace. Adam lay down on the sofa and was quickly asleep, his father placed a blanket over the young man and closed the door.

Elsbeth picked the cup up and poured herself some tea in the kitchen; she had left Tom sitting with his mother for a while. The gravity of what had gone on hit her all at once as the cup tumbled from her hand sending porcelain and hot tea splattering on the tiled floor with a noise that resembled church bells chinking in chaos.

"Oh, my love. This has been a terrible time for you too. Come here."

Tom wrapped her in his arms as she sobbed unashamedly. Geraldine stood watching from the hallway, fury filling her inside at what one wretched person could do to so many.

"Go into the parlour Tom, it's warmer in there and I'll bring you a fresh pot in. Come on now, I'll clear this up."

"I have to go and sit with Grace."

Sobbed Elsbeth.

"No, dear. The doctor is sitting with Grace, now go and get yourselves 5 minutes. Off you go." instructed Geraldine.

Tom and Elsbeth sat in front of the fire in silence, there was little either of them could say but it helped to be in each other's company.

Taking his hand in hers, Elsbeth stroked with her thumb the warm fingers that she held. It was going to be a waiting game that they may not win. The door opened making the pair turn, their expectant expressions obvious as the doctor came through.
"How is she?"
Tom asked as he got to his feet. The doctor frowned, his eyes desperately trying to avoid contact with those of the pair in the room.
"I can't tell you any more than I did earlier Tom. I have checked your mothers pulse and various other things, and she remains extremely weak. The sooner we can transfer her the better in my view. Which brings me to my question; do I have your permission to move her now? I would have preferred not to, alas, we don't have that luxury."
Tom looked at Elsbeth for help, she squeezed his hand.
"If this gives Grace the best chance, I think we should allow it my dear."
That was all Tom needed to hear as he nodded to the doctor. Without haste the doctor left the room and began to make his arrangements with the help of one of the constables.

Grace looked so pale as the 2 men carried her down the stairs and into the doctor's buggy. Tom was to follow as he knew more of his mother's details than anyone else, leaving Elsbeth and Geraldine standing at the door in the dark.
"Come on dear, let's get back inside. There's little more we can do for now."
Geraldine ushered the woman in and closed the door.
"Do you believe she will pull through this, Geraldine?"
Elsbeth hadn't dared to ask this question while Tom was in the house.
"We have no idea how long she has been down there to start with, nor do we know what she has ingested or when. All we can do is pray, now off to bed for you."

Elsbeth didn't argue, she needed to sleep and to be on her own for a while. Kissing Geraldine on the cheek she made her way up to her room, stopping only to look in on the children as they slept.

The morning sun came soon enough and with it Billoughby stirred in his bed. It had been a fretful night, but his recent illness had made him more tired than usual and so as guilty as the man felt, he had slept. The lane was quiet as he looked from the window and thought about the day he had first brought Grace here. It seemed such a long time ago now and so many things had happened over the years. In his mind, Billoughby had always worried that it would be his profession, if anything, that would put his family in jeopardy, but this hadn't been the case at all. The woman was a stranger to their small community, and it had been sheer bad luck on their part that she had decided to land here. Billoughby dressed and went down to the kitchen, he expected Adam to be awake but there was no sign he had made breakfast, so the Inspector set about boiling some water for tea and slicing bread to toast. He quietly peered into the sitting room where Adam slept soundly still with the blanket around him, not wanting to disturb his son he closed the door once again.

Daisy tapped at the back kitchen door and pushed it open to see the Inspector sitting at the table taking his medicine. The comforting smell of toasted bread filled her nostrils as he beckoned her in.
"Help yourself."
He said as he pushed a plate and mug forward.
"Don't mind if I do, it does smell wonderful, and I haven't had a chance to eat this morning. I came to tell you that during the night the doctor thought it best to move Mrs. Billoughby to the hospital in Hythe, he felt her chances would be better there. Tom accompanied her and I have come to fetch you and take you over, if you're alright with that?"

Billoughby swallowed his medicine down and nodded as Daisy buttered some toast.

"How did all of this happen? I can't get my head around any of it." He muttered to the young woman.

"I don't know, Inspector. I have been asking myself the same thing, kicking myself to be honest that we didn't do more or well, something."

She replied, her face sad and confused.

"I should have been here, I should have never got myself so cross with Gracie. She was only speaking her mind, she's entitled."

"You can't have known, none of us did. Will Adam be coming with us?"

"I know, still…The lad's still sleeping, he's flat out. I'm thinking best we leave him to rest, he's had a shock as much as the next man."

Daisy agreed, he had looked terrible last night when they came back to the cottage. Seeing one's mother like that would be enough to shock anyone.

"Makes sense to me, we can stop at Cate's and let her know he's fine."

They finished eating and the pair set off for Hythe.

Mr. Hirst arrived back at Mr. Gregory house quite early and after giving a brief explanation he packed up his case and said his goodbyes, promising Mr. Gregory that he would call by and visit again soon. The old gentleman was somewhat sad to see his guest leave but understood the urgency at which he must go.

"If you need any help, please let me know. It has been nice to have a guest, I hope to see you again soon."

They shook hands and Mr. Hirst left the large house.

Sitting on his horse he thought long and hard about what and where he would go if he were in Nora Howards position. She would not risk the port of Dover, he was sure of this. London perhaps, but then that would not get her out of the country, and he guessed this would be her aim. The sea looked calm and peaceful as he rode along the coastline, the odd person here and there that bid him a good day. He liked this place, he imagined quite happily living here one day but right now he had more important things to do than daydream.

Nora Howard sat in her carriage as she looked out one last time over the sea in Hythe, unaware that the man who had come to track her down was no more than 50 feet away from her. She had settled up with the Inn and sold off many of the items stolen from the hall to a character that dealt in silver and ornamental fineries of the wealthy. She had secured the carriage from a seller down on his luck financially for a very decent price. The man had recommended a young lad to take her on her journey as long as he was fed and watered on the trip, all in all she felt pleased at what she had accomplished as she smiled to herself.

The carriage had slowed as the lad talked with someone, she couldn't quite make out what they were saying with the sound of the sea breeze and the thick heavy curtains that covered the doors and windows.

Mr. Hirst was enquiring what kind of trip the lad was taking. The lad said he had some woman that had bought the carriage in a hurry and employed him to take her to Liverpool. Mr. Hirsts' mouth fell open, the hair on his neck tingled as he felt the oddest sensation down his spine. He passed a few coins to the lad and spoke quietly then rode away quickly.

"Who were you talking to, boy?"
called Nora as she poked her head through the heavy velvet.
"Farmer, miss. Tells me to watch out for his sheep on the roads ahead."
The lad smiled as he slipped the coins into his pocket.
"I don't pay you to chatter, let's get along shall we?"
She called impatiently as she sat back in her seat.

Saving Grace | D M Roberts

Mr. Hirst knew it had to be her, he rode ahead and doubled back to get behind them. He stayed far enough back so as not to be detected by the occupant. The lad had said she wasn't from round here and it was then, at that moment, he knew. The carriage went for a good few hours before it came to a stop in another village. Mr. Hirst stayed back as he watched the woman alight and enter an Inn. He had no intention of going inside, he would simply watch from a safe distance.

Grace was still not awake, and her colour had not improved overnight. The nurses fussed around the bed leaving little space for Billoughby to get near her. There was no more they could do, they had told the man, other than to wait and hope. Eventually the nurses left Billoughby alone with his wife having wiped her face and adjusted the contraption that they assured him was giving her the fluids she needed if she was ever to stand a chance of recovery. He pulled his chair closer and spoke softly, oblivious to anyone around him.
"Hello my love. Well, this is a bit of a to-do you've gotten yourself into and no mistake. The boys send their love as do Cate and Maisy. Maisy is missing her grandma, she isn't used to going this many days without seeing you. Truth be told Gracie, love, that goes for me too. Right then, here's what needs to happen, you need to get yourself well and I know you can hear me so hear me good, get yourself well and give me that sweet smile of yours so I can go back and tell young Maisy that Grandma is on the mend."
His eyes filled as he struggled to take in that he might never get to see that smile again.
The hand that rested on his shoulder was Robert's, he had stood and watched long enough the struggling Inspector and felt he needed to make the man aware he was there for him. Billoughby looked up,

Robert saw the pain in this once strong and competent man's eyes and it was all he could do not to shed a tear himself.

"She's made of good stock Milton, she will get through this." Even as he spoke, Robert knew that his words were mostly to boost the man and were most likely not true. Yes, Grace was a strong woman but whatever she had been given could be the end of her and he knew it as surely as Billoughby did.
"Any news from the village?"
The inspector asked as he tried to focus.
"Nowt as yet, but I hear that chap Hirst has gone off to see if he can find the woman that likely did this. Not sure of his chances myself, she seems a devil of a person by all accounts."
"At least he's doing something. I feel I should be out there looking but I can't leave my Gracie."
"You're right where you should be for now, nothing more important than being by Grace's side for when she wakes up, you know it and I know it."
"I do. Has Adam been to the farm today? I left him sleeping this morning, he looked done in." Robert shook his head.
"No, I figured he had other things on his mind and we're quiet at the moment, he needs a few days as do a lot of folk."
The pair sat and talked in hushed voices, nurses coming through often to check on Grace who lay there in her deep state.

Cate tidied away the lunch things as Maisy slept peacefully on the rug, she looked through the window again but there was still no sign of Adam. Maybe he had gone to work, he always liked to keep busy when he had things on his mind. He may well have gone over to the hospital, Tom had probably picked him up on his way, yes that was likely what had happened. Cate had decided that when Maisy woke she would take a walk into the village and see the Reverend, there were often times that Cate went to the church as a form of comfort, and she needed that now. Back in Ireland Cate and her family had been regular visitors to their church and she had missed that. The reverend had assured her that she was welcome any time and once she had gotten used to the village and the people she had made good use of his offer.

Mrs. Nash was standing outside of the grocers when Cate walked down the lane.
"Afternoon, dear and hello there little missy."
She called to Cate and Maisy.
"Mrs. Nash, nice to see you. How are you?"
"Oh, you know dear, people worse off than me. Is there any word on Mrs. Billoughby yet? I've been standing out here hoping to catch a sight of anyone that might know but it's been quiet as the grave this afternoon."
Cate crossed the path to the grocers wife.
"I've had no news either way, Mrs. Nash. I think my Adam must have gone over there with Tom; I was expecting him home but I'm sure he must have gone to visit his Ma."
Mrs. Nash shook her head.
"I don't think so my dearie, I saw Tom and that Mrs. from the hall heading over Hythe way lunchtime but I don't recall seeing your Adam with them."
Cate wasn't too worried; he must have gone to work as she originally thought.
"Ah, he'll be home when his stomach tells him to, I'm sure so he will, hey little Maisy?" Cate replied half to Mrs. Nash and half to her daughter.
"If he passes I'll tell him you're, where?"
"Off to see the reverend. Thank you Mrs. Nash."
Cate replied as she went on her way.

Reverend Moore opened the door and smiled, he enjoyed his visits from the parishioners especially when they were as bright as this young lady.

"Do come in, and hello to you little lady."

Maisy gurgled as the reverend tickled her chin playfully.

"I'm ever so sorry to drop in on you like this Reverend Moore, I felt I might go a little mad on my own today, what with no news on Mrs. Billoughby yet and Adam being at work."

Cate placed Maisy down on the rug in the parlour and sat on the chair.

"No apology needed Cate, I always enjoy your visits. Can I tempt you to tea and a slice of cake? I was about to have one."

Cate nodded, she felt comfortable in the reverend's presence.

"That is very kind of you. I don't suppose Miss Harvey has brought any news back?"

She asked hopefully. Tobias shook his head.

"Sadly no, they are doing all they can, so I hear but it's in God's hands now. I'll be a moment." Tobias went into the kitchen and returned swiftly with the promised tea and cake.

"Ah, and here was I thinking you were being kind reverend, you really were stopping for tea and now I don't feel so bad."

She laughed. Once the tea was poured Tobias became very serious.

"Have you given any thought to Maisy's baptism? We spoke briefly about it I know but with everything that's been happening I'm afraid I lost track of my duties."

Cate sipped the hot sweet tea. It was a tricky one, her parents had been adamant that the child be baptised in Ireland, and they weren't backing down. They had told Cate and Adam it was the least they could do considering they didn't get to see their grandchild as often as they would like to now that Cate had moved so far away.

"I've written to my parents again, I told them that we want to do this as soon as we can and their idea, as much as I see their side of things, might not work for us. Well especially now, what with the new one on the way."

The reverend gasped and only then did Cate realise that they had still not mentioned the coming event.

"Oh, my dear girl, I am thrilled for you, for both of you. Yes, it would be an arduous journey at the best of times but now, well I think you are wise to wait."

"What with Mrs. Billoughby being the way she is too, I don't think Adam would agree to a trip so far away."

"Quite right, your home is here now with your family. I see no reason that your parents can't travel to see you. Were they not planning to do this at some point?"

"They were too Father, my Mammy said it was better that they wait for calmer seas, them having to go on the boat and the crossing can be terrible rough in the colder seasons."

replied Cate. Tobias smiled at the woman, it was strange that when she spoke of her family her accent was even more pronounced than other times.

"It will all work itself out, have no fear. Now, cake?"

He sliced the cake without waiting for an answer and handed the side plate to Cate.

Sally chased young William around the table. He was not going to eat the vegetables and she couldn't make him.

"Master William! Please, will you sit back down at the table with the other children and eat your supper?"

William shook his head with vigour.

"I hate green things, you can't make me eat them. Dolly and Lily don't have to eat them."

He shouted as he dodged the woman's arms once again.

"Dolly and Lily are babies; they don't eat the same things as we do but when they get bigger they will."

Geraldine came into the room.

"Young man! What is the meaning of this? Do we speak to Miss. Sally in that loud and angry voice?"
William stopped in his tracks and shook his head.
"No, Miss. But, I don't like the vegetables."
"You want to grow as tall as David?"
She asked the child, her voice lower now.
"Yes, Miss."
He answered as he retook his seat at the table.
"Then I suggest you might get to starting with the liking of your vegetables."
"Yes, Miss."
He muttered as he stared at David who was happily shovelling carrots and beans into his mouth.
"And what do we say to Miss. Sally?"
William looked over, his face still holding its sulky stare as he apologised to the bemused woman.
"Sally, can you go up to the nursery and check that the house girls have fed the little ones? I will stay here with the children."
Sally nodded and as she left the room, turned and stuck out her tongue at William. Ruby, Martha and Doris chuckled at the funny older woman as they sat at the table.
"Tisn't funny."
Scowled William as he pushed a green bean around his plate.
"Is too."
replied Doris.
"It is a little funny, dear. I, for one, did not know Miss. Sally could run as well as she did."
Said Geraldine as she cut up Jacobs potatoes and tried very hard not to laugh.
"She didn't catch me; I can run much faster than she can."
William was not letting this one go.
"Can't run as fast as I can, that's because you don't eat your green food."

Said David, matter of factly before placing another carrot into his mouth.
Geraldine looked around the table as the children chattered and ate, she was glad they remained unaware of what was going on. The less they knew, the better.

Tom and Elsbeth arrived back at the Hall later that evening. They had stopped off at the farm to try to catch Adam, but he wasn't there. Billoughby had decided to stay over at the hospital, the nurses made him up a cot next to Grace as they felt, under the circumstances it was kinder, just in case. Geraldine, along with the other adults at the Hall were pleased to hear that although no better, Grace was no worse. Cook and Sally left together, they had offered to stay on, and this touched Elsbeth.
"Go home, you are so kind for all the extra help you have given. We will need you both as fit as possible in the coming weeks. I am going to have a devil of a time trying to get someone I can trust to help with the children."
The women agreed and left for home.
"What will you do? I know it isn't my place, but they are a handful when they want to be." asked Geraldine.
"I wondered if I might rely on your good graces a little while longer in truth. I may ask Sally if she would rather keep on with the children and employ one of the village ladies to take her place in the kitchen and house. I don't know, Geraldine. What do you think I should do?"
Geraldine patted her friend's hand gently.
"You know I will stay as long as you need me to. Sally will jump at the chance; she is many things but she is fond of them and she does deserve a better position after all the help she's given and she hasn't questioned it once."
Elsbeth nodded, Sally had proven her worth many times over in the past weeks and so it was decided that they would put this to the

Saving Grace | D M Roberts

woman the next day.

Chapter Ten

The scream was so loud that the neighbour from the cottage opposite came running through the garden and into the kitchen. The kitchen was empty, and it was only then that the neighbour wondered if they had been foolish to rush in when they didn't know what was happening. Daisy walked from the sitting room, her legs trembled, and her face was as white as a field freshly snowed on. She tried to speak, her mouth opened but no words came out. Instead, she slumped to the floor. The man from across the lane tried to catch the young constable but was just not quick enough. Crouching down next to her he pulled a cushion from the dining chair and eased it under her head.

"Miss, miss are you with us. Miss?"

He sat there calling to Daisy not knowing what to do for the best, he had never had anyone faint in front of him before. He continued to talk, his voice now sounding quite panicked as she lay there, motionless. The noise from the other room startled him, and standing up he peered forward to where it came from.

"Who's in there? I'm not on my own you know, you best come out here if you know what's good for you."

He knew as soon as he said it that they could well come out and be dangerous, what was he thinking?

"It's only me Mr. Charter, it's Adam. You remember me?"

The old man heaved a sigh of relief as Adam came out of the sitting room. Straight away Adam could see Daisy on the floor.

"Hell's bell's, whatever is going on?"

He said as he knelt beside Daisy. Mr. Charter shook his head.

"Buggered if I know, I heard the young miss scream and came running over, then she must have fainted."

Daisy was now beginning to stir. She opened her eyes and stared at the 2 men peering down over her.

"Adam, you're alright? I thought you were dead!"

She muttered, still quite dazed as she tried to sit up.

"Whyever would you think that?"

Asked Adam with confusion clear in his voice.

"I tried to wake you; Cate has been going out of her mind with worry as you haven't been seen for 2 days."

Adam scratched his chin, then his head.

"2 days you say? I remember coming back here with you and not much else. How is Ma? Is she…is she?"

Adam couldn't bring himself to say the words.

"She's hanging in there. I can't believe you have slept all this time. Had you taken anything?"

"Not that I know of. I had a sip of tea at the Hall, it tasted awful but please don't tell Miss. Geraldine, I felt a bit off after that and then, I don't know."

Daisy was now standing, she wondered if Adam might have had whatever Grace had.

"I think we should let Cate know that you're alright and then maybe have you checked over by the doctor. Mr. Charter, thank you so much for coming to my aid. It was very good of you."

"Wasn't nothing Miss. You're alright then? Only my breakfast is likely getting cold."

Daisy smiled at the man.

"Go and have your breakfast, I'm quite fine."

Nodding to the pair Mr. Charter went back to his house.

"Well, you gave me quite a fright. It has been a terrible week and I'm not one for drama, but I really did think you were, well you know."

Daisy was still a little rattled, she sat down at the table as Adam handed her a cup of water.

"Here, drink this. Has Pa not been back home?"

Daisy gulped down the fresh liquid and shook her head.

"They made him a bed at the hospital, they didn't have the heart to send him home and I think the doctor might have asked them to keep an eye on him too after his recent illness. They are in the best place. Mr. Hirst has taken off to track that woman down as he feels he has a good knowledge of where she is headed for. I sent the constables back to Ashford last night, not much more they can do here."

Daisy paused for another mouthful of water.

"I can't say I am happy about this fella Hirst taking the lead on this, we don't know him and only have his say so that he is who he says he is. What do you think, Adam?"

Adam sat down; he had wondered why his father had been happy to let this stranger deal with things that Billoughby would normally deal with himself.

"Maybe we don't know the whole story, it isn't like Pa to be so trusting especially in a situation like this, that involves his own wife."

"True, I know the Inspector had some quiet words with the man, he didn't share the conversation with me. Mr. Hirst also spoke with the Reverend in private, I imagine they know more than we do."

Daisy concluded.

"It will all come out when the time's right."

Adam replied.

"Now, we best get you over to your wife and then off to see the doctor."

Daisy could be quite forceful when she wanted to be.

Mr. Nash looked twice as he saw Adam and Daisy leaving the cottage, he shook his head and continued on his round. When he got back to the shop he was quick to tell his wife what he saw.

"I expect she was there so early to see the Inspector, I didn't know that the young Billoughby lad was staying at the cottage though. You would think he would be at home with his wife and the little one at a time like this."

He said as he packed away the crates in the back room.

"You don't think…"

Began his wife, always one for a little village gossip.

"Now, love. I didn't say anything of the sort, and don't you go repeating what I said."

Mrs. Nash tutted her tongue.

"Besides, I hear that Miss. Harvey is to be wed soon enough."

Mr. Nash came back into the shop front as he spoke.

"Such a thing as cold feet my lovely, lots of women get it right before their wedding. One last how d'ya do before they tie the knot."

Her husband scowled; he could see he had done the wrong thing by telling her.

"Did you have cold feet then? Before we were wed."

"Don't be daft, I'm not that kind of woman and well you know."

"But you think our Miss. Harvey is?"

This was more a rhetorical question however his wife saw fit to answer all the same.

"If the cap fits, them folk from London aren't like us lot. They have their own peculiar ways."

"I'll have not another word said on it, I wish I never told you now. Hear me wife, say nothing about this."

Mr. Nash made his way from the shop, passing Cook as she went in.

"Morning."

She said with a smile.

"How do."

Replied the man as he stomped off.

"What's the matter with his face this morning?"

Said Cook as she placed her basket on the counter.

"Well, if you must know, this is between you, me and the gate, he just caught sight of that young Adam and Miss. Harvey coming out of the Inspectors cottage bright and early. Said they looked right up to no good and close, he did."

Cook gasped, that couldn't be right. Not with his mother in the state she was in and all.

"No! I can't believe that."

She protested as she pointed to the piece of boiled ham. Mrs. Nash began to slice the meat for her as she talked.

"Believe what you like, he's not a one for tales my husband, as you know. Bold as the daylight he said."

"Probably there on police type errand I expect."

Added Cook as she put the meat into her basket.

"That's what I said, no he says, not the way they were acting and so early too."

Cook passed over her coins and shook her head in disbelief.

"That poor young lass of his, her with a little one too."

"Beggars belief doesn't it. Here's hoping she doesn't find out about it, that fiancé of Miss. Harvey's neither."

Cook made for the door.

"They won't be hearing it from me, that's for sure."

The bell tinkled as the shop door closed behind her. Mrs. Nash told 3 other people that morning, each time she added a little more. When Mr. Nash returned he put an arm around her shoulder.

"I know I was a bit off with you this morning, you're not the kind to spread rumours and I'm sorry, love."

He pecked her on the cheek and started on his afternoon chores. Mrs. Nash was very quiet for the rest of the day, she knew that she had started something, and it would not be easy to get out of this one.

Mr. Hirst watched the driver of the carriage stagger down the lane, it was obvious he had drunk too much for his young age. He must have received quite a tidy payment for the journey he was to take but as is the way of some, he most likely spent the larger part on ale and women. He followed the lad as he went around the back of the Inn.

Saving Grace | D M Roberts

Taking off his cap and too large overcoat the drunken driver laid them on a straw bale and sat down on another. He was soon asleep, giving Mr. Hirst ample time to take the items from the bale. He checked quickly through the pockets, removing what was left of the young man's coins and placing them carefully into his waistcoat pocket. He didn't want the lads money, he merely wanted his outer clothes. Pulling on the cap well down over his head and throwing on the large coat he wondered if he would be able to cope with the stench that emanated from both, he would have to if his plan was to work. He sat against the back of the carriage and waited for the woman to come out. He didn't have too long to wait, she obviously wanted to make an early start. There she was, flinging the overnight bag at his feet and barely looking up.
"Well don't just stand there! Open the door and sort my luggage out, you ungrateful oath."
Mr. Hirst kept his head low as he pulled the door wide, glad that it hid his frame from her. He coughed and made a low growling sound.
"Did you drink a little too much last night? I don't care, let's get back on the road. Well hurry up about it."
She pulled the door from his grasp and slid the curtains across. Mr. Hirst quickly tied his own horse to the front of the carriage and climbed onto the high platform. The lanes were uneven and twisty, but he made good headway as the power of an extra horse soon came into its own. Inside, Nora Howard was happy that this lad had finally picked up some speed and she did not mind too much the occasional bumps if that was the price she had to pay for such haste.

They had been going for some time now, almost a day or so. He could hear the woman shouting for him to stop, he paid her no heed, as he geed the horses to go faster. In the carriage Nora Howard was furious, she needed to stop and stretch her legs. Maybe she had been too stern in her voice when she had insisted to the lad that they shouldn't dawdle. She slumped back against the seat, none the wiser as to what was happening. Mr. Hirst went as fast as the horses would allow, he needed to get her back to the Inspector at any cost if he was ever to be free of this wretched woman's slur on his name. He went a further hour and a half and could feel the thuds as she frantically hit the carriage ceiling with her stick, he smiled as he spotted the familiar markings of the Marshlands. The horses were slowing, and he felt bad that he had worked them so hard, but he just couldn't give up now that he was so close.

Daisy and Tobias were standing in the churchyard when they heard the sound of thundering hooves coming down the lane.
 "Good heavens, it sounds like the devil himself is after somebody!" Exclaimed Reverend Moore as the carriage thundered toward them. The man at the helm called a loud 'Woah' as the horses slowed to an abrupt stop. The door flew open, and an infuriated Nora Howard jumped out, stick in hand as she rounded the carriage to berate the driver. Her mouth dropped open as she caught sight of Daisy and Tobias.
 "WHAT HAVE YOU DONE? WHY HAVE YOU BROUGHT ME HERE?"
She screamed as the man jumped down from his high seat. Taking off the cap Mr. Hirst lunged forward to grab the woman. Nora Howard thrust at him with her stick, catching him on the jaw. Mr. Hirst was not so easily halted, grabbing the stick from her hands he threw it to one side and made his way toward her. Nora looked like a cornered beast as she kicked out and thrashed her arms in a bid to escape him. Daisy leapt forward now, the realisation of who it was had hit her like a ton of bricks. Between them they tussled with the woman, pinning her face down on the floor, Reverend Moore removed his stole and handed it to Mr. Hirst who proceeded to bind the woman's hands together to stop her escaping further.
 "YOU CAN'T DO THIS TO ME! I WILL HAVE THE LAW ONTO YOU."

She cried out in fury.

"We can and we have. I am the law, a constable of it at any rate and I am placing you under arrest. You do not have to say anything but anything you do say will be taken down and may be given in evidence."

Mr. Hirst smiled at Constable Harvey, his face perspiring and red but happy to have at least brought the woman back. Reverend Moore helped them get the woman to her feet and they took her into the church.

"We have a room at the back with a very sturdy door that locks if you need to make use of it." Offered the Reverend.

"That's what I was thinking, thank you Reverend."
replied Daisy as they moved the woman who continued to squirm and kick.

"We shall need to inform Inspector Billoughby as soon as possible. She will need to be transported to Canterbury, but I am sure the Inspector would love a few words first."
Said Mr. Hirst. Nora Howard began to laugh, it was loud and it had a nasty ring to it.

"Dead is she? What a fool, she drank it down like a good 'en, then out like a light she went." Her voice cackled as Mr. Hirst thrust her into the brick room, slamming the door shut and bolting it across. He handed Tobias his stole back and the three of them wiped their brows with the sound of Nora Howard ringing in their ears.

Tom could not believe what he was hearing about his own brother.
"Who told you this?"
He demanded as the woman stepped back. She had known this lad all his life but never had she seen this wild and angry look in his eyes.

"It was one of the women in the village, she said she heard it on good authority. I haven't mentioned it to anyone but you, Tom. I thought it only right to tell you, he is your brother after all and that poor young wife of his, well if she hears it I don't know what she will make of such nonsense."

Tom nodded.

"It isn't true, I won't have it. I will get to the bottom of this. You can bet your life on it and when I do…"

"All I know is there was mention of the grocer, you know, seeing them both early in the morning at your house. Speak to Mr. Nash, lad."

The woman scurried away like a frightened rabbit leaving Tom standing shaking in the lane. He stared down toward the village, this would not keep, he thought as he ran down to where Mr. Nash was closing up for the night.

"Tom, you made me jump lad. What's the rush, if you need something you best be quick before I get off for my supper."

"What have you been telling people about my brother?"

Mr. Nash shook his head, he didn't know what the lad was talking about at first. He looked quizzically at Tom.

"I don't know what you mean lad. What about him?"

"That you saw him coming out of our house all cosy with Miss. Harvey."

The expression on Mr. Nash's face changed from that of confusion to annoyance.

"That bloody woman! I told her to keep her mouth shut, but can she? No, she cannot. I said that I saw young Adam and Miss. Harvey, that is true enough. I said no such thing as them being cosy or any such like."

"Where is Mrs. Nash? I would like a word with her."

Tom asked, trying not to raise his voice at the older man.

"Now Tom, you leave this to me, I'll not have you bellowing at my wife no matter what she might have said. I will set her straight, no fear on that."

"You best do, I don't want to hear any of this nonsense again and Cate best not get to hearing it neither."

Tom stalked off, he felt irritated at the mere small mindedness of his neighbours.

The loud voices coming from inside the Nash's home echoed down the lane as Mr. Nash made it clear to his wife that this kind of gossip had to stop, and it wasn't the first time, he added.

Billoughby was surprised at the sight of not only his son but Mr. Hirst and Daisy. He smiled at the small group as they approached the bedside.

"Any news, Pa?"

asked Adam as he bent to kiss his mother's forehead.

"Shh, you'll wake her."

said the Inspector.

"Isn't that the idea?"

Asked Daisy as she patted Grace's hand affectionately.

"Yesterday, maybe. Today we have had a small miracle. Today Gracie opened her eyes and had a drink and a little bite to eat."

Billoughby gushed with happiness as the trio stared wide-eyed at the woman.

"Oh, my word, that is good news."

Said Mr. Hirst, his voice low.

"Not the only bit of good news today, Inspector. Mr. Hirst here, well he only went and caught that woman, brought her back to the village where at the moment she is safely behind lock and key at the church."

Daisy knew this would please him.

"That is a weight of my mind, thank you and well done. What are you intending to do with her, now you have caught her?"

Asked the Inspector.

"I am arranging transport to Canterbury, from there she must surely be placed into custody where she cannot hurt another person. I feel that taking her back to Redruth will prove more of a risk, knowing her cunning ways as I do. What are your thoughts, Inspector? After all, it was your constable that arrested the woman."

Billoughby stroked his chin, it wasn't worth her getting loose again if the man happened to slip up on the journey to Cornwall.

Billoughby realised that Mr. Hirst was a competent man, but this woman was a sneaky individual as they had been pained to see.

"We think Adam may have accidentally ingested some of the same thing that Mrs. Billoughby was given, he has been asleep for the last few days. I almost thought he was, well, you know? I called at your home this morning and he was just lying there, it put the wind up me I can tell you."

Said Daisy, her frown showing that she had not altogether gotten over the shock.

"The doctor has checked me out, Pa. He said I should be fine and if I get any problems to go back and see him straight away. Poor Cate thought I had gone off, as if I would."

He grinned. Grace stirred in the bed, her eyes flickered as she tried to make sense of the voices around her.

"They said she might be like this for a week or so, best to let her rest."

Billoughby spoke in a quiet voice as he held her warm hand.

Tobias sat in the parlour, he did not like the idea of having that creature so close to him especially as the Inspector, Daisy and Mr. Hirst were currently away from the village. True enough a constable had turned up, but he did not like this one bit! Tobias had been at the mercy of an unstable person before, he remembered it vividly not only in his nightmares but in his waking hours too. The constable they had sent along was a large chap, and no doubt he could take care of himself should the need arise…that said, who knew what might happen.

The knock on the door startled him, causing the beverage to spill slightly as his body jerked.

"Darned fool! Pull yourself together man."
He spoke out loud as he went to answer the door.
"Who is it?"
He called, not wanting to be as careless as the last time.
"It's Tom, Tom Billoughby. Can I have a minute of your time, Reverend?"
Tobias pulled open the large door, he smiled at the young man, his relief obvious.
"Who were you expecting? You look right jittery Reverend."
"Strange times, strange times Tom. Do come through."
"I hope you don't mind me calling so late, mostly I wanted to check you were alright with the one you've got locked up in the church. I promised Mrs. Stanhope that I would call in."
"Very kind of you, I have to confess that all of this has shaken me a little. I will feel much better once the wretched woman is far away from here."
"The others should be back soon I imagine. I know it isn't much but having some extra bodies around you tonight might help."
"It will. I'm afraid I am getting too old for all of this excitement."
Tom shrugged, he wasn't nearly as old as the reverend, but it seemed that none of them should underestimate the woman that was under lock and key.
"Some folks are just not right, that's the top and bottom of it Reverend. There was something else I wanted to talk about, if you have time?"
"Oh, of course. You know I will help where I can."
Tom took a deep breath, he wasn't used to talking about personal things with anyone, not even his family.
"It's about me and Mrs. Stanhope, do you think I am too young for her?"
Tobias sat back. Well, that was a question he hadn't expected from the lad.
"Do you?"

"Makes no difference to me Reverend, I worry you see about what folk will say and I know Elsbeth does too, even if she doesn't say too much on the subject."

Tobias most often had an answer for most things, but this was not one of those times.

"Tom, this is a small village with folk that are set in their ways and have nothing better to do than gossip. If it isn't about you it will be about someone else. I have no right or wrong answer for you, except to say that you will have to do what you think is right."

That wasn't what Tom wanted to hear but he figured it would have to do.

"Aye, you have that right. I had to set someone straight only tonight on my way over here. Can you believe there are stories about Adam and Miss. Harvey! It is ridiculous when a person can't call on another in times of need to have people making up tales about them."

Tobias sat up in his seat.

"No! Really? I find that hard to believe, who would say such things?"

Tom shook his head.

"It's dealt with now Reverend, and I hope the person thinks long and hard before doing it again."

The sound of the door opening interrupted the pair and Daisy called through to say they were back.

"I may well put a few words in my sermon on Sunday regarding telling tales and untruths. Thank you for stopping by Tom and remember what I said; Do what you think is best."

Tom got up to leave, he had spent far longer than he intended at the rectory. After a very brief talk with Daisy and Mr. Hirst regarding Grace's wellbeing, Tom made off for home to see his father and brother.

Saving Grace | D M Roberts

Nora Howard paced up and down in the small room. She had tried to reach the tiny window at the top of the wall, but it was in vain, not that she would fit through it even if she had. She called out to the constable that had sat outside the room for most of the night and at first he replied, upon realising she was merely taunting him the chap stopped listening and carried on reading his newspaper and eating his sandwiches. Mr. Hirst quietly approached him, his steps light and his voice low.
"Over here."
He beckoned to the constable. The man walked over to the other side of the church.
"Everything as it should be, Sir."
He said in an equally hushed voice.
"Excellent, if you need to stretch your legs or get a hot drink from the rectory I suggest you do it now before the Reverend turns in for the night. I can keep watch here until you get back. It might be an idea to ask the reverend for a rug, it gets pretty cold in these places at night."
The constable nodded and made his way outside.
Mr. Hirst sat in silence, he didn't want to draw attention to the fact that he was here, but she knew, she recognised the smell of those cigars anywhere and there was only one place that she knew of where they could be bought, and it certainly wasn't in this God forsaken village.
"Missed me did you?"
Her voice echoed through the building. Mr. Hirst sat perfectly still, how did she know? Nora Howard continued to shout.
"I am talking to you. I know you're out there, I can smell those cigars from here. If you let me out I will tell them it wasn't you, that's why you're here isn't it? You help me and I'll help you." For a second he wondered if she would but discarded the notion all but instantly as he walked softly back to the door.
"Lively that one."

Whispered the constable as they passed each other.

"Yes she is and make no mistake that she's a dangerous one into the bargain. I suggest you stay up this end and don't speak to her. She'll soon tire of her own voice."

The constable didn't need telling twice, he had dealt with women the likes of Nora Howard in the past and he had no intentions of entering into a conversation with the likes of her. Mr. Hirst tipped his hat at the man and went back to the rectory. It had been arranged that he would stay there for the night and accompanied by Constable Harvey and the constable now standing watch, the 3 of them would escort Nora Howard to Canterbury first thing in the morning.

Billoughby seemed brighter when he woke to the smell of breakfast that morning. It took him a moment to recall what had happened and that it was likely Tom in the kitchen. The hour was early, but the sun was bright as the Inspector sat up in the large bed. It felt strange that Gracie wasn't lying beside him and yet he was cheered on knowing that she was doing better. Tom poked his head around the door.

"You awake Pa?"

He called quietly as he balanced a tray in his hand.

"What's all this then son? Breakfast in bed, eh! Best not get used to this."

Tom laughed; he placed the tray on the empty space where his mother would usually be.

"I thought I should make sure you eat something before I get off to work. We can't have you fading away on us now, can we?"

"Size of my stomach son, I'm hardly likely to fade for some time yet."

"All the same, I've been given my instructions. It was worrying, you know, when you took bad."

Tom looked down as he spoke.

"Worried me too son. I don't mind telling you it put the frights on me and then all this with your mother. I hope there's no more to come, not sure I could take it."
"Let's hope not. I hear she'll be taken to Canterbury this morning and let that be an end to it." Billoughby nodded as he ate, he couldn't help thinking that there was more instore for the small village, but he brushed the thought from his mind.
"Good cook you are son, take after your Ma you do."
"If a man wants to eat well he has to cook well. Right, I'll be downstairs for a while, give me a shout when you've finished with the tray Pa."

Tom had reached the door when his father spoke again.
"Son, do you have a minute or 2?"
"I think so. Was there something you wanted me to do?"
Billoughby shook his head.
"No son, I wanted a quiet word with you, if you are alright with that?"
Tom came back in and sat in the chair. Had his father heard about the gossip concerning his brother?
"Yes Pa, that's alright with me."
"Is everything well with you and Mrs. Stanhope? What I mean is, are you certain this is what you want? Makes no odds to me as long as you're happy with it."
Billoughby felt awkward now that he had raised the subject and knowing that his son could be as emotional as his wife.
"Everything is just fine, Pa and yes, we are certain this is what we want. I know it isn't going to be easy and that people will talk, it's a small village. I really am hoping that Ma will come around but if she doesn't…I love her Pa, that's as simple as I can put it."
Billoughby smiled at his son, he admired the fact that Tom was willing to deal with whatever gossip or issues that may come along for the woman he loved.

"Right then, that's good enough for me son and all I had to say if I'm honest."

In the church Daisy, and Mr. Hirst were making the final checks and preparations for moving the woman Nora Howard. The constable had told them it had started off a noisy night with the woman shouting and cursing for some time but after some time she had quietened, and he hadn't heard a thing from her since.
"Do you think she's still sleeping?"
Asked Daisy as they approached the door.
"I don't know, could be I suppose. Don't be fooled by her is all I say, she is quick and strong." Replied Mr. Hirst as he turned the key. The woman stayed still as the 3 people went into the room. The constable put himself in front of Daisy, he didn't want to take any chances as Mr. Hirst poked Nora Howard's shoulder.
"Time to go, come along now."
Said the man, his voice loud and unwavering. Nora didn't stir.
"Wake up Miss, time to go."
Echoed the constable as he leaned forward over her frame.

Nora leapt toward him like an unleashed tiger, her nails sinking deep into the skin on his face. The constable barely flinched as he grabbed her forearms and thrust her against the wall. Daisy watched the man with blood running down his face as he pulled Nora's hands behind her back without hesitation and placed the handcuffs on. Mr. Hirst was impressed, he had been a little concerned regarding the man's competence when it came to dealing with the woman's manic state and sighed with relief that his concerns were unfounded.
"Well done constable. Right then, shall we get on our way?"
Daisy shot Mr. Hirst a look that said she was as impressed as he was with the quiet constable from Ashford.
"You won't keep me for long, you wait. I'll not stay locked up forever and when I get out I'll be coming for you."

She jeered and then spat in Daisy's direction.
"Hush now, nobody wants or cares to hear what you have to say." Replied Daisy as they walked out into the churchyard.

Tobias watched from the rectory, he was relieved that she was no longer going to be his burden as the trio bundled Nora Howard into the cart. Walking back into the kitchen he poured a large mug of tea and closed his eyes as he gave thanks to the Almighty for removing this vile creature from their small village.

Chapter Eleven

Elsbeth had gotten to the hospital earlier than most visitors would, the night nurse happily let her in before she finished her shift.
"There's tea on the trolley my dear, help yourself."
Elsbeth thanked her and quietly poured herself a cup of tea. Sitting in the chair now she wondered if it had been the right thing to do, visiting a woman that most likely despised her. Grace looked so pale, for a woman that had a beautifully glowing complexion on any given day of the week her skin was ghostly white in a way that Elsbeth had never seen on a person other than dear Esther. Grace stirred, her low voice letting out a weak moan.
"Do you need something dear?"
whispered Elsbeth as she pulled the chair closer.
"Where am I?"
Her voice barely audible and yet Elsbeth picked up every word.
"You're in the hospital Grace. Would you like some water?"
Grace nodded her head, her eyes glinting as she recognised her friend. Grace slowly stretched her hand out letting it come to rest on the hand of a very startled Elsbeth.
"Milton is Milton alright?"
her eyes beseeched Elsbeth's.
"He's doing well Grace, he has been sent home to regain his strength. Would you like to sit up?" Elsbeth stood behind carefully easing the woman into a better position against her pillows.
"Tom and Adam?"
Grace was weak, her voice quiet and breathless. Elsbeth handed her some water and sat on the edge of the bed.
"Don't try to talk too much just yet, know that everyone is safe and well, naturally they are worried about you, but they are alright."

Saving Grace | D M Roberts

The footsteps of the nurse could be heard coming down the ward as the day started to unwind.

Jacob and Martha were first down to breakfast. The staff were bustling about as they did every morning. Sally greeted the children with a cheery 'good morning' and placed porridge down in front of the pair. It was a school day, and the rest of the children came down in dribs and drabs.

"Come along you lot, we don't want to be late. David, where are your shoes dear? And William, don't forget to take your book with you."

Sally chattered as she passed out more bowls of porridge until they all had one.

"I have a test today Miss. Sally."

Ruby was a confident child, but tests caused her a sense of anxiousness.

"And you will do fine little Miss, remember what I told you?"

Replied Sally as she poured water for the group around the table. Ruby nodded as she stirred her porridge around the bowl.

"Do your best and that is enough Miss Sally."

"That's right, you don't have to tie yourself up in knots young Ruby, as long as you do your best."

Sally didn't hold with tests at their ages, she thought it was all too much for youngsters and that they had plenty of time for learning when they were older.

Breakfast finished, Sally made sure all of the children had what they needed for school, and they began their walk down to the village.

"Good morning Cook, has Sally left already?"

Elsbeth asked when she returned to the hall.

"Good morning Ma'am, she has. They were lively this morning and eager to get going. Would you like your breakfast sent through Ma'am?"

Saving Grace | D M Roberts

Cook was already preparing the tray for Elsbeth as they spoke.
"That's good of you Cook, I wasn't sure I was hungry when I got back but now I see it I'm sure I will manage to work my way through it. I went to see Mrs. Billoughby before the hospital got too busy."
Elsbeth sat down at the table in the kitchen, not something she would often do. Cook looked at the woman, she looked tired and in need of a talk.
"If you don't mind me saying Ma'am, you are welcome to join me as I was about to have mine. How is Mrs. Billoughby?"
Elsbeth smiled, she welcomed the company today.
"I would like that, thank you Cook. Shall I pour?"
Elsbeth put back the teacups and saucers and instead put a mug onto the table next to the cook's. She poured them both a hot drink as Cook served the breakfast onto the plates.
"Thank you Ma'am"
"Mrs. Billoughby sat up this morning, she spoke to me, and asked after her family. She sounds and looks ever so weak. I do hope she gets through this for her own and everyone else's sake. It would have been Wilf's birthday today; it is a very odd day in so many ways."
Elsbeth began to eat, her eyes misty as her thoughts ran away with her.
"It's good to hear that Mrs. Billoughby is sitting up, the Inspector must be out of his mind with worry. It's nice that she spoke, I hope I don't speak out of turn, but she was a bit frosty with you last time she came here. It was very good of you to visit knowing this. I am sorry Ma'am, I didn't know that about your husband. If you want to talk about him, I am happy to listen?" Elsbeth continued eating, nodding as she did. She was surprised at just how hungry she felt.
"It was very encouraging to see Mrs. Billoughby awake. I can't imagine what she must be thinking or feeling, or how scared she must have been. It will take her some time to see me as a friend

again, if she ever does, but I would settle for her being well again and never speaking to me than the alternative. Thank you for the offer Cook but I wouldn't know what to say regarding Wilf, all I know is that I miss him every day and I imagine I always will." Elsbeth's face had such a sad expression that Cook felt compelled to go to the woman and put her arms around her. Cook knew this was not right given her status in the house, but she also knew that as a compassionate human it was exactly what she must do. Elsbeth leant against the older woman and sobbed quietly against her apron. Cook didn't speak, she let her employer grieve for it was a long time coming.

Nora Howard was charged and booked into the police headquarters in Canterbury. Mr. Hirst, Daisy and the constable heaved a sigh of relief. There was an amount of paperwork that Daisy took care of and the 3 of them went over the road to eat a well-deserved lunch.
"My goodness, is that you Miss. Harvey?"
The familiar voice called across the room, Daisy turned to see Dr. Joseph Lyons the medical examiner.
"Dr. Lyons, I haven't seen you for quite some time. How are you? You must join us, that is if you aren't with company."
Daisy was on her feet as she greeted the man.
"No, on my own as it happens my dear. I am quite well. So, you must tell me news of the village."
Joseph shook hands with Mr. Hirst and the constable as Daisy introduced the men and he sat down to join them.
 Daisy filled Joseph in on everything happening regarding Grace and Milton Billoughby and was somewhat surprised to find that the man was completely unaware of the difficulties his friends had been facing.
"I felt sure you would have been informed Sir, I feel rather foolish to have blurted these things out in the manner I have."
"I was not. I must visit, are you returning to the village today?"

asked the concerned man.

"We are, you are more than welcome to travel back with us." Offered Daisy.

"That is most kind of you, I happen to have a free afternoon as Beryl has gone to stay with her mother for a few days. Why did Milton not call me, or indeed you Miss. Harvey, why did you not call me? We have been friends for a long while."

"I think that because everything has happened so fast the Inspector has had little chance to contact anyone. I myself have left word with Janet and Henry to let them know of Mrs. Billoughby's current health problem."

said Daisy. She was beginning to feel a little hemmed in by the questions and Mr. Hirst could sense this as he looked at the 2 acquaintances as they talked.

"If I may say something?"

He began, well aware that this man did not know him and may well take exception to his input. Joseph nodded and Mr. Hirst continued.

"This has been a particularly perilous time for all concerned and with the Inspector himself in the hospital we had little chance to put everyone in the picture. Constable Harvey has performed her duties admirably and if I may add, as good as any higher officer in the constabulary could have hoped to. I understand how upsetting this may be to you as a close friend but sometimes we have to work within the perimeters we are set."

Joseph sat back and looked at Mr. Hirst. He admired a man that stood up to him, he knew his no-nonsense attitude could appear a little intimidating to some and the last thing he had meant to do was criticise the woman.

"Quite so, the constable is and always has been very capable. Now, I don't know about all of you, but I am famished. Shall we eat?"

Tom worked harder than normal today, he was trying to catch up on chores he had missed over the past few days and truth be told he needed to keep his mind occupied so that it didn't run down that spiral of darkness he was often prone to. Robert and Mary stood at the gate as they watched the young man toil tirelessly in the field.

"He didn't come in for lunch dear, could you go and have a word? It isn't good for him to go all day without eating."

Mary asked her husband, the concern obvious in her voice.

"He's a fit young fella Mary, he'll be alright. Sometimes a man needs to get stuck in when he's got a problem or 2 to sort in his head. Tom will be in when he's good and ready."

"Don't you men need to talk about things?"

She asked with a bewildered tone.

"We do, only when we're ready mind, and only when we know we can trust another body. It's how our mind works, we're the problem solvers."

"I don't see how that can be good for anyone, we can't always solve things on our own."

She argued as they went into the farmhouse.

"It's the way it's always been my love, stubborn and private we are and that's likely how we'll stay."

In the field Tom was beginning to feel the hunger pangs in his stomach. He looked around and gave a satisfied nod to the work he had done so far and sat down on the soil. Pulling out an apple from his pocket he began to crunch through the juicy and sweet fruit. What a time it had been, he thought as he chewed on his apple. He thought about his time away from the Marsh, it seemed an age ago now and yet it hadn't been that long. Closing his eyes he remembered the night that his Elsbeth had come to him in his lodgings, his lips curving up into a soft smile as the images ran through his head.

"If you sit there too long you'll root yourself lad. Come on, tea's on the table."

Shouted Robert from across the fence. Robert didn't wait for an answer this time and Tom duly got up and followed the man into the house.

"There you are Tom, now you might not be hungry, but you must have a drink of something, we don't want you coming over with sun sickness. Sit down and I'll fetch the pot."

Ordered Mary as she darted around the large kitchen.

"Thanks Miss. Mary, I reckon I might be feeling more like a bite to eat now."

Mary thrust the bread board and cheese toward Tom.

"Help yourself, you know the rules."

She laughed as she placed a drink in front of Tom.

"I do. It's quiet here today, gives a fella space to think."
he said as he carved a slice of bread.

"It is. Seems quieter since young David went home, I have to admit I miss that boy."
replied Mary wistfully.

"Maybe Elsbeth will let him stay a little longer next time. I can speak to her if you like, I have to call in tonight on my way home."

"Oh, would you Tom? That would be kind of you, it's selfish of me I know but I do so love having the children here."

"It isn't selfish, they give you a sense of light-heartedness that grown-ups just don't have."

He laughed.

"I'm light-hearted, aren't I Mary? Why, only this morning I cracked a joke with the young lad in the stable. He didn't get it mind you, no sense of humour."

Mary chuckled at her husband.

"Of course you are my love, you make me laugh on many occasions."

She winked at Tom.

"I saw that Mrs."

He retorted as he sat down with Tom.

"You were meant to dear. Now, I've been thinking. Daisy and Julian have their wedding coming up soon and as Daisy has left her gown at your house Tom, I wondered if I might fetch it over here. I know it's the last thing on young Daisy's mind right now, but it does need to be altered."

"Hell's bell's, I had forgotten about that with everything, of course I will bring it over tomorrow if you like. It won't do if the dress of the bride is not ready."

"I know it hasn't been the best of times, Tom and I know your mother would do a much better job than I could hope to, but it does have to be dealt with."
replied Mary.

"You are just as talented with these things as Ma, I'll not forget, you will have it tomorrow. Shall I call and ask Miss. Harvey to come and see you for a fitting?"

"If you could, dear, that would be a help. I will be here all day for the next few days. I won't be here on Monday as I have a trip to Ashford, but any other day is fine with me."

"I don't think Miss. Harvey will mind about the day as long as she knows the dress is being done. It is so thoughtful of you."
And Tom meant it, after all he knew how much Daisy was looking forward to her special day.

Billoughby opened the door and for a minute he stared at the red faced man and then he realised who it was. His smile went from ear to ear as he embraced his old friend in a bear hug.

"Heaven's man, let me in the door before you cause a stir."
Laughed Joseph.

"It is so good to see you, dear friend, come in. What brings you over this way?"
Billoughby asked as he stepped back to let the doctor through.

"Dear chap, what do you think brings me here? How did I not hear about all of these going's on?"

Joseph glared at Billoughby; he wanted answers.

"It all happened so fast if you want the God's honest Joseph, and no sooner I'm about to be sent home my Gracie is poisoned by this crazed woman. I tell you my friend, if she doesn't get through this I don't know what I'll do."

Billoughby could feel himself starting to shake, it had been the first time he had said these thoughts out loud. His heart was thumping fast as he struggled to compose himself.

"There now, sit yourself down. Do you have any brandy in the cottage? Of course you do, same place as always?"

Joseph called over his shoulder.

"Y-yes, over there."

Billoughby pointed toward the cupboard.

"Right then, get this down you. It might help to steady your nerves. Are you taking your medicine?"

asked Joseph as he sat facing the man.

"I am, I think it's helping. I feel so useless, Joseph. She's my wife and I am a police Inspector, yet I wasn't here to help her. Took some fella from halfway across the country to do that, what does that make me? What will folk say about an Inspector that catches crooks for a living that couldn't save his own wife?"

Billoughby let out a sob that Joseph had never heard before from the man sitting there, he had known the Inspector a long time and had not once seen the man in such a state as he was now.

"Seems to me that you are being too hard on yourself Inspector. People get sick, that's unfortunate but that is also part and parcel of life. I have no doubt that had you been here this woman would still have done what she did, and dear Grace would still be in the predicament she is now in. I intend to see her, Grace that is, with your permission of course. See if I can't help in some way. Will you be visiting tomorrow; I could stay at the Inn tonight and we could travel down there together in the morning?"

Joseph knew a fair deal about poisons and his intention was to do all he could to get Grace fit and well.

"I was going to, and you are very welcome to come with me. I don't see the need for you to stay at the Inn, we have the spare visitors room in the back, it's not grand but it's clean and warm."

"Then I shall accept your gracious offer my friend. Now, you must allow me to cook as a thank you. Beryl says I am quite the gifted person in the kitchen area!"

Joseph announced proudly.

"If that suits you I won't put up any argument."

Daisy gasped when Tom mentioned Mary's offer, she was so happy to finally be getting married to her beloved Julian and yet one of the most important items of the upcoming day had been completely forgotten in her mind!

"How could I have not given it a thought? Is that a bad omen do you think Reverend, that it slipped my mind?"

Tobias laughed; she had the oddest way at times.

"My dear, do you recall the upset of the past few weeks? You are a fine constable and you put your duty to the law first when you needed to and helped to catch a criminal. It is not a bad omen my dear, it is a sign that you put duty before personal matters."

"You don't mind taking the dress to Mary, Tom? I am ever so grateful and if you say that I will call tomorrow in the afternoon. I am so excited; I shall soon be a wife!"

Daisy skipped around the parlour with a happiness that neither the reverend nor Tom had seen in some time.

"I will be happy to, I have to get going now. I promised Elsbeth that I would call and see her on my way back. Cheerio."

As Tom left he could hear Daisy talking excitedly to the reverend about her special day and wondered if he and Elsbeth would ever be accepted enough to have one of their own.

Saving Grace | D M Roberts

The hall was quiet now that the children had gone to bed and the staff had retired to their rooms, Elsbeth stared out of the large windows as she waited for Tom. The dusky sky was a stunning mixture of reds and purple as the sun had begun to set over the countryside view. The solitary silhouette walked down the long path and Elsbeth smiled to herself as she watched him. He was such a handsome man, kind too and with the most gentle and loving soul. How could anybody not love him? For every reason Elsbeth gave herself that this was wrong her heart and soul gave her 2 that told her it was right. She would be 47 years old this year, but she did not feel that when she was with Tom, he had a way of making her feel like a young woman again and she never questioned her feelings when he wrapped his arms around her. Today she needed the reassurance of his love, today had been a difficult and painful day.
"Shall we sit in the gardens, it's such a beautiful evening."
Asked Tom as he embraced her. Elsbeth nestled her face against his, he always smelt so good like the sweet grass itself.
"That sounds perfect. I have missed you so much."
Tom felt the emotion in Elsbeth, her arms gripping him tighter and for longer than she would ordinarily.
"I have missed you too, my love, as I do every second I am away from you. Do you want to talk about what it is that's on your mind?" Tom asked softly as he stroked her hair.
"I think first, we should get you something to eat. I imagine you haven't eaten yet?"
Elsbeth looked up into his eyes.
"Don't go to any trouble for me my love, I am just happy to see you."
Tom tightened his hold as they stood against the sunset for what seemed an eternity until eventually he felt her relax.
"Come, let us get you fed. I'll bring it out to you; I'll fetch some throws too."

Elsbeth made her way into the house leaving Tom to find a seat in the gardens away from prying eyes. He still felt the need for privacy when they had time alone even though they were now becoming common knowledge. Elsbeth returned laden with blankets around her shoulders and a tray.

"You will make someone a fine wife!"

Laughed Tom as she set the tray down.

"Do you think so? I have had a small amount of practice, and what of you Tom Billoughby, will you make someone a fine husband I wonder."

Her smile was like the fresh air that he breathed and like that air he could not live without her.

"I will, if I am given the chance to prove it. Who do we know that might offer a poor farm hand the chance to show what a devoted husband and father he could be?"

Tom's eyes burned into hers as he bit into the pie Elsbeth had served him.

"Who indeed!"

Elsbeth replied.

"Would you, my sweet and beautiful Elsbeth? Would you let me prove to you that you are the only woman I want and need?"

Tom's face was serious now, the frivolous grin had been replaced with a look of longing.

"You would be willing to give up the chance of having your own children and the looks you, we, would get from all that know us and those that don't?"

Tom took her hand in his.

"I would cross oceans and mountains, walk through fire and swim through ice for you my love, you know I would. We have all the children we will ever need, maybe we will have more who can say. They will be ours, yours and mine and we will love them as our own. As for other people, they will tire of us one day but until that day comes they will never change how I feel for you."

"Oh Tom, then you would make me the happiest woman alive." Elsbeth cried for the second time that day, but this time they were tears of joy.

Mr. Hirst knocked on the rectory door. It was mid-morning, and he had a friend with him that he wanted to introduce to the Reverend Moore.
"Good morning, please come in. Oh, hello again."
Tobias was confused, why was Mr. Hirst with one of the gentlemen that had come to see him weeks before?
"You know each other?"
Asked Mr. Hirst as he walked through to the sitting room.
"We have had the pleasure of meeting on a somewhat tricky occasion, however today I am merely here as your companion."
Replied the man.
"And may I ask how you know each other? It seems peculiar to me that 2 people from different parts of the country with dissimilar careers should be friends."
Enquired Tobias, who was wondering if this could be the person who had written to the clergymen in the first place!
"It was pure coincidence Reverend Moore, nothing other than that. Today, as I said, I am here at the invitation of Mr. Hirst. He speaks very highly of you and your village including all the good work that you do on your parishioners' behalf. I insist that today you call me Mitchell, or if you would rather, Mr. Gregory."
Tobias was not sure about this, he had heard of the underhanded ways that some would use to catch a fellow out.
"That is most kind of you, Sir. Can I fetch you a beverage of some sort?"
Offered Tobias as Mr. Hirst and Mr. Gregory sat down.
"Only if we aren't interrupting your day, Reverend. I had no idea that you 2 fellows knew each other in any capacity, it's fair to say

that until now I had no clue that Mr. Gregory was connected to the church."

By the awkwardness of Mr. Hirst's voice, Tobias felt at ease that he probably wasn't the person that put the complaint in.

"I try not to bring my religious undertakings into what I hope to be a friendship."

The older man smiled as he spoke, and Tobias caught sight of the warmth in his face that he had seen once before.

"Quite right, it is a pleasure to have you here again."

Tobias disappeared to the kitchen to make some tea, his heart beating a little steadier than it had been now that he knew he wasn't being studied.

"Help yourselves. You say you met quite by accident, was this in Canterbury?"

Tobias continued as he sat back in his chair.

"No, as a matter of fact we met in Dover. Andrew here was staying at the same hotel as I was and we got to talking, he then came to stay with me at my house in Hythe. A true and honest man that is easy and good company can be a rare thing to find, don't you agree?" Replied Mr. Gregory.

"You are too kind, Sir. I am ever in your debt for such wonderful hospitality. Do you know, Reverend, that Mr. Gregory is quite the fisherman? I have to say, I am envious of a man that possesses as much patience as a fisherman has."

Laughed Mr. Hirst.

"Is that so? You must accompany our small group some time when we have a fishing trip, maybe share a little of your knowledge."

Tobias enjoyed the fishing trips as he grew older, the calmness gave him a sense of tranquillity and he cared little whether he caught a fish or not.

"I would be delighted. Now there is a reason I asked to come here today, as I understand it Andrew is going to need some help in regard to this frightful business. The man has still to be cleared of any and all involvement in the wicked crimes perpetrated by this woman. Would you be willing to make a character statement on his behalf Reverend Moore? I imagine you have gotten to know him as well as any other during his time in your village."

"Surely now they have the woman the facts will speak for themselves? I mean, yes, of course I am happy to do this, without a doubt. Are you saying there is a chance that you may be charged as some kind of accomplice?"

The thought had never occurred to Tobias before this moment, and he shuddered to think what could be. They could well hang the man!

"As we all know, in matters such as these the law can be mercilessly narrow minded. I have seen it with my own eyes so any help you can offer would be gratefully received Reverend Moore."

Tobias recognised that glimmer of fear in Mr. Hirst's eyes, he had been there.

"Of course, anything I can do to help. Will you be travelling back home or will it be dealt with in London as these things often are."

"I suspect it will be London, I have a few contacts in the Canterbury Headquarters keeping me abreast of what is happening. The woman has made a full confession of her crimes although she is now claiming that the devil himself had possessed her mind."

Replied Mr. Hirst as he rolled his eyes. It wasn't that he didn't believe in evil, but he knew her acts were her own.

"You think she will likely get away with what she has done?"

Asked Mr. Gregory with concern sounding in his voice.

"It wouldn't be the first time. Many innocent men have been found guilty and many guilty men have walked free."

Mr. Hirst replied.

"Then we need to make sure this isn't going to be the case with Nora Howard. What else can I do?"

Asked Tobias.

"I feel that a meeting should be had with Inspector Billoughby, Constable Harvey and me, I would be obliged if you were also present Reverend and anyone else that you feel might be connected or helpful. If we can get all of our evidence and facts in order it would at least be a start."

Mr. Hirst was a man that did things by the book, it wasn't his intention to coerce the others, but he would be damned if he didn't do his best to have all of their paperwork in order.

"That's what I like to hear, a man who takes action in the face of adversity."

Added Mr. Gregory.

Joseph and Billoughby arrived at the hospital where Joseph promptly insisted that he speak to the doctor dealing with Grace. The nurse, a little put out at first, scurried off to track the man down.

"You are impressive once you get going."

Laughed Billoughby as the pair walked quietly down the ward to find Grace.

"What are friends for?"

Chuckled the man, his smile fading when he caught sight of the pale and fragile woman being helped to sit up by an orderly. Her normally rosy complexion gone and replaced with a greyish yellow tinge. Joseph had to swallow hard as he approached Grace.

"Well then Mrs. Billoughby, what has been going on my dear woman?"

Grace tried to smile as the kindly friend sat down and took her hand. Billoughby kissed Grace softly on the forehead, he was happy to see her sitting up and awake again. That had to be a good sign he thought to himself. Grace leaned forward, her voice still weak as she spoke to Joseph.

"It is so good to see you, Joseph. Is Beryl here?"

"I'm sorry to say she isn't, we had no idea of the torments you have both suffered but when Beryl returns from her trip I will be sure to bring her for a visit. Now, I would like to examine you if you are okay with me doing that? Not that they aren't excellent here, they are, but you know me Grace."

Grace nodded, if there was one thing she knew it was that Joseph was exceptional in the medical field and if he could do anything to help her feel better and get her home she would allow it. Joseph instructed the orderly to pull the curtain around the bed and began his examination of Grace. He had not always been a doctor of pathology, Joseph had started his career as a general practitioner, he moved on to become a surgeon but felt his calling was in pathology and research.

"May I ask what you th…Oh my word! If it isn't Joseph Lyons himself. What on earth brings you over this way and pray tell, what are you doing with my patient? It will be a very long time before you get your hands on this particular lady if I have anything to do with it."

The doctor laughed as he grasped the hand of Joseph and shook it vigorously.

"Monte! Why, I haven't seen you for, what is it, 10 years? How the devil are you?"

"11, but who's counting? Now, why are you going over my work? You must tell him, Mrs. Billoughby, that you are not quite ready to meet your maker."

"If I had known it was you, dear boy, I would not have dared interfere. As it is I didn't so please accept my most humble apology. Time for a quick chat?"

Asked Joseph as he nodded to the orderly to return the curtain to its rightful place.

"Always time for you Joseph, you know that. Please excuse us Inspector, Grace, I'll be back shortly."

The 2 doctors walked a way down the ward then stopped to talk in whispered voices. Billoughby watched them, bemused that no matter where Joseph went, everybody seemed to know him and what's more, everybody loved him.

There was a lot of nodding and head scratching going on between Joseph and the doctor, Billoughby wasn't sure whether that was a good thing or not. He turned to Grace, she too was watching the men standing at the end of the ward.
"What do you think they are saying?"
She said quietly.
"Oh, you know Joseph, he's likely picking the man's brains about something or other. They did say it had been over 10 years since they last spoke, I expect they have a lot to catch up on. Now let's see if we can't finish some of this porridge my love."
Billoughby handed the spoon to Grace then did another backward glance to Joseph at the same time the 2 doctors looked over to Grace.

"Arsenic? Do people still use that, and do we have any idea how much she might have ingested?"
Said Joseph, his worried expression not visible to the patient or her husband.
"I would stake my career on it. It's difficult to say how much, Mrs. Billoughby had vomited a fair amount from the reports we received but then she was also starved of food and water for a good few days too and you know what it's like Joseph, a lot of vomit to one person is not necessarily a lot to us. She is certainly taking a long time to regain her appetite, not to mention her pallor. I am concerned that there may be something else going on that is totally unrelated to this incident. I was going to look at her blood samples this morning, if you would care to second me on this?"
Joseph knew that his old friend was thorough in his work and didn't doubt his professional opinions in the slightest, but he would take him up on the offer all the same.

Chapter Twelve

Daisy stood in her under slip as Mary lifted the beautifully crafted gown over her head. It was as well they had remembered its importance because Mary could instantly see that it would have to be taken in quite a lot.

"Oh dear, it's so big Mary! Whatever will I do and only a week until I'm supposed to wear it. I don't remember it being this big the last time I tried it on."

The poor girl's face crumpled as she imagined herself holding the thing together as she walked down the aisle.

"Now, now Daisy, don't worry. I will have it fitting you like a glove in no time."

Mary smiled, although secretly she wondered if she had taken on a task that exceeded even her talents with a needle.

"Are you sure you can do something with it? I can easily get something else if it proves too much, not that I think you aren't capable, you understand. I know you are but it's a big ask at such short notice."

Daisy decided to stop talking, she felt if she continued all she would achieve was to insult the woman that was doing her a kindness.

"It will be just fine, now hold still while I pin it in a few places."

Mary set about pulling and pinning in all the places that stood out the most. There would be enough material over to make all the bridesmaid dresses too at this rate she mused as she continued. After what seemed hours, Mary stood back and pursed her lips.

"It feels better already, maybe we should leave it pinned."

Laughed Daisy.

"Don't move too much my girl, we don't want any blood on it from a stray pin! How would you feel if we took a couple of the layers off, there are so many, and times have moved on since this was last in fashion. I think we could get away with making it a more modern dress."

"Do you think you could do that Mary? I did promise Julian that I would wear it, even though it wouldn't be my choice but if you could change it a little I can't see that he would mind that."

"I think I could, it would be easier for you to wear, and you wouldn't feel so hot in it. Don't forget the day is likely to be a warm one. I shall keep all the remnants so that if he needed me to I could put it back to how it was afterwards. What do you say, Daisy, are you willing to take a chance?"

Daisy grinned, she was all about taking chances and she hadn't relished wearing the heavy-set gown in the first place.

"Let's do it."

She said as she stepped from the gown.

"I have all the measurements that I need, and it's pinned up securely. When you next try it on in, oh let's say, 2 days? It will be transformed."

Mary smiled; she had a sense for fashion even though she spent most of her time in work clothes.

"Do you think Mrs. Billoughby will be better by then?"

Daisy asked as she got back into her own clothes.

"I do hope so, the news from the hospital is encouraging in some ways but her recovery is very slow. The doctor says slower than many cases he's seen but then better than a hundred more." Daisy nodded, she knew that poisoning could be fatal in far too many people so Grace was lucky to some degree.

"I asked the Inspector if I should call the wedding off until we knew Mrs. Billoughby was in the clear, but he wouldn't hear of it, Julian and I wouldn't have minded."

"And that's as it should be! This is your day Daisy, yours and Julians, the Inspector was right to tell you no."

Cate was not feeling good again, she had escaped the morning sickness with Maisy but this child inside her was more than making up for that. Adam could be heard downstairs trying to soothe the little one's cries as she wondered where her mammy was. Between bouts of sickness Cate tried to get up so that she could tend to her daughter, who was now wailing louder than a hungry seagull.

"Bring her to me, Adam, Adam."

Cate shouted down to her husband.

"She's alright love, you get yourself feeling better and I'll look after little Maisy."

Cate groaned; God love him he tried but the child would surely burst a lung if she kept this up.

"Adam please! Bring her to me."

Adam relented and carried the child up to her mother, still wailing for all the world to hear. The minute Maisy saw her mother she stopped, her small mouth curling into a smile.

"That's how it is, Eh! All girls together, well I know where I stand." Said Adam as he placed the child with her mother.

"Don't take on love, she most likely knows I'm feeling under the weather."

Cate tried to soothe her husband's ego with her words.

"Is it normal for you to feel this sick every day? I am starting to get a little bit worried about you love."

"Quite normal. I asked the doctor, and he said each baby can be different but hopefully it shouldn't last too long. Besides, it's said that sickness is a good sign."

"I hope so, I don't like seeing you unwell."

Adam stroked her face as he spoke.

"I'm not unwell my lovely, I'm having a baby, our baby."

"Should I send word to Aunt Janet, do you think? She would want to know about Ma, and she might be able to offer us some help until you are feeling better?"

Cate didn't like asking for help but with Adam at work and Maisy being much more active than she was, it definitely sounded like a good idea.

"At the very least they should be told about your Ma and Pa, they won't be happy to find out later on. It would be a help to have someone here when you're at work."

"That's settled then. I'll send word over to them."

Adam replied. Cate sighed under her breath, maybe Janet would have more luck amusing Maisy.

The officer arrived at the Hall as arranged and Sally was first to be questioned before making her statement. She retold the episodes involving the children that she witnessed and the morning that Nora Howard had dismissed the staff claiming it was on the Mistresses instruction. Sally didn't embellish as sometimes could be her way, she didn't feel she needed to considering what a wicked woman they had unknowingly let into the house. The officer thanked her and asked that Cook be sent through, and so it continued for the rest of the day until he was satisfied that they had everybody's statements.

"What happens now?"

Asked Elsbeth as they drank tea in the parlour.

"We have a couple more people to visit in the village and then I shall take the statements back to London, there a judge at the Old Bailey will read the charges. If the woman pleads guilty she will be sentenced, if not then I am sure there will be a trial judging by the statements. I have met Mrs. Howard and although she has confessed I get the feeling she will change her mind on the day."

"How can she do that? Surely there isn't a possibility that she will get away with this?"

The officer shrugged; he had seen her like many times.

"It happens Miss, not altogether there if you want my opinion and she will try to wriggle out of it if she can. Still, we shall see."

Elsbeth saw the officer to the door, he would be in touch he assured her as he left for the village.

Daisy was stunned when she saw the dress. It exceeded all her expectations and more. The bodice was smooth and seamless with the skirts so much lighter now that Mary had removed the cage and at least 3 layers. The train was attached at the back with a large satin bow. Mary had removed the flouncy sleeves and replaced them with slimmer sheer fabric that had been part of the underskirts. Daisy twirled as she admired the miracle that the woman had performed in such a short space of time.
"You approve?"
Asked Mary with a smile.
"Oh Mary, it's perfect! How on earth did you manage it?"
Gushed the bride to be.
"Do you love it, I hope so. It was tricky, I will admit that, and I'm convinced dear Grace would have done a better job, but I did pay a recent trip to London, and you know they are the first to wear new designs."
"I do love it. Thank you so much Mary."
Daisy hugged Mary hard, a weight now lifted from her.
"It will be a beautiful day and you will be the most beautiful bride."
Daisy carefully removed the gown, handing it back to Mary who would do the final finishing touches before the big day.
"Will Julian be here for the rehearsal?"
"Yes, he has been given a month off work so that we can spend some time together in our new cottage. He arrives on Friday and his family will arrive the day of our wedding. I believe they are staying with a close friend of the family in Hythe. He has a huge home and kindly offered to accommodate them."
"That's very generous of them. Are you nervous about married life? I hear you are going to continue in your work."

Mary said as she stored the dress in the cupboard and the pair headed into the sitting room.

"I am a little, but I'm also excited. Julian is modern in his thinking and believes that women should have the choice to work or join the society wives, I don't imagine myself a society wife Mary, do you?" Daisy laughed, not because she mocked society wives but because she knew she would be bored rigid.

"Too much energy young Miss, that's your problem. I like that you will continue to follow your path, and who knows, one day you could be the first woman Inspector!"
The pair chuckled at what they knew was something that would never happen.

Joseph returned to the hospital a few days later, he had arranged with his old colleague Monte to be present when the doctor spoke to the Billoughby's that morning. Grace had been given a new medicine tonic that Joseph had recommended, and she was beginning to feel a little better. The morning saw her disagreeing with the nurse at having to remain longer than she wanted to.
"Can't you talk to them Joseph?"
Her voice still quieter than usual.
"My dear, it was I that insisted you stay longer. You are not well enough to go home and under the circumstances it is best you do as you are asked."
Grace lay back against the pillow, her head shaking in annoyance at the man who was supposed to be their friend.
"Is there something you aren't telling us, Joseph?"
Billoughby had picked up on the phrase his friend had used even if Grace hadn't.
"The doctor will be here soon, and we can discuss Grace's condition then. In the meantime, please be a good patient Grace, it would make your stay so much more pleasant for everyone." Joseph smiled as he

spoke, he meant what he said but did not like the idea of telling a close friend how to behave.

It wasn't long before Monte appeared, he was smiling as he beckoned Joseph to him. The pair had a brief quiet talk and when Joseph came back to the bedside he had lost the look of despair on his face.

"Well hello Grace, Mr. Billoughby. I had imagined the news I was about to share with you both today would be grim but after doing some extensive testing I, and Dr. Lyons here, are very happy to tell you that you should be perfectly fine Grace with a lot of rest, naturally."

The man patted Billoughby on the shoulder and gave Grace a warm smile.

"What did you think the problem was?"

Asked Billoughby as he squeezed his wife's hand.

"In cases like this there can be dire complications with organs such as the liver, kidneys etc but we have been testing Grace's blood on a very regular basis over the past week or so and it is picking up remarkably. We will need to give you ferrous salt to make sure you continue to build yourself up in the meantime."

He explained.

"When can I go home?"

Asked Grace.

"Not just yet I'm afraid, I want to be certain that you are heading in the right direction. Now I must get on and see my other patients, but I will call by and see you again before I leave."

"That is good news."

Said Joseph as he sat in the spare seat next to Grace.

"I am so relieved, Joseph. I can't tell you how much your help has meant to us."

Billoughby could feel that lump rising again in his throat but this time it was with gratitude.

"Hush now man, it's what we do, and I can't think of better people than you 2."

Tom and Elsbeth walked behind the children in the field, the day was bright and warm, and it wasn't often that they got to spend time during the week together. Ruby and Martha skipped through the tall grass holding hands and singing a nursery rhyme while David, William and Jacob raced each other across the meadow.
"Don't you want to have a run with the others, Doris dear?"
Elsbeth asked the young girl.
"No thank you Miss. Elsbeth. I like walking just fine."
Tom chuckled, he remembered how at her age he was a similar soul whereas Adam would be tearing around like a startled cat.
"That's alright Doris, it's too hot for all that running around. Have you spotted anywhere we might stop for our picnic?"
He asked as Doris picked daisies as she walked.
"Over there, Mr. Tom. There's a flat piece of grass."
She pointed at the clearing near the trees in the distance.
"Perfect dear, would you like to help me set the blanket and baskets out?"
Asked Elsbeth.
"Can I?"
replied a smiling Doris.
"Of course! I would ask the others, but you know the boys would likely eat the goodies before they had a chance to be set down."
She laughed.
"Hey, we are growing boys!"
Sniggered Tom as he set the baskets down on the ground. The children ahead of them turned to see that the grown-ups had come to a stop and raced over knowing that it must mean time to eat.
"Is it time for lunch?"
They cried almost simultaneously as they clambered for the best spot on the blankets.

"Oh, I don't know…have we enough for everyone, that's what I'm thinking."
Said Tom in his most serious voice.
"Don't be silly Mr. Tom, there's loads of food."
David said his face showing a small amount of worry as he surveyed the array that Doris and Elsbeth had laid out.
"He's teasing, David. There is more than enough food for everyone."
Giggled Doris as she bit into a triangular sandwich. The children sat contented as they laughed and ate in the afternoon sun.
"Are you looking forward to Miss. Harvey's wedding on Saturday, children?"
Asked Elsbeth as she poured the lemonade out.
"Oo, I am. We get to wear our pretty dresses again like when Miss. Mary got married."
Said Doris, her eyes wide.
"You will, and ever so pretty you looked in it too."
Replied Elsbeth.
"I didn't like the tie; it made my neck itchy."
Said David as he tugged at his collar to replicate the feeling.
"It's only for one day, David. Imagine when you're older and have to wear one every day!"
Said Tom with a goofy look on his face.
"Then we will have to wear them again when you and Miss. Elsbeth get married!" Said William as he munched on an apple.
"Manners, William. We don't speak with our mouths full dear."
Said Elsbeth as she rolled her eyes in Tom's direction.
"Yes, you're right William. 2 whole days when you will have to bear the torture of a tie. Argh, whatever will we do."
Tom chuckled out loud as the children laughed at his dramatic reply.
"Are you going to marry Mr. Tom, Miss?"
Martha asked with concern.
"Is that a problem, dear?"

Elsbeth replied.

"Oh no, Miss. I think that's lovely."

Martha liked the idea of them all being one big family.

"Well, that's settled then."

Said Tom as he jumped up, pulling Elsbeth up to her feet. The children watched with bewilderment and Elsbeth grinned, she too was a little confused as to what Tom had up his sleeve. Tom kept her hand in his, his knee touching on the ground he stared up into her eyes.

"My dearest Miss. Elsbeth. You would make me the happiest man in the whole wide world if you would marry me. I love you and I love our family, now and always, will you marry me?" The gasps echoed through the quiet summer meadow as the children bounced up and down with glee.

"Shush you lot, she's going to answer!"

Ordered Jacob in his loudest yet still quiet voice. Elsbeth had to fight the tear that began to escape from her eyes.

"Oh, Thomas James Billoughby! That is the most perfect proposal a woman could ask for, and yes, yes I will marry you. Won't we children?"

The children roared an emphatic yes as Tom took Elsbeth in his arms and hugged her tight, whispering in her ear.

"Thank you my darling."

Julian had arrived with his best man, Mr. Edward Cavendish and the pair reacquainted themselves with the village before attending the rehearsal.

The rehearsal itself went as well as these things can but the real treat was that everybody got to relax for the night in the company of old friends and new.

Daisy and Julian were suitably kept at a distance from each other on the request of Reverend Moore, he took his duty as chaperone very seriously and with Mr. Gregory in attendance it seemed prudent for him to do so.

Grace was missed, of course, and Billoughby took great delight in sharing an update about his wife and her health.

Mr. Hirst spoke at length with Edward Cavendish regarding the upcoming trial of Nora Howard, Edward was a good friend of the judge and saw no reason for the man to worry.

"Cases like these are often quite clear cut, and if the woman has confessed once that should be enough. Theoretically you have nothing to worry about officer, and you will likely be reinstated to your previous post."

It was the theoretical that concerned Mr. Hirst and he wouldn't settle until the woman was sentenced.

"Thank you for taking the time to talk with me, now you must go and join the others and enjoy the evening. It will be a big day tomorrow."

Saturday arrived and the parish women's group were busy arranging flowers in the church and setting out the scene for the wedding of Miss.Daisy Harvey, a woman they had come to admire and love like one of their own. Daisy had insisted on paying for the arrangements, but they would hear nothing of it, it was their gift to the happy couple.

"Oh, look at this! Splendid ladies, utterly splendid!"

Reverend Moore was fussing around like a mother hen. He wanted everything just perfect for the young woman he had come to care about as if she were his own daughter. The guests began arriving and soon the church started filling up.

Back at the cottage Daisy was staring at her reflection as Mary fixed the veil at the back.

"You look so pretty, but you always do. What do you think, dear?"

Mary stepped back to take another look at the young woman.

"I am so happy, Mary. It looks beautiful and I am getting married!"
"We best start making a move then my girl, we don't want your man thinking he's been left at the altar now, do we?"
Mary wiped a stray tear from her face, she remembered this exact feeling from her own wedding day.
"Is dad here yet? They should be here by now."
Mary smiled.
"Of course they are, now stop worrying. You will hear the carriage when it arrives, sit yourself down and try to relax and whatever you do, don't spill anything on that dress!"

When Daisy walked down the aisle the congregation turned and looked at what must have seemed to them, the most beautiful bride that had ever graced the small church. The children smiled proudly as they walked behind her holding the train. David's eyes were as wide as saucers as the vision passed by. Cate and Adam held hands as they stood to witness the bride in her new chapter.
"Doesn't she look lovely?"
Sobbed Sally into her handkerchief, Cook nodded to her friend, words failing her. The dress was a glowing success with Mary watching with pride, and Robert whispering to her what a clever woman she was to have created it in such a short space of time. Billoughby stood with Tom and Elsbeth, he wished that Grace could have been here to see this.
Julian looked up nervously as Edward prodded him discreetly.
"Look at her, am I not the luckiest chap?"
He whispered to his best man with a smile as big as his love for this unconventional and brilliant woman that was soon to be his.
"You are indeed my friend."
Replied Edward as they stepped forward. Daisy smiled through her veil as her father gave her delicate lace gloved hand to her future husband, wiping away a tear as he stood to the side. Reverend Moore

began the ceremony of the year, unaware of the 2 men standing at the back.

Grace was confused, Joseph and her doctor had told her not a couple of days ago that she had to stay in the hospital for a good while and yet the nurse stood before her with a wheelchair telling her she was being discharged! Grace looked around the ward, but it was quiet, and her usual nurse didn't seem to be anywhere in sight.
"Come along, we have other patients to care for without you being difficult."
The stern and strange voice bothered Grace. Her heart started racing, she felt odd, and she didn't want to go anywhere with this nurse.
"I need to see my doctor."
She argued as the woman tried to pry her from the bed.
"Why? Don't you think you have wasted enough of his and everybody else's time, he does have plenty of other patients. Patients that are very sick, I might add!"
She was certainly not the compassionate type, thought Grace as she reluctantly climbed into the chair. The nurse pushed the chair hastily down the quiet ward and Grace couldn't help but feel that something wasn't right.
"Are you to take me home, nurse?"
she asked, keeping her voice steady.
"Yes, it appears that I am. A cart has been ordered and should be waiting outside for us."
"That is very kind of you, I'm sure my husband would have come had he known."
Replied Grace as they continued down the empty corridor.
"Well, he didn't so now it's down to me and I don't mind telling you that it isn't part of my duties so if you could stop asking questions we can get on with it."

When the nurses came out of the side-room they looked down to the bed where Mrs. Billoughby should have been. It was common at weekends to have less patients on the ward.
"Where could she be? She knows she isn't to get out of bed without our help."
The young woman said with panic in her voice.
"Maybe she went to the w.c.? She is very independent, you know. Go and have a quick look and I'll check in the nurse's office."
The nurses went off in opposite directions. The bathroom was empty, as the nurse came walking out she heard a screech from the office. She ran down the ward to find the senior nurse kneeling beside the doctor who lay on the floor. It didn't take long for the dazed doctor to come round. It appeared that he had been hit on the back of his head and knocked out cold.
"What the devil happened?"
Helped to a chair the doctor put his hand up to feel his head, his fingers touching on the damp, warm blood. The nurse quickly tended to it as she explained that Mrs. Billoughby had gone.
"You don't think she would have done such a thing do you, doctor?"
Asked the senior nurse.
"No, beside the fact that she wouldn't have the strength, I was watching her through the window as I worked. I assure you she was asleep in that bed when I felt the whack on my head."
"Then who, and where on earth could Mrs. Billoughby have gotten to?"
She asked. They had never had anything like this happen in their quiet little hospital and it shook the trio.
"First thing we should do is contact the constabulary, this cannot go unreported. I suggest we call together the orderlies and do a thorough search of the premises for our missing patient, if she is still here we will find her."

They searched every inch of the hospital, but Grace was nowhere to be seen and when the officers arrived the hospital staff were at a loss as to what they should do next.

Chapter Thirteen

Grace was well aware that they were not going in the direction of her village, she was also aware that this woman was not a nurse. Grace kept quiet, she had no intention of letting on that she knew anything. Nora Howard called back to her captive every now and again to ask if she was alright to which Grace would merely say 'Yes thank you' giving Nora no clue that she had been discovered. They were headed toward Aldington, Grace recognised the area from the frequent trips they had made with the boys when they were younger and subsequent trips she and Milton had made to visit friends. One of their friends in particular was an old colleague of Milton's; they had a cottage set back into the woodland area of its village.

Grace imagined the woman was going to try to escape the country via a different route. How did she escape? That was the other thought that ran through her mind now. The alarm would soon be raised when the nurse's came to give out lunch. Grace shook her head, there were so many different thoughts going through her head right now and she couldn't concentrate on them all at once.

"How has this happened? You tell me how one woman, who doesn't know the area let alone the station house, has managed to not only get past all of the officers in the building but get herself to Hythe without money or help? Tell me that, because I would dearly like to know."

Try as he might, Billoughby could not keep his voice low as the 2 men stood before him in the back room of the rectory.

"Sir, if I may say, we were not there at the time. I understand your concern and anger, I do, we both do."

Saving Grace | D M Roberts

The officer said, his voice low and measured as he tried to diffuse the situation.

"YOU DO NOT!"

Bellowed the Inspector as he paced frantically around the small room. The door opened behind him, Daisy stared at him.

"What is going on, Inspector? And please, don't tell me nothing as I know better."

"Go back to your guests, love. It's your special day and I won't stand for anyone or anything ruining that for you."

Billoughby's voice was shaking but he managed to lower it as he spoke to the woman that had barely been wed 5 minutes.

"I will not! If something has happened, and judging by your upset it clearly has, then I want to know about it."

Daisy was not going to give up easily.

"Now, Miss. Please do as the Inspector asked and run along like a good girl, this is police business and no concern of yours."

Billoughby shook his head at the officer, he had no idea who he had just insulted.

"GOOD GIRL! How dare you speak to me in such a manner. I am a constable, and I will NOT be spoken to in that manner. Do not let my attire or my pretty face fool you into thinking that I am some dumb woman that only troubles herself with flowers and poetry! Now I asked a question officer, what is going on?"

The man looked at Inspector Billoughby, possibly for some sort of back-up but it wasn't forthcoming. Daisy stomped her foot on the hard stone floor impatiently as she looked at them in turn.

"Sir?"

The officer gestured to Billoughby, in turn Billoughby nodded his approval and the situation was explained again.

"How? Did you get any reasoning as to how this occurred?"

Asked Daisy as she patted the Inspector's arm. What must he be thinking? He stayed away from the hospital today only to attend her wedding!

"Apparently the woman assaulted a female cleaner early this morning when she entered her cell, banged her head off the wall and swapped clothes then had it away out of the door, constable. That's all we know as to the how. We have nothing to say that she's the one that has taken the good Inspector's wife, if indeed anyone has. All we know is that Mrs. Billoughby has gone missing this afternoon."
Billoughby slammed his fist against the wall.
"Of course she has, damn it man, these kinds of things aren't coincidence!"
Billoughby was not in the mood for flat-footed optimism.
"What can I do?"
Asked Daisy to Billoughby all the while glaring at the man who was now staring at the floor.
"You can do one thing, if you wouldn't mind?"
Replied the Inspector.
"Name it."
Daisy was happy to do anything she could to help her mentor.
"I know you want to help, but right now you have a hall full of guests that expect to see the bride; not to mention your new husband. Now, I don't want any arguments out of you, but I would feel much better if you could go and enjoy your day. You have more than held the fort for me constable, and for that I am truly grateful, but I feel it's time I get back to what I do best, starting with finding my wife and an escaped murderer."
His smile softened as he spoke, and Daisy knew she had lost this particular battle.
"Very well, I shall but only because I know if anyone can sort this mess out it is you, Inspector." Daisy stretched up giving the Inspector a brief kiss on the cheek as the 2 officers watched open-mouthed.

Mary and Elsbeth rushed to Daisy's side when she returned to the hall.

"Whatever is happening, dear and who were the 2 men that the Inspector went off with?"

Daisy shook her head, should she tell them? Billoughby hadn't asked her not to.

"Yes, I didn't recognise either of them and they didn't appear to be wedding guests."

Elsbeth added.

"They weren't."

Whispered Daisy as she guided the women to a quieter space.

"Then who are they?"

Asked Mary, her voice low and urgent.

"They are constables from Canterbury. I am not certain I should be saying this, but, as you have been involved with these matters I don't think the Inspector would mind. The woman, Nora Howard has escaped her custody in Canterbury, worst still, Mrs. Billoughby has gone missing from the hospital. The doctor was knocked unconscious and when the nurse's returned Grace was gone."

Daisy breathed with relief when she finished telling what she knew.

"Oh, good God, No! This is terrible news, whatever is wrong with people. Do Tom and Adam know?"

Elsbeth said, shocked that for a second time Grace could be in serious danger. Daisy shook her head, until now she hadn't thought about Tom and Adam.

"Do you think we ought to tell them?"

Asked Mary.

"It is their mother; they have a right to know but then I think it might be better coming from their father."

Elsbeth added after a pause. She wasn't too sure if she would be able to keep this from Tom.

"I think for now, at least, we say nothing to anyone. The Inspector knows what he's doing, and he did say I should come back here and enjoy the rest of my day…Not that I feel much like celebrating with what I know."

Daisy waved over to Julian who had been watching the women huddled together with curiosity.

"Off you go, dear. It doesn't pay to keep your new husband waiting."

Smiled Mary as she ushered the young woman back to the waiting throng of well-wishers.

Grace looked around her, the area was coming up soon and she didn't want to miss her chance.

"Nurse? I'm sorry, I didn't catch your name."

Nora grinned at the sheer stupidity of the woman behind her. If she only knew who she was she would certainly not be sounding so calm. Nora was good with accents, it was something she prided herself on and this Scots accent sounded so convincing even if she thought so herself.

"I didn't tell you my name, we aren't meant to build personal friendships with the patients. What is it?"

"I wondered if I might stop for a moment, I need to…well, you know?"

Replied Grace.

"What! Out here, in the woods?"

Nora knew they had odd ways in the countryside, but she hadn't realised just what animals they were.

"I'll make it quick, growing up it was how we had to do things. There were no lavish rooms for us children, so I suppose I'm used to it. It doesn't bother…"

"Could you please just get out and get on with it, for heaven's sake do I have to listen to you consistently prattling on, I told you it is not part of my job."

"Could you help me, nurse?"

Grace almost knew what the answer to this would be as she steadied herself in the cart.

"I will not! It is your choice to behave like a heathen, it is my choice not to bear witness to it."

"I'm sorry, I didn't mean to upset you. I will be a moment, just behind the tree, there?"

Grace pointed as she stepped from the cart.

"Fine, just hurry up about it."

Snorted Nora as she looked in the other direction. She had no concerns of the woman making a run for it, why would she? They were in the middle of nowhere and she didn't have a clue. The twisted smile spread across her face as sounds of Grace humming quietly to herself rang through the air.

It had been a few minutes when Nora realised that the humming had stopped, blast that do-gooder of a woman! No doubt she had fainted or some such drama.

"Are you finished back there?"

There came only the chirping of the birds in the trees.

"I SAID ARE YOU FINISHED?"

Nora screamed at the top of her lungs. She didn't wait for an answer, she sprang down from the cart and headed into the dark woods, her head spinning this way and that in a desperate bid to spot the Inspectors wife. Nora did not like the woods, they gave her the creeps. She wandered further in, calling out as she went.

"THINK YOU'RE CLEVER DO YOU LASSIE? I WILL FIND YOU, AND WHEN I DO YOU WILL BE SORRY. DO YOU HEAR ME?"

Grace sat perfectly still in the bushes, the thorns and brambles scratched her body, but she could stand it. Knowing that she would never outrun Nora Howard in the feeble state she was in, Grace knew her only chance was to wait it out as quietly as she could. It would be dark soon, she knew the pathway well from so many visits over the years.

Nora stood and listened, she heard nothing but the sounds of nature. She would go back to the cart, the Inspectors wife had to come out sooner or later and when she did Nora would be ready!

Adam was raging, he pushed through the merry crowd that danced to the band Julian had arranged to come from London and play in the evening at his and Daisy's wedding.

"Son, wait!"

Billoughby ran after him, catching hold of his jacket sleeve.

"No, Pa. Why are we just hearing this? We could have been out there, looking. What is wrong with this woman that she has taken against Ma so much? I don't get it."

Tom caught up with the pair.

"Adam, you'll do no-one any good getting so worked up. It isn't Pa's fault this has happened." Adam stood back, his anger burnt from his eyes.

"No, it isn't! If it wasn't for the upset you have caused Ma, she would never have been at the Hall that day, she would never have been known to that murderous witch! You're right, Tom, it isn't Pa's doing, it's yours, and hers!"

Adam pointed at Elsbeth who had just reached the garden. Elsbeth stopped in her tracks, her expression going from that of concern to hurt.

"You take that back, brother. Take it back right now."

Tom started toward Adam; their anger now matched in the humid evening air.

"Why should I? It's true, you know it, I know it. Bloody hell Tom, even Pa knows it, don't you?"

Adam levelled the question at his father.

"Adam, be quiet. This is nonsense and it won't help in getting your mother home."

Replied Billoughby as he stepped between his sons'.

Elsbeth was halfway down the lane with the words sticking in her chest like a dagger.

"Are you alright, Miss?"

Edward was walking back the other way when he spotted the woman who seemed to be in distress. Elsbeth dabbed her eyes and smiled, she didn't want to draw any more attention to herself than she quite obviously had.

"Yes, thank you. I felt the need for some air."

Her voice low, Elsbeth continued to walk.

"I could walk with you?"

Edward was a gentleman; it was his nature to be courteous and he wasn't about to change now.

"Really, it's not necessary."

"Maybe not but my father taught me manners and I try not to waste them."

He smiled as he turned to walk beside Elsbeth.

"You are Mr. Cavendish? Julian's friend from London."

Asked Elsbeth as the moonlight shone onto his face.

"And you are Elsbeth Stanhope, friend of the newly betrothed Daisy Richardson from right here."

He laughed. Elsbeth couldn't help but smile, he certainly was charming.

"May I ask what seems to have upset you? Or, is that something you would rather not discuss with a nearly new friend."

Edward stopped to rest on the wall, he patted the space next to him and after a moment Elsbeth relented and sat down.

"Inspector Billoughby's wife, Grace, has been taken again by a woman that we thought was in a custodial cell in Canterbury. This has caused a great deal of angst, understandably and I'm afraid I got caught in the crossfire."

Edward listened intently as Elsbeth poured out the events of the past weeks, he didn't interrupt, nor did he stop her. Elsbeth sighed, had she divulged too much to this man?

"Where were you going? Just now, when we met."
He asked gently.
"Home. I said I wouldn't stay too long. The children had a long day, they went back a couple of hours ago so I must go home and give my staff a chance to come and enjoy the festivities, they have helped me so much they deserve the night off."
"That is very kind of you, I'm sure they will appreciate it. Quite the party, don't you think?"
"It is indeed. Please don't let me keep you, I can make my way home on my own."
"You are not keeping me. I will let you in on a little secret, I am not a party person. By the time I reached 16 I had attended enough parties and balls to last a lifetime. As for escorting you home, I insist. Now Miss. Stanhope, I think it only fair that my chivalry be rewarded with a decent cup of tea. Is that agreeable with you?"
Elsbeth smiled, she certainly had a captivating smile Edward noted.

Sally and the 2 housemaids barely noticed Mr. Cavendish going into the parlour, their main concern was getting to the village before they missed all the fun. Sally reported that the children had all gone out as soon as their heads hit their beds.
"They had such a nice time, Ma'am. They behaved like angels when we came back and went to bed with no problems. If there's nothing else Ma'am?"
"Nothing else, enjoy yourselves and thank you."
Elsbeth called as the buggy pulled away.
"Tea? I believe that was the order of the day."
Said Elsbeth as she took off her wrap and placed it along the back of the settee.
"Unless you have a decent glass of brandy, not that you wouldn't. Oh dear, that was not what I meant to say."
Edward blushed at his clumsy attempt of levity.

"I do believe we have some very fine brandy. Would you prefer it in your tea, or on its own?" Elsbeth asked as she approached the cabinet.

"On its own if you don't mind?"

He watched as her skirts swished in an elegant manner while she busied herself pouring 2 large glasses of the liqueur.

"There we are, enjoy."

She said as she handed the glass to her guest.

"Thank you. Tell me about yourself, Miss. Stanhope. Is there a Mr. Stanhope?"

Edward settled back into the chair and took a gulp of the strong drink, nodding his approval.

"There was, he died. There was also a husband before I became Mrs. Stanhope, my Wilf." Elsbeth paused as she said the name she felt a tinge of sadness sweep through her body. Edward noticed her expression change and without explanation he knew that Wilf was no longer.

"I am sorry to hear that, on both counts. It must have been a tough time for you, and still so young."

Elsbeth took a large swallow of the brandy, she wasn't accustomed to drinking the way most were but felt she needed it after the night she had experienced.

"It was, on both occasions. My children more than make up for my lack of a husband."

Elsbeth smiled as she thought of the joy that they brought to her life.

"Ah, you have children! They must miss their father?"

Edward couldn't imagine being without his children or how they would cope if he were to die.

"Oh, I should explain. The children I took in, they were living in the most appalling conditions at a home for orphans. I have this great big home that was calling out for them, it seemed selfish not to share my home and my heart with those that needed it."

Did this woman's heart have no bounds he thought as he watched the warmth emanate from her face as she spoke about them.

"You are truly an incredible woman, Miss. Stanhope. I am in awe of your generosity."

"It's nothing special, I'm sure that most would do the same if they were in my position."

She blushed. Elsbeth had always found it difficult accepting compliments, especially from one as handsome as Mr. Cavendish.

"Oh, but it is special. You are special and it would be quite remiss of me not to tell you while I have your ear."

"They bring so much to my life that it is I that should be grateful to them for sharing their lives with me. Do you have children, Mr. Cavendish?"

It occurred to Elsbeth that she had asked nothing about the man or his life.

"I do, I have 2 beautiful daughters. We wanted 2 of each in truth, sadly Amelia passed last month giving birth to what would have been our first son…He didn't make it either."

A shiver ran through Elsbeth, this was truly tragic, and the pain was more than evident on the man's face as he swallowed back a larger helping of brandy.

"I am so very sorry to hear that. It must have been dreadful for you, and your girls."

Edward grinned, it was put on, of course.

"The church tells me there's a reason for it, part of God's great plan I do believe the phrase was. Do you believe in the great plan, Elsbeth?"

The way he said her name gave the woman the strangest sensation unlike any she had experienced. It wasn't polite to call a person by first name terms when they had only been introduced recently and yet he said her name as though he had been speaking it for years.

Saving Grace | D M Roberts

"It depends, if it is to save us some way down the road from a far greater tragedy or, to make a path for a happier life perhaps? God's plan is beyond my capabilities of knowledge, Mr. Cavendish."
There, thought Elsbeth, she had put them back on a formal footing.
"Please, call me Edward. It has been a while since anyone has used my name other than Amelia, and she has now gone. It will surprise you to learn that even my parents fail to use my Christian name, it's either dear boy or dear son, never Edward."
He stared into the flickering flames that danced in the large fire.
"Edward, it is a fine name."
Her voice softened in sadness for the man.
"You say it so well. Another drink, perhaps?"
Edward got up from the chair, taking Elsbeth's glass with his own to the cabinet. He filled them a little higher than his hostess would have, he needed a companion in his despair. Elsbeth feared that this amount of alcohol may well lead her to a trouble she would have difficulty getting out of, but she took the glass with a warm smile.

Cate was furious with Adam, she was aware that he had consumed a fair amount of ale and that he was in fear for the safety of his mother, but this!
"You go to your brother this instance and beg his forgiveness that you would say such a hateful thing Adam Billoughby! Do you hear me? And when you are done saying your sorries you go straight up to that hall and apologise to Mrs. Stanhope. What must she be thinking that you lay the blame at her door for the acts of this wicked person?"
Adam shrugged, yes he knew he had gone a step too far, but it was nearly midnight and all he wanted to do was sleep.
"I'll do it in the morning, love."
"You'll do no such thing! You'll do it now or you'll have me to answer to."

Adam shook his head; he knew she was right, but hell's teeth could it not wait a few hours?

"Cate, I hear what you're saying, I do, but it's late and I imagine Tom has gone home with Pa and Elsbeth, well she's likely tucked up in bed if she has any sense."

Cate stared at her husband, God how she loved this man but sometimes! Adam grabbed his jacket off the back of the chair.

"Good man."

Said Cate as he made his way into the village hall.

Tom sat with Julian, they had both drunk a good deal and it looked like they were propping each other up. Rolling his eyes Tom muttered when he caught sight of his brother coming toward him.

"Here we go."

"What's that you say friend?"

asked a very intoxicated Julian. Tom motioned with his head toward Adam. Billoughby watched the pair from a distance as Sally talked non-stop in his ear about, well who knows, certainly not the Inspector as his mind was elsewhere.

"Tom."

"Adam."

"I'm to apologise."

mumbled Adam.

"Are you indeed?"

"I am. Now let that be an end to it."

Said Adam with some measure of relief in his voice.

"Thank you brother."

replied Tom. Adam left the pair and went back to Cate. Julian opened his eyes wide and looked at Tom in disbelief.

"Was that it?"

He asked.

"What more is there?"

Replied Tom, confused at the man who had clearly witnessed the apology.

"Oh, nothing my friend."

Julian supped a little more from his mug, his mind wondering now why all conflicts could not be solved in such a simple way.

Adam escorted Cate home, on the way he tried to persuade his wife that the apology to Elsbeth could surely wait until the morning, Cate disagreed saying it wasn't right to sleep on such bad terms and the sooner he went there the quicker he could be home and in bed. Reluctantly Adam set off to the hall.

His horse was swift enough, and it took no time at all for him to reach the large house. Tying the reins to the gate post Adam was pleased to see there were lights on in the parlour, he didn't want to disturb the whole house by ringing the bell or using the large doorknocker, instead he made his way to the large windows to tap for attention. Sure enough he could see Elsbeth sitting on the settee, he was about to knock on the window when he saw a man he recognised from the church. The man who had stood as Julian's best man now seated himself next to Elsbeth, passing the woman a large glass of something. Adam stepped back, he didn't know what to think but he knew it wasn't proper that this woman who had stolen her brother's heart should be sitting with such closeness to another man, and certainly not consuming that amount of alcohol they appeared to have. No, this was not proper at all, and no chaperone either!

Adam returned home, his mind whirring as he climbed into bed.

"You saw Elsbeth?"

Asked a sleepy Cate.

"Aye, I did that."

He replied.

"Thank you my darlin'"

Cate rolled over and went back to sleep, satisfied that her husband had done the right thing.

Grace was beginning to feel cold in the woods, the damp night air and the humidity of the trees sent chills through her bones. The cottage wasn't far, and had Grace not fallen asleep she would have attempted to make her way there earlier, as it was she would have to go now and risk the occupiers being asleep. Grace kept low, almost on her front as she crawled over mud and stones to keep out of the sight of Nora Howard. The only sounds heard were Owls that hooted back and forth to their young with the occasional rats and mice that scurried through the undergrowth looking for food. The warm blood that oozed from the tears in her skin served only as encouragement to Grace that she must keep going, she wasn't coming this far to give up now. She would see her husband and her boys again and she would see that woman hang if it was the last thing she did.
The cold hand covered her mouth and Grace cursed that she had dared to imagine the ordeal was almost over. She wanted to scream or bite but she couldn't. Grace was pulled to her feet and frogmarched deeper into the woods and she knew, her heart sank as she realised that this was it, this was where she would meet her final end.

Chapter Fourteen

Nora sat in the cart, she was beginning to feel tired, and she didn't enjoy being so far from what she considered civilisation. Pulling the wrap tighter around her shoulders she shrugged.
"Well then, that's that. Time to go."
The horse began to trot when she shook the reins with force, the road was difficult to navigate in the daylight but in the enveloping darkness it was becoming nigh on impossible. She could hear something; she slowed her pace in an effort to listen to the noise that she almost recognised.
"Hey, you, hey you stop."
The voice called out behind her. It must be a type of highway robber; she had heard about these kinds of people. Nora screamed at the horse to go, thrashing the whip against the beasts back in a blind panic. They would not steal her money or her trophies, not after everything she had gone through to get them. The whip cracked continually as the person pursuing her shouted louder and louder.
It took one wrong turn to send the horse, cart and occupant tumbling with an almighty screech and crash down the steep ridge in the darkness of the unforgiving Kent countryside. The rider slowed his horse to a standstill, he knew this terrain like the back of his hand.
"That's what you call God's own justice my girl. Come on then, let's you and me get back. Nothing we can do 'til light."

Mrs. Daisy Richardson stretched her arm across the bed to where her husband lay. She wore a smile as big and as wide as the bright blue sky that peeked through the drapes. Julian snored quietly, a trait he had divulged to his new wife before they had married. He had quickly added that this only ever happened if he had consumed too much alcohol, to which Daisy had merely shrugged and assured him that this was not a thing that overly concerned her.

"Good morning, sleepy head."

She whispered as he blinked his eyes open.

"Good morning my love. What time is it? You're dressed, was I that terrible on our first night together?"

Julian sat up.

"No, you were perfect as I knew you would be. I have a small task to see to and then we can set off for our Honeymoon, if that is alright with you my love?"

Julian nodded; he was aware that Daisy had a duty as much to him as she did to her job. Daisy placed the breakfast tray down onto the bedcovers and poured 2 cups of tea.

"Oh, you are a good wife! You did all of this while I slept?"

"I did, I never start the day on an empty stomach. Has Edward gone back to London already? He doesn't seem to be in the house."

Julian scraped marmalade across his toast and shook his head.

"No, he would have said. I imagine he went back with the fellows to Billoughby's cottage."

Elsbeth stared at the man lying in her bed, she felt sick. What had she done! It was still early, and she doubted that anybody would be awake yet. Her hand touched his shoulder in an attempt to wake him and the whole frisson of what had happened the previous night came flooding back to the forefront of her mind. He groaned as his perfectly proportioned body rolled over revealing enough flesh that the woman blushed and looked away. She had drunk so much of the brandy and if she was honest with herself she was more than a little angry that Tom, who professed to love her, had said nothing in her defence to his brother. It was no excuse! She was a fool, and this would be the undoing of what she and Tom had. Edward opened his eyes and for a moment he struggled to remember where he was.

"Did I, er, did we…"

"Yes. You have to go."

"I don't want to go."

He looked at her now in the morning light, her hair tumbling wildly over her shoulders and her eyes as wild as a tigers. She was a beautiful woman inside and out and he would happily stay here for eternity and damn the consequences.

"Please, Edward, you have to. I have no excuses or explanations for what we did."

Her face looked sad; he didn't want her to be sad.

"Does there have to be excuses, or explanations? We did nothing wrong Elsbeth, we are both adults and we have both suffered great losses in our lives. Surely we are owed happiness when it presents itself. Were you not the one that told me God's plan can be there to make way for a better life? Did you not say those very words to me in this very house?"

He stared at her; his gaze unwavering.

"We have others to consider. I have been reckless; I am never reckless."

Elsbeth did not know what to think, she needed to be on her own to think things through.

"I shall go, I shall go before anyone gets sight of me. But I want you to hear me when I say, I will come back, and I give you my word that when I do it will be to stay."

Edward dressed quickly and left through the morning room doors.

Adam sat across from his brother at the kitchen table while Billoughby set about making breakfast.

"You're quiet this morning; did you have a bit too much of the ale?" Laughed Tom. Adam shrugged, he had come around to find out of any news on his mother, and to have a quiet word with his father regarding what he had witnessed at the hall. He hadn't expected Tom to still be there but then it was Sunday.

"Adam? Lost your tongue lad?"

Called Billoughby from across the room.

"Too much ale, yeah that's what it is."

He replied.

"Cate's alright this morning and the little one?"

"Aye, Pa. All good."

"Miss…Oh, I do mean Mrs. Richardson, will be here soon. We are meeting with Mr. Hirst to see what the next step should be in finding your Ma."

Adam and Tom knew that their father was trying to put on a brave face even though his heart was being torn in 2.

"What can we do, Pa? We don't want to just sit here when we could be out looking, tell us where and we'll go."

Said Tom as he took the hot plates from his father.

"That's the thing, son. Until we have a sit down and talk I have no clue where to start. Mr. Hirst might be better at knowing what the woman might do next."

Billoughby stabbed his fork into the steaming sausage on his plate, his eyes red with the worry of his missing wife, not knowing if she was still alive or had succumbed to the crazed actions of a mad woman. He thought that he would know, he would get a feeling? He had heard tales of such things when 2 people were as close as they were and up to now he had no such feeling.

"We'll fi…that must be Daisy."

Tom was interrupted by the rattling of the front door.

"Daisy normally uses the kitchen door. Mind, she's a married lass now."

Laughed Billoughby. Tom went off to answer the door leaving Adam and his father to continue their breakfast.

The footsteps could be heard as the front door closed. Billoughby glanced up to greet Daisy, he looked back at his plate, shook his head and jumped from his seat.

"Well bless my soul, would you look at what the winds blew our way!"

He darted forward and pulled the early morning visitor into his arms.

"Bloody hell, Connie!"

Cried Adam as he too got to his feet.

"Hello you lot. I see you are still on those amazing breakfasts, got any spare? I'm a growing girl as you can see."

Connie took off her coat revealing a perfectly round stomach.

"Oh, my word, congratulations! Whatever brings you here? Not that it isn't great to see you, still looking as pretty as a picture too."

Billoughby had a very soft spot for the young woman, it showed.

"Sit, sit and tell us all your news. The news right there we can make an educated guess at." Chuckled Adam. Tom stared in wonder, there was something different about her. She had always looked good but now, she looked radiantly beautiful.

Connie tucked into the plate with relish, it had been quite a journey, and she was famished.

"I saw Dr. Lyons in Maidstone and he told me everything. Is Mrs. Billoughby on the mend now?"

The young woman rested her fork on the edge of the plate as she waited for the news.

"Sadly, the woman Nora Howard has likely taken my Gracie again, from the hospital."

Said the Inspector with despair in his voice. Connie stretched her hand across the table and gently patted his hand.

"She'll be okay Mr. Billoughby, you'll see. She's a tough woman, always has been even when I was a little one."

Billoughby nodded.

"And you? When did this happen?"

Tom pointed to the growing bump in Connie's stomach. She smiled, but it wasn't the happiest of smiles one would expect from an expectant mother.

"The little one is due to arrive in 6 weeks. My husband passed. There, I said it without crying! I usually always cry when I say it out loud. He caught the influenza; it was very quick, and he didn't suffer too long which was merciful."
Connie stared at the plate; her smile now faded from her face.
"Oh, love. I am that sorry. How will you manage?"
Asked Billoughby.
"I will have to Mr. Billoughby, I have no other option but to get on with things for the sake of the little one."
Adam stood behind her and hugged the woman as she sat.
"You need to come home, that's what you should do. We can all help you, can't we Pa? We, Cate and I, have tons of baby things that we won't be needing for a good 8 months or so. There's work to be had locally if you're happy to leave the town?"
Adam had it all figured out.
"I couldn't ask people to do that Adam, they have more than enough things going on in their own lives, never mind a woman with child and no husband."
Billoughby scoffed.
"Nonsense missy, we've been your family a long time now and that doesn't stop because you're having a spot of bother. The guest room is still where it always was, and you are welcome to stay as long as you like."
The kitchen door opened, and Daisy popped her head around it.
"Room for one more?"
She smiled.
"Come in, constable, Mrs. Richardson, which do you prefer?"
Daisy laughed.
"As it's a work-related visit I suppose we should go with Constable Harvey. How are you doing, Inspector? Oh, and Connie! My goodness I didn't see you sitting in the corner there. How are you, we must have a catch-up, you are staying a while aren't you? Please say you are."

"Can I come in?"
Mr. Hirst was standing at the door now.
"Yes, yes. Please do." Called Billoughby.
"I'm going to leave you to it for a while, Pa, it's getting pretty crowded in here. Tom, come on, let's go for a walk."
Adam knew he had to do this now.
"Can I tag along and stretch my legs a while?"
Connie stood up.
"Of course you can."
Replied Tom, much to Adam's frustration.

Julian was in shock. This man who had come to be his best friend had done what no gentleman should do, and in the village where he was to eventually make his home.
"Why?"
he asked as he poured a glass of lemonade and slumped down into the garden seat.
"You of all people should know that I never do anything lightly and what's more I never do anything that I don't intend to follow through and believe me my friend, I thoroughly intend to follow this through to its nth degree."
Julian shook his head again. He knew that his friend had been hurting since the loss of his son and wife, but this behaviour was unacceptable by any standards. Mrs. Stanhope was not some London flossy that he could pick up and drop at his whim. She was a respectable lady with responsibilities. And then there was her part in this madness. Had the woman lost her mind? He had heard snippets of a marriage proposal from the Billoughby man only last night for heaven's sake.
"Please stop shaking your head in that manner, Julian. I know what I am doing, and I do believe that the lady in question does too. It is fated, and no, I have not lost my mind. I have merely lost my heart."

Saving Grace | D M Roberts

Edward walked across the lawn and back again. He realised he would have a hard time convincing his friend that he was sincere in his feelings, but he cared not for being spoken to like a teenage boy in the first throes of romance.

"You have known her but a day and a half. Do you know what that could do to her reputation in such a small village? It is fine for you, you can simply scuttle off back to London. Think about her, Edward."

"I will be scuttling nowhere! I have no intention of ruining her reputation, if anything I can enhance it. I have heard the stories about this young man. As you said, it's a small village and people are only too happy to talk. That kind of thing would never work out, Julian. You know it as well as I do. I can give Elsbeth Stanhope the chance to not only be blissfully happy, and God knows she deserves it, but I can steady her reputation once and for good."

Julian scratched his chin, it had to be noted that when put in this way it didn't sound as outlandish as he first thought.

"What of young Tom Billoughby? Do you not think he might take umbrage at you stealing the woman from right under his nose?"

Edward shrugged; he had not given the lad much of a second thought in all of this.

"He is young, he will get over it and eventually he might even thank me."

Edward replied.

Elsbeth called Geraldine into the study. She had to talk to someone, and it had to be now.

"Is everything alright, dear?"

Geraldine stood in the doorway.

"Come in please, Geraldine. Close the door."

Geraldine sat on the high back chair; she could see that Elsbeth seemed quite distressed about something.

"Is it Grace, have they found her? Oh, dear God it's bad news isn't it. I knew there was something when I woke this morning, there was a strange and disquieted feeling in the house."

"No dearest, it is not about Grace. I have heard no news as yet. I wanted to talk with you on a personal matter that I feel I cannot talk to anyone else about. I would need your solemn word and absolute secrecy if I am to share what I have to say."

Elsbeth's eyes looked beseechingly into Geraldine's as she waited for her answer.

"You know you can trust me, Elsbeth. Unless you have killed a person of course but I doubt that you would so that wouldn't be relevant."

Elsbeth smiled, a faint smile as she sat forward.

"No dear, I have not done that. I shall explain it to you, you may judge me, and I am ready for that, but I would desperately appreciate your wisdom and your friendship if, after hearing what I have to say, you still feel able to continue our friendship."

Geraldine nodded and sat back as Elsbeth told her everything.

Geraldine sat upright in her seat. She thought she knew this woman well enough by now to be able to say that this was out of character, and yet she also detected a fresh vigour in her voice when she spoke of this man. It was obvious there was some kind of strong physical attraction but there was more than that. Geraldine saw a sparkle in Elsbeth's eyes that she had never seen before. It was a vibrant shine that not even Tom had managed to bring out in the woman. It was the same shine that she had glimpsed when Elsbeth spoke of Wilf.

"What are you going to do about it, dear? You should speak to young Tom; you owe him that much. I have no great words of wisdom except to say that you know as well as I do that life is precious, you must seize your happiness with both hands when it comes your way. You are an intelligent woman, Elsbeth, you don't

need mine or anyone else's approval my dear, but you have mine if that is of any comfort to you."
Elsbeth clasped her friend's hands in hers.
"You have no idea what that means to me. Of course I shall speak with Tom, I never intended to do otherwise. He is a wonderful young man, maybe that is the problem. He is so young, who am I to deny him all the joys that this world will have to offer him?"
Geraldine nodded, he was young, and he would love again.

Billoughby had the maps spread across the tables, the 3 of them poured over the various areas that were possible sites they could concentrate on. Daisy informed the Inspector of the officers out of Canterbury that were following up possible sightings in villages along the coast. It was decided that each of them would take a couple of the men from the village, and they would begin their search. Billoughby insisted that Daisy was to call it a day if she turned nothing up by the afternoon, he would not hear of her wasting well-earned time off when she had a new husband waiting on her. They set off down to the village to collect the helpers, leaving Connie and Tom free to return to the cottage.

"Do you want to talk about your husband?"
Tom was awkward when it came to Connie, but he felt he should give the woman a chance to unburden if she needed to. Connie smiled the smile that had always turned his legs to jelly, some things never changed he thought to himself as he pulled out a chair.
"You are very sweet, Tom Billoughby, you always were. He was a good and honest man, and he was taken way too soon, like poor Esther. I have to remember that he left me with the greatest gift a man can give a woman."
Connie rubbed her stomach bump, her bright face shone with the hope of what was to be.
"You will stay?"

He asked, it was almost a plea, and he couldn't figure out why.

"As long as I am welcome I will stay, Tom. I have felt very much alone the last few months. I don't mind telling you."

Connie's eyes glistened with un-spilt tears, her hands twisting as she tried to keep her composure. Tom could not help himself; he pulled the young woman to him and held her tight in his arms, she didn't cry she simply let the man comfort her and it felt good.

"Am I interrupting?"

Tom and Connie turned to see Elsbeth standing at the door. She didn't wait for a reply as she continued.

"I did knock but you mustn't have heard me. Hello Connie, it is good to see you again. My, you're expecting. How wonderful for you."

Elsbeth was surprised that the pangs of jealousy she had once experienced with Esther had vanished. Connie freeing herself from Tom's arms gave the woman she had known as a younger girl a hug, then kissed her on the cheek.

"Mrs. Stanhope. Yes, I am expecting. You look so very well."

Tom stood in silence, not sure what to say.

"Mr. Billoughby, I called to find out if there is any word on your mother?"

Tom shook his head, he wanted to speak but he couldn't.

"Would you like tea, Mrs. Stanhope?"

Offered Connie.

"Thank you dear but no, I have so many things to do today. Mr. Billoughby, should you get any news would you keep me informed?"

Tom nodded, what the hell is wrong with me? He thought as he watched Elsbeth leave.

"She looks well, mind she was always a pretty one, don't you think?"

Tom sat down, what was that?

"Maybe I should catch her up and let her know that Pa and the others have gone out searching. I didn't think."
Connie nodded as she filled up the kettle.

"Wait, Elsbeth. I am sorry about that; I don't know what got into me."
He was breathless after the run down the lane and with his heart thumping from the rush of adrenaline Tom clasped his hands to his knees as he took in a deep breath.
"It's alright Tom. It would never have worked, you and me. I know that now and that is what I came to tell you. I will always carry a piece of you in my heart and I would hope that you would do the same. I am not the one for you Tom, I wish I could have been, so very much, but I'm not." Tom was speechless, a small part of him wanted to grab the woman right there and tell her she was wrong, a small part was not enough, and he knew that.
"Is that what you want?"
He asked, his eyes boring into hers.
"It is, and what's more Tom, it is what you need and what is right."
She touched his face gently and he closed his eyes for a moment. She was gone.

The man peered over the ridge, he had contacted the local constabulary, and the officers carefully lowered the experienced climbers down over the edge. The shattered cart was visible as was the large corpse of the horse that sadly went with it. The men reached the remnants of the accident and swiftly scanned the area.
"There's nobody down here, Sir."
Came the call from below. The man shook his head.
"Impossible, look again man!"
They looked a little further and still they found no person in the debris.

"Sir, Sir. There isn't anyone down here, wait a minute. Oh dear. Sir? Can you hear me up there?"
"Yes. What is it?"
"Under the horse Sir, a woman, Sir."
"Can you move the horse? Between you, can you move the horse and get her up here?"
"Yes, we can do that, Sir. Won't be a pretty sight mind."
"Just get her up here, man."
It took them a good hour to get the body back up to firm ground, a sheet was used to wrap the woman in until the medical examiner arrived. He was due at any time according to the Sergeant.

Joseph Lyons walked carefully along the edges of the ridge; he wasn't overly confident when it came to heights such as these.
"You have something for me, officer?"
He asked as he stepped across rocks and tree roots.
"Just in that clearing, Doctor. Mr. Jones was the one that reported it, we only got the word today, but it appears it happened sometime late last night. Mr. Jones was a member of the constabulary a few years back. He also has someone at his cottage, if you wouldn't mind taking a look when you're done here?"
Joseph nodded. He set to his examination and quickly concluded what was obvious to all, the woman had died due to injuries sustained in the fall, and about 100 lb worth of horse into the bargain!
"You can take her now men. If you could point me in the direction of Mr. Jones?"
An officer walked Joseph through the wooded area to the cottage, Joseph looked around. Not a bad place to live if you liked solitude, he thought.
"Mr. Jones, the doctor is here."
Called the officer through the open door. Mr. Jones came outside, he grinned.

"Well bugger me! Joseph, you're still at it then? Come in, second thoughts, a quick word first. You remember that Inspector, Milton Billoughby? We stayed friends once I left the job. I have his wife here, she's in a bit of a state mind you. I found her in the woods last night, frozen to the bone she was. My missus has cleaned up her cuts and scratches best she can but there's something going on that had her out there and I reckon it was likely to do with that horse and cart that took a tumble off the ridge. Now, she's sleeping, and I didn't want to disturb her. Can you?" Joseph sighed so hard with relief that he startled Mr. Jones.
"Show me."
He said. Mr. Jones led the way through to the sitting room. Sure enough, there lay Grace on the large settee next to the fire. Joseph knelt by her side on the floor.
"Grace, Grace wake up dear."
Grace stirred, she opened her eyes and tried to adjust to the dimly lit room.
"Has she gone?"
She whispered.
"Quite gone my dear. Can't guarantee she's gone up there, but she has most definitely gone." Replied Joseph. Grace flung her arms around his neck, she sobbed loudly with relief that the ordeal was finally over.

Mr. Hirst made his way back to the Billoughby's cottage. He was desperately upset that he had no news on the Inspector's wife, he stood outside the front door not wanting to enter. He thought about his own wife and son, he would be tearing the countryside to pieces if he thought they were in this type of danger but now, having experienced such a search he knew that it was easier said than done. The voices from inside the quaint home became louder as the door opened before him.
"Mr. Hirst. Did you knock? I didn't hear it if you did."

Robert was just leaving with Mary, and they seemed overly jolly considering the circumstances.

"I was about to, then you opened the door."

He mumbled.

"Must have sensed you were here, go in man."

Replied Robert as he stepped out of the way.

"Mr. Hirst."

Mary smiled at him as she too got out of his way.

"Yes, you must have. I'm sorry that I haven't returned with better news."

He said, his head bowed almost in shame at what he considered failure. Mary laughed, as did Robert. Had they all gone stark staring mad? He thought to himself.

"Get yourself inside and you'll see that we aren't as insensitive as we might appear."

Said Mary pushing the door open further. Taking off his hat he entered the house. The Inspector was bustling about in the kitchen, voices came through from the parlour that he didn't recognise.

"Inspector?"

He asked, puzzled.

"They found her, they found my Gracie. What's more, that woman is dead. It's all over Mr. Hirst, finished with. You best come through; Joseph will tell you all about it."

Mr. Hirst couldn't believe what he was hearing. It was finally done with? How could this be?

Cate and Adam had invited Connie over for supper, they thought Milton and Grace could do with some time alone after their ordeal. Adam was sent to the rectory to pass on the good news while Connie and Cate talked babies and prepared the food. Elsbeth was on her way out of Reverend Moore's home as Adam rounded the corner.

"Oh, Mr. Billoughby I do beg your pardon."

Elsbeth moved out of his way.

"I wanted to speak to you?"
Said Adam. He meant to get this off his chest and have his say.
"Of course. What is it you wanted to speak about?"
Elsbeth asked, she imagined that Tom had mentioned their talk.
"I saw you. Last night, at the hall I saw you and that man from London. Now, I haven't said anything to my brother, but I think you should."
Adam kept his voice low; he did not care much for this woman's reputation anymore but his brother, well that was something altogether different.
"What exactly did you see, Mr. Billoughby? I had a guest call over for a nightcap, I wasn't aware this went against some kind of code. As for your brother, I have called off our relationship. It is nobody's concern but Tom's and mine. Tom can see it is for the best and I have only his interests at heart, other than that I really do not see what it has to do with you, or anyone else for that matter."
Adam stepped back; this was news to him.
"Oh, I didn't know that.Tom hasn't mentioned it to me."
"Maybe Tom has been too busy worrying about your mother, I also called over to your parents today to find out if there was any word on Grace, Tom was quite busy with your latest guest. Shall we also make something of that?"
Adam gulped, well played Mrs. Stanhope.
"No, as you pointed out, a person's friends are their own business. Right, now that's done with, I am very happy to tell you that Ma is home and Mrs. Nora Howard is deceased. Pa has all the information and I'm sure he will fill you in on it when you go to visit Ma. I hope you do; you were good friends once."
Adam smiled as he looked at the woman and could now see what his brother saw.
"I would be happy to, it is the best news I have heard in a long time. Good evening, Adam." Elsbeth walked away and Adam realised it

was the first time in a long time that she had called him Adam. Maybe things were getting back to how they should be.

Epilogue

What lies in store next for Billoughby? Has Elsbeth sacrificed her true love to save the reputation of a young woman, and a valued friendship. Why is Geraldine back in the village, can Tobias hold onto his post?

Find out in the next exciting instalment of Billoughby.

About the Author

Mother to 3 amazing Adults and 2 grandson's, Dee is happily sharing her life with her partner in Kent.
Dee decided it was time to do the thing she had always wanted to do and write.
Dee enjoys many hobbies and pastimes including but not limited to, field archery, DIY, crafts, dancing, car shows and reenacting.
Currently working in the care sector Dee is kept very busy.

Other books in this series

Billoughby – The Long Shadows
Billoughby 2 – Petticoats and Bowler Hats
Billoughby 3 – Lost Souls

Books by this Author

Ria
Words Out
Ladies Preference
Billoughby, The Long Shadows
Billoughby 2, Petticoats and Bowler Hats
Billoughby 3, Lost Souls
Billoughby 4, Saving Grace

Printed in Great Britain
by Amazon